Praise for the novels of Heather Gudenkauf

"Masterful, terrible, and absolutely addicting...
Tense, taut, and terrifying."
—*Kirkus Reviews*

"Fully realized, wholly absorbing, and almost painfully
suspenseful... The journey is mesmerizing."
—*New York Times*

"With a brilliant structure, an authentic sense of
place, and gorgeous storytelling, Gudenkauf proves
she is the queen of the rural thriller."
—Hank Phillippi Ryan, bestselling author of *Her Perfect Life*

"A chilling and heart-stopping stunner."
—Kimberly Belle, bestselling author of *My Darling Husband*

"If you haven't read Heather Gudenkauf yet,
now's the time."
—Lisa Unger, *New York Times* bestselling author
of *Secluded Cabin Sleeps Six*

"Heather Gudenkauf has created a special thriller
with a unique and brilliantly effective hook that
I simply could not put down."
—C. J. Box, #1 bestselling author of *Treasure State*

Also by Heather Gudenkauf

The Weight of Silence
These Things Hidden
One Breath Away
Missing Pieces
Not a Sound
Before She Was Found
This Is How I Lied
The Overnight Guest

LITTLE MERCIES

HEATHER GUDENKAUF

PARK
ROW
BOOKS

PARK
ROW
BOOKS™

ISBN-13: 978-0-7783-3388-3

Little Mercies

First published in 2014. This edition published in 2024.

This is a work of fiction. Names, characters, places and incidents are either the product of the author's imagination or are used fictitiously. Any resemblance to actual persons, living or dead, businesses, companies, events or locales is entirely coincidental.

Park Row Books
22 Adelaide St. West, 41st Floor
Toronto, Ontario M5H 4E3, Canada
ParkRowBooks.com
BookClubbish.com

Printed in U.S.A.

Recycling programs for this product may not exist in your area.

For my brothers and sisters.

Chapter 1

When people find out what I do for a living their first question is always about the most horrendous case of child abuse I've encountered. I can be at a backyard barbecue or at a New Year's Eve party or in the waiting room at the dentist's office, or my husband's baseball game. *You must see so much,* they say, shaking their heads, lips pursed in something like empathy, like *I* was the one who might have endured the beatings, the burns, the torrents of hateful words. Of course I don't share any details about my clients and their families. So much has been stripped from the children that stagger in and out of my orbit; the very least I can do is honor their privacy. *Come on,* people urge, *tell me. It's bad, isn't it?* Like I'm dangling some salacious gossip in front of them. Like I'm keeping mum because I don't want to offend their tender ears, upset their perfectly ordered worlds where all children are touched with gentle hands, spoken to with loving words and tucked warmly into beds with full stomachs.

Close your eyes, I once told the shortstop's mother and she did, almost quivering in anticipation of the gory details. She nodded in compliance, cocking her head in my direction, preparing for what I will reveal next. Will I tell her about Mariah Crane, the seven-year-old whose mother held her head under water until there was no chance that her damaged brain could ever catch up with her growing body? Or will I tell them about the twins? Everyone has heard about the *Twin Case,* as it's still known. Everyone wants to know more about the twins.

Now imagine the vilest things that can be done to a human being, I say. I let her think about this for a moment and I can see the slight spasm of revulsion skitter across her face. *That's what I've seen.* She opens one eye to see if I'll say anything else. But that's all I have for her.

The only people I talk to about the Twin Case are my husband and Joe Gaddey. I was a newly minted social worker, just out of graduate school when I moved back to my hometown of Cedar City, the second largest city in Iowa, just behind Des Moines with a population of about one hundred ninety-five thousand. My husband moved to Cedar City to teach high school history and coach baseball, having grown up in the tiny town of Broken Branch, Iowa, where everyone is related, if not by blood then by marriage. We met through mutual friends and eventually settled into married life, ready to change the world. In the end I have struggled to not let the case change me.

Adam and I hadn't even met yet when I was assigned my first social work case involving a set of six-year-old twin boys, a five-year-old girl, their mother, their father and a baseball bat. Only one of the boys survived. The family wasn't new to the system; I had inherited the case from my predecessor and arrived for the first of my scheduled visits just as the emergency personnel were bringing out the first stretcher. Joe Gaddey was the officer positioned outside the front door. In a daze I moved toward him.

"And you are?" he asked. I couldn't even speak, could only look up at him. I peeked around his solid girth, trying to peer into the house and was greeted with a terrible sight. I teetered on my high heels and grabbed on to his sleeve for support. "Whoa, now," he said, steadying me. "You don't want to see that."

"I'm their social worker," I said in a small voice. "What happened?"

"Their dad happened," he said in that wry way I have grown to appreciate over the years. I swallowed back the bile that had collected in my throat, willing myself not to vomit. I knew this job would be difficult, even heartbreaking, but nothing, nothing, had prepared me for this. I felt the police officer's gaze on me. He was massive. Six-three, two hundred and ten pounds of muscle, a thirty-six-year-old with a baby face and a sharp tongue. "You going to be okay?" he asked. We stood there for a moment. Me nodding my chin up and down like some maniacal bobblehead doll and the officer standing there uncomfortably. "You should probably call your supervisor," he finally said as the second, third and fourth stretchers emerged, shrouded in black body bags, two of which were child-sized.

"Yeah," I said, still nodding.

Every day I chronicle the monstrosities inflicted upon children in volumes of paperwork, in endless meetings, while testifying in court. I rarely talk to my husband about my clients anymore. He can see what kind of day I've had by the look on my face, the sag of my shoulders, how quickly I make a beeline to the bottle of pinot grigio I've reserved expressly for the more difficult days. On these days, Adam understands that there are no words and will gently replace my wineglass with our eleven-month-old daughter. Avery will wrap her chubby arms around my neck and press her petal-pink lips against my cheek so that I can smell the scent of apples on her breath. Whenever I come through the door it's like Christmas, her birthday and the Fourth of July all at once, she is always so happy to see me. I could take comfort in this, and I do, but I see the same delight on the faces of the children I work with who are reunited with a mother or father. The same mothers or fathers who once slapped them so hard that teeth were loosened or grabbed them so roughly that bones were broken. In Avery I see the same spark that's in their eyes, the eruption of the same joyful grin. *I knew you'd come back to me,* their faces say. I know the psychology behind this—why an abused child will run into the arms of their abuser—but it makes me sad.

There is one case I do not talk about anymore, one that I am not able to speak of, not to Adam, not even to Joe. It was a case that I knew would end badly... I felt it in my bones the moment I walked into the home, and I was right.

Madalyn Olmstead did not have an easy entrance into this world, nor did she have a gentle exit. Madalyn was born at Cedar City Hospital six years ago and spent the first ten days of her life in the Neonatal Intensive Care Unit for respiratory issues. I became involved when Madalyn was one and a home health-care nurse called my supervisor at the Department of Human Services and asked if someone could check in with Madalyn and her mother at their home. I was assigned the case. When pressed for details, the nurse was vague. "Madalyn needs to use a nebulizer for her asthma, but her mother has a hard time remembering what I tell her. I think she might have trouble reading but is a quick learner when someone shows her what to do. She seems great with Madalyn." The nurse was quiet for a moment. "Honestly, it's the husband I'm worried about. It's like when he comes into the room all the air is sucked out. She becomes tense and all her attention goes right to the husband. He acts like a jealous sibling or something. He has no interest in Madalyn but to complain about how much time his wife is spending with her. She seemed scared of him. Can't you just go over there and check? I'd feel so much better."

As a social worker, I was obligated to follow through, though based on what the nurse shared, I didn't think I'd find anything that was actionable, but at least the father would know that someone was paying attention to the way he was interacting with his wife and his daughter. Three years later Madalyn was dead and I knew James Olmstead had killed her and he got away with it.

Most often Madalyn comes to me in the violet-tinged mornings. That middling space between night and day. She has the sweet, unformed features of a toddler and sparkling gray eyes recessed above full, pink cheeks. Surprisingly, considering the way she was found, it wasn't the most gruesome of deaths—very little blood and only a few bruises marred her perfect little body. It was the hidden, internal injuries that killed Madalyn. Still Madalyn's short time on earth began with the violent expulsion from her mother's womb into the cold, unforgiving earthly air and ended in violence, as well. It just couldn't be proved. I knew differently and I think her mother did, too. Though she was too blind, too scared, to say so.

When I wake up in the mornings, as the memory of Madalyn creeps beneath the covers with me and my snoring husband, my children sleeping soundly in the rooms down the hall, over and over I try to parse out just how her father, James Olmstead, got away with murder.

I'd been in and out of the Olmstead home for years because of suspected abuse by the father. Neighbors to the Olmsteads would call the police because of loud fighting coming from the house. Twice Madalyn had to be removed from the home because the father had beaten the mother so badly. Twice, the mother didn't press charges. Twice, Madalyn was returned to the home. There were contusions on Madalyn, but the kind you find on all children: skinned knees, bruised elbows, purple knots on the forehead. All explained away by Madalyn's mother. *Such a busy little girl. You have children, right?*

She was right, I do have children. Just before Madalyn died, Lucas was four and Leah was seven and they had the exact same kind of bruises. But as social workers, we know. We know which homes hold the addicts, the predators, the abusers. We just can't always prove it.

Two years ago, on a beautiful May afternoon, Madalyn Olmstead tumbled out of the third-story window of her apartment building and fell to the concrete sidewalk below. The only other person in the apartment at the time was her father.

"She was out of my sight for only a second," her father claimed. "She thought she could fly," he cried convincingly to the news cameras. During the autopsy, besides the traumatic head injury, the medical examiner found suspicious bruising on Madalyn but not suspicious enough to call it murder. Because of his neglect, Madalyn's father was arrested for child endangerment that resulted in the death of a child and was facing up to a fifty-year prison sentence.

Even though I was convinced this was no accident, at the time I was satisfied that James Olmstead was being tried for the lesser charge and would have been content just having him put in prison. I prepared to testify against James. Over and over I reviewed the documentation of my visits to the Olmstead home, practiced describing the injuries I saw on Madalyn's mother, the suspicious bruises I saw on Madalyn. The jury never heard my testimony. It can be very difficult for the prosecution to get a defendant's prior bad acts entered into evidence, and the judge in this case felt that the facts would prejudice the jury too much. Our only hope was that the defense would open the door by providing testimony that it was all a mistake, that James's character was much different than what he was alleged to have done. That he just wasn't capable of hurting his daughter. The defense didn't open that door, didn't bring James's moral fiber into testimony, didn't have his wife or his co-workers at the foundry where he worked, nor the parents of children he coached in Tiny Tot T-Ball, speak on his behalf. Didn't have James testify on his own behalf. As a result, the jurors were not allowed to hear of James's abusiveness. He was acquitted. Too much reasonable doubt, the jury foreperson explained after the trial was over.

Three months later, James and his wife sued the owner of the apartment building for not insuring that the window screens were safely installed. They won a tidy sum of money and were from then on known as the victims.

I just knew that James had beaten his daughter and then panicked. In my gut I knew he made it look like she had climbed onto the windowsill, fallen through the screen and tumbled three stories to the sidewalk below. Madalyn was a fear-filled little girl. She was afraid of water, was afraid of dogs, was afraid of strangers, and was, most likely, afraid of heights. There was no way that Madalyn Olmstead would climb onto a window-sill and press her little hands against the screen. Never once in all the time I spent with her did she ever tell me she wished she could be a bird, wished she could fly. One thing I knew of for sure was that Madalyn was afraid of her father.

Months after the trial, not Caren, my supervisor, not Joe, not even my husband would listen to me rant and rave about my suspicions anymore. "Didn't the medical examiner say her injuries were consistent with an accidental fall?" Adam asked when I brought up my concerns for about the millionth time. I tried to explain that the medical examiner at the time was overworked and had a reputation of taking the lazy way out in determining his findings. Adam wasn't sympathetic. "Ellen," he said, "you're making yourself sick over this. You need to stop worrying about this kid. No one else seems to be."

Adam's lack of concern irked me a bit, but Caren's and Joe's dismissal truly hurt. In social work and police work, too, we not only deal with facts but gut instinct often prods us into action. I thought they would listen to my worries and would back me up when I suggested another in-depth investigation into Madalyn's death. They were sympathetic, made all the right noises when I made my case to them, but in the end they said they were satisfied with the jury's decision and I needed to drop it.

In the end all that was left was the man who got away with murder, the woman who chose to protect him, and me, the social worker who was powerless to protect a four-year-old little girl named Madalyn Olmstead, who will forever be known as *Little Bird, the little girl who thought she could fly.*

Chapter 2

In the evening's fading sunshine, ten-year-old Jenny Briard, on her knees, sweating and scraping at the hard-scrabble dirt, did not have a reliable lucky charm, but she was determined to find one the first chance she got. Maybe a four-leaf clover or a horseshoe. Even a dusty old penny would do. Her father, Billy, in one of his rare moments of clarity a week ago, gave her a rabbit's-foot key chain for her tenth birthday. No matter that he gave it to her two weeks late, Jenny wanted to cherish the silky white limb. But try as she might, the thought of a rabbit relieved of its paw to enhance the good fortune of others made her stomach flip-flop dangerously.

"What the hell? What're you doing out here?" her father mumbled when he came upon Jenny trying to bury the rabbit's foot in the weedy area behind the motel where they were currently staying. Jenny tried to hide behind her back the pocketknife she had lifted from her father's jeans for use as a shovel but it was too late. "That's my pocketknife. Give it here!" Jenny quickly tried to brush away the dirt before sheepishly handing over the knife. Her father peered into the shallow hole.

"Hey, that's your birthday present! What are you doing that for?" he exclaimed, his hair still wild from sleep, his voice laced with cigarette smoke.

Jenny didn't know what to say. She hadn't wanted to hurt her father's feelings, to seem ungrateful for the gift, but in the five whole days she'd been in possession of the charm her father had once again lost his job, they had been evicted from their apartment, their truck had broken down for good, and her father had succumbed to what he called his weakness—twice. "It just seemed like the right thing to do," she finally said, not able to meet his gaze.

Her father stood there for a moment staring down at her, his shirttail flapping like a flag in the hot Nebraska wind, his jeans hanging low on his hips, the band of his boxers peeking out. "Guess I can't argue with that line of thinking," he said at last, lowering himself into a sitting position next to her. "I'm thinking that wasn't the best birthday present for a little girl, was it? You probably wanted new shoes or your ears pierced. Something girlie like that."

"No, no," Jenny protested. "It was a great idea for a present. I just felt...sorry for it."

They both looked down into the small trench. "Well, how about we commence with the ceremony and then go to the Happy Pancake for supper?" her father asked, looking at her with weary, bloodshot eyes. Together they filled in the tiny hole covering the white paw with dusty earth. "Would you like to say a few words?" her father asked solemnly.

"I've never been to a funeral before," Jenny admitted. "I'm not sure what I should say."

"Well, I've been to my share of funerals and mostly there's a lot of praying and crying. You can say whatever comes to mind and it's all right."

Jenny thought this over for a moment. "Do I have to say it out loud?" she asked.

"Nope, some of the most powerful words ever spoken are said right here." He tapped his tobacco-stained fingers sagely against his chest.

Jenny stood silently over the tiny grave for a moment and then her father took her by the hand and they walked the quarter mile to the Happy Pancake, both retreating to the restroom after the waitress raised her eyebrows at their dirt-encrusted fingernails.

"The Chocolate Chip Happy Stack is $4.99, if that's not too much," Jenny said hopefully, scanning the prices on the menu. "And you can have my bacon if you want it."

"Get whatever you want, Peanut. We're celebrating today," her father said buoyantly. Jenny peeked skeptically at her father from behind the plastic folds of the menu. Usually, whenever her father announced a celebration, he said he was going to invite two friends over and two friends only. Brew and Ski. Her only consolation was that the Happy Pancake promised a strictly family atmosphere complete with thirty-seven kinds of pancakes and a man who dressed up in a smiling pancake costume and made balloon animals on Sundays. Beer and his problematic friends were nowhere to be found on the menu.

"I guess I'll have the Happy Hawaiian Stack then," Jenny decided. She had already tried three of the thirty-seven pancake varieties and was determined to try each.

"A fine, fine choice, *madame,*" her father said in his fake French waiter accent, causing her to giggle.

"So what are we celebrating?" Jenny asked in her most grown-up voice after their orders were placed and they were both sipping on tall frothy glasses of orange juice.

"Hold on to your hat…" he began, and Jenny indulgently clapped her hands atop her head. "We are going on a trip!" her father said, emphasizing each word with a hand slap to the Formica tabletop.

"What kind of trip?" Jenny asked, narrowing her eyes suspiciously, thinking of their truck leaking dangerous black smoke from beneath the hood the last time her father tried to start it.

"I got a call from my old friend Matthew," her father said, pausing when the waitress appeared with their plates and slid a pile of steaming pancakes topped with pineapples, whipped cream and a brightly colored umbrella in front of Jenny. He waited until the waitress retreated before continuing, "You wouldn't remember him, you were just a baby the last time we saw him, but Matthew called and said they were looking for some workers at the John Deere plant over in Iowa." He looked at his daughter hopefully.

"That doesn't sound like a trip," Jenny said miserably, staring down at her pancakes, the whipped cream already sliding from the stack in a buttery sludge. She pushed her plate to the middle of the table. "That sounds like moving." She suddenly wasn't hungry anymore.

"It's right on the Mississippi River. We can go fishing, maybe even buy a boat someday. Imagine that, Peanut." Her father stabbed his fork at a piece of sausage, a wide grin on his face. "We could live on a houseboat if we wanted to."

This was an interesting thought. A houseboat. But Jenny pushed the thought aside. "What's the name of this place," Jenny asked grumpily, pulling her plate back and pinching off a piece of the pancake with her fingers.

"Dubuque. And besides the Mississippi River, there's a dog track and a river museum with otters and alligators and all kinds of cool things."

Silently, Jenny began eating—she wasn't sure when she and her father would get their next decent meal. Eight hours from now they would most likely be splitting a bag of chips and a stick of beef jerky. Her belly felt uncomfortably full, her tongue thick with syrup. Her father was going on and on about how great Iowa was going to be, how the John Deere plant paid fifteen dollars an hour, how they'd move into an apartment, but just for a while. Once they were settled they could move into a house where she would have her own room and a backyard. Jenny wanted to ask him if there would be a breakfast nook. It sounded so cozy and comfortable, a small corner of the kitchen, surrounded by sun-filled windows. But her stomach hurt and she didn't want him to think that she approved of his plan in any way. Jenny licked her syrupy fingers one by one. "When do we leave?" she asked in resignation.

"How 'bout tonight?" her father asked, smiling broadly, his right cheek collapsing into a deep dimple that women loved. Then, leaning in so closely that she could smell sausage intermingled with this afternoon's beer, he lowered his voice. "You run on home and start packing. I'll pay and catch up with you in a few minutes. We got a bus to catch at midnight."

Jenny knew that her father wasn't going to pay for their supper, but at least he was letting her get out of the restaurant before embarrassing her to death. He was thoughtful that way.

Chapter 3

I creep down the hallway, the wooden floor sighing creakily beneath my bare feet. I peek into the kids' rooms. First Leah's and then Lucas's. Leah is tented beneath her thin white sheet, her bright pink comforter covered with multicolored peace symbols kicked to the end of the bed. A faint glow shines through the cotton and I'm hoping that she has a flashlight beneath the covers reading a book like I used to when I was little. But I know my daughter too well. It's her handheld video game, one that Adam's parents, Hank and Theresa, gave her a few months ago for her ninth birthday. A confusing game where the avatar goes back in time, trying to save the stolen prince and return him safely to the enchanted kingdom. *It's a lot like what you do for a living, El,* Hank told me happily after Leah opened the brightly wrapped package, whooped with joy and called to thank her grandparents.

Now *that* would be a superpower, I think to myself. To be able to step into a time machine and travel back a week, an hour, a minute, a second before some indescribable thing happens to a child. To stand before a parent brandishing a cigarette, a stepparent with a lurid leer, a caregiver with a raised fist and say, "Do you really want to do this?"

"Hey, Leah," I whisper, closing the bedroom door behind me and trying not to wake Lucas who, across the hall, is buried beneath his own blanket like a wooly bear caterpillar, even though it's still eighty degrees outside and the air conditioner is less than reliable. Neither Adam nor I have had the time to call the repairman. I peer beneath her sheet and smile at my firstborn daughter. She looks up guiltily at me from beneath a forelock of dark hair damply pasted against her forehead.

"It's nearly midnight, turn that thing off," I chide, holding out my hand for the game. She presses a button and suddenly we're plunged into darkness but for the star-shaped night-light plugged into the receptacle next to her bed.

"I can't sleep though," she protests in her gravelly voice.

"Want me to rub your back?" I ask.

"Too hot," she answers grumpily.

"Sing you a song?"

"Um, no," she says shortly. I'm not surprised at this response. My singing is a long-running family joke. Still, I hum a few bars of a song that is Leah's current favorite and wiggle my hips. Even in the dark I can tell that she is rolling her eyes.

"How about a cold washcloth for your forehead and another fan brought up here?"

"I guess," she says with a jaw-breaking yawn.

By the time I go downstairs, lug up the oscillating fan, wet a washcloth beneath the cold-water faucet and return to Leah's bedroom, she is fast asleep. I slap the washcloth on the back of my own sweaty neck, plug in the fan and position it so that the marginally cooler air is focused squarely on her sleeping form. I lean over and lightly press my lips to Leah's cheek and she doesn't stir. I tiptoe across the hall to Lucas's bedroom, stoop down to kiss his forehead and he waves a hand as if trying to swat away a pesky mosquito.

I pull the washcloth from my neck, its coolness already absorbed into my hot skin, and I turn to see my husband's silhouette in the doorway, a sleepy Avery in his arms. "Ellen, everything okay?" Adam whispers.

I put a finger to my lips and silently cross the bedroom, step out into the hall and pull the door shut behind me. "I'm okay, it's too hot for anyone to sleep." I lay a hand on his arm and brush Avery's hair from her forehead and she smiles sleepily up at me.

"Thanks for coming to the game tonight," he says as we move through the hallway toward Avery's room.

"Oh, I like watching the boys play. They're really improving." Adam is the coach for East High School boys' varsity baseball team.

"Yeah, they are," Adam says proudly.

Though I've been a social worker for nearly fifteen years, the job weighs heavily on my chest. I've thought about quitting, thought about getting a job where I wouldn't hear the voice of a client shouting in my ear or weeping for the children I've taken away from them. One where I wouldn't hear the cries of children in my sleep. But of course I don't. I know my job is important, I know I help children.

Adam presses Avery into my arms and, as I hold my daughter, I kiss the fine, silky strands of the dark hair that tops her head. She wraps her plump arms around my neck, and her even, steady heartbeat is a metronome, calming the galloping thud against my chest. I push away all thoughts of the children I work with and focus on the one in my arms and the two that are sound asleep just a few steps away. Despite the craziness of life, the long hours, the endless housework, the sleepless nights, for now all is right in my world and for this I am so grateful.

Chapter 4

Jenny sat on the wobbly chair at the bus station, her red backpack at her feet. Inside it held all her worldly possessions: some clothing, a few toy figurines, a cheap plastic wallet and an old birthday card from her grandmother. Closing her eyes, she could almost imagine the swaying porch swing they would have once they were settled into a house in their new town. Though it was nearly midnight and her eyes felt scratchy and heavy, Jenny felt a bubbling anticipation that came with something new. She rocked back and forth in the lopsided chair, punctuated with a satisfying thunk each time the chair legs hit the floor, until the old woman sitting next to her started making impatient clucking sounds with her tongue. Jenny reluctantly opened her eyes to find the tsking woman wearing a red-and-pink-flowered sundress and a scowl. The woman was frowning so deeply at Jenny that the corners of her down-turned mouth seemed to have collapsed into her thick neck.

Jenny pretended not to notice and rocked the chair a few more times for good measure and then hopped to her feet to join her father, who was deep in conversation with a young woman with midnight-black hair, an intricate tattoo that crept up the woman's arm and a nose ring. Jenny was accustomed to this, her father striking up conversations with strange women. Jenny always knew when he was going to make his move. He would run his fingers through his shaggy, brown hair shot through with copper and rub his palms against his cheeks as if checking the length of his stubble, and there was always stubble. Women loved her father. At least for a while anyway. He was almost movie-star handsome, but not quite, which made people like him all the more. His nose was a bit too prominent and slightly off center. His skin was tanned and deeply trenched lines scored his forehead and the corners of his blue eyes, making him appear much older than his thirty years. In the past six months a parade of women had come in and out of their lives. There was the checkout girl at the grocery store that always slid a pack of gum into their bag for Jenny. "My treat," she said, not even looking at Jenny, keeping her smile brightly focused on Billy. There was the bank teller, the lady who decorated cakes at the bakery and even the nurse at the emergency room, who spent more time chatting with Billy than attending to the three-inch gash that Jenny got when she ran into the metal frame of the opened screen door. The nurse, a lively redhead with the pretty face and the curves Jenny knew her father favored, pressed a wad of gauze into Jenny's fingers. "Hold that against your head, sweetie. The doctor will be here in a few minutes to stitch you up," the nurse told her while glancing surreptitiously at her father's ringless left hand.

"Stitches?" Jenny squawked.

"Won't hurt a bit," the nurse assured her. "We're

good here." The nurse was right—it was, for the most part, painless. Instead of stitches, the doctor applied a thin layer of medical glue to her forehead, fusing the wound together. The worst part was lying on her back waiting for the glue to dry while her father stood on one side of the examination table and the nurse on the other, making plans to meet after her shift was over.

Then there was Jenny's favorite friend-girl (she refused to call them his girlfriends), Connie, who he dated last winter. She was a curvy woman who always wore a sweet, dimpled smile and her curly brown hair pulled back in a high ponytail. Connie had long, perfectly shaped fingernails that she had manicured every single Thursday after she got off work from her job at a hardware store. Holding Connie's small, feminine hand in his, Jenny's father used to laugh that such pretty fingers could handle a hammer much better than he ever could. Sometimes Connie would come from the salon with her nail tips painted a crisp white; sometimes they were lacquered neon-green or painted in a shimmery blue. Jenny's favorite was when she came from the salon and there would be tiny jewels inset into each of her nails. One day, to Jenny's surprise, when Jenny had finally gotten used to finding Connie blow-drying her hair in the apartment's small bathroom or coming home from school to the smell of the turtle brownies that Connie was baking, Connie invited Jenny to go with her to the salon. Jenny picked out a pearly lilac-purple shade and minuscule silver gems that formed a butterfly on the nail of each of her thumbs.

By the time the last of the sparkling jewels fell away, the polish chipped and peeling, Connie was gone. Jenny demanded that her father tell her what had happened.

Did they have an argument? *Say you're sorry.* Jenny asked her father if he was drinking again. *You said you weren't going to do that anymore!* Her father winced as if Jenny had slapped him when she asked him if Connie left them because of his drinking. He insisted that wasn't the case and Jenny knew that he was telling the truth. He got up each morning, walked her to school, went off to work as a painter for an area contractor, came home each night by six. Connie would often join them for supper and they would watch TV, even play board games together. And even though his hands shook sometimes and once in a while his eyes flashed desperately for a brief moment, he didn't act like he was drinking. *Then what was it?* Jenny asked. Did Jenny do something that made Connie leave? *I'll say I'm sorry.* Jenny knew that some of her father's friend-girls thought she was a pest, always in the way, but not Connie. She always made a point to invite Jenny on their outings even when it was clear that her father wanted Jenny to skedaddle.

For about six months, Connie and her father had been inseparable and Jenny thought that they actually might get married. Though she never said anything to her father, Jenny imagined being the flower girl in their wedding and living together in Connie's tidy little house. Unfortunately, their relationship ended as all her father's relationships did. Badly.

"No," her father had said when Jenny worried out loud that she was the one who had driven Connie away. He pulled her into a tight hug. "It has nothing to do with you. It just didn't work out." Jenny remembered stiffening against her father's embrace, not quite believing him.

A few days after Connie left, Jenny discovered the real reason for her departure. She tumbled out of bed and padded out of her little room into her father's bedroom to wake him up for work. She found him in bed intertwined with a slim, pale-skinned woman with curly hair that fell down her naked back. The room smelled of sweat and beer and of something that Jenny knew had to do with being naked and in bed. She tripped out of the room and ran to the bathroom, slammed the door and locked it. She turned on the shower and sat on the lid of the toilet and cried.

But still, Jenny found herself looking for Connie's face among crowds of people, hoping to see her again if even for a minute.

Jenny stepped in between her father and the tattooed woman who were talking about how it was too bad that they were both leaving Benton tonight on different buses. Jenny tugged on her father's sleeve, but on and on they went.

"Hey, Jenny Penny," her father finally said, dragging his eyes away from the woman. "Why don't you see if you can find our seats on the bus?" He handed her a ticket and his heavy duffel bag.

Jenny had never been on such a big bus before. School buses and city buses, certainly. But this enormous silver-and-blue bus with the sleek dog on the side was very different from her typical modes of transportation. The mustard-yellow school bus that squealed, groaned and belched black smoke when it picked her up on the corner of Fremont Street, just down the road from their last apartment, always smelled vaguely of peanut butter sandwiches and body odor.

This bus was three times as big as the motel room

they left behind and smelled, Jenny realized happily, breathing in deeply, like nothing. Jenny, setting her book bag and her father's duffel bag in the aisle, slid into one of the high-backed seats that was covered in peacock-blue fabric and looked out the window. Her father was still outside talking to the lady with the tattooed arm, so she turned her attention to her immediate surroundings and stepped out into the aisle that intersected the two halves of the bus.

Jenny, surprised that so many people had somewhere to go at midnight on a Monday, surveyed the passengers already seated on the bus: a woman with skin the color of cinnamon and a hopeful smile, a sad-eyed woman with four children, three of which needed a tissue, a man in a black suit and red tie already slumped in sleep. And to her dismay, the frowning old woman in the red-and-pink sundress. Before the woman could notice her, Jenny, clutching the book bag and duffel, dashed to the rear of the bus and plunked into the last seat on the right and waited for her father. From behind the high-backed seat, Jenny watched as the final cluster of passengers boarded the bus. There was a dazed-looking grandmotherly type with sugar-spun white hair, a blissfully happy-looking young man holding the hand of a pretty girl wearing jeans and a diaphanous bridal veil, and a stooped elderly man with thick glasses and an intricately carved wooden cane. Jenny pressed her nose against the cool, tinted window to see if her father was still talking to the tattoo lady. She was still there, leaning against the brick building, illuminated beneath the parking lot lights, but there was no sign of her father.

The bus was steadily filling with people and, despite her reluctance, Jenny was beginning to feel excited about the trip. The prospect of her father having a steady, well-paying job meant that there would be no more mortifying trips to the food pantry, no more of the teacher's helper who scanned her lunch ticket at school and slipped bags of Goldfish Crackers and baggies of carrot sticks into her locker each day. No more collecting and rationing foodstuff for when her father was having one of his bad spells.

As the passengers embarked, Jenny braced herself for being kicked out of her seat, relegated to sitting next to the frowning woman or the old woman with hair so white that Jenny had to wonder what had frightened her so badly that it would turn her hair that color. To her surprise, no one tried to rouse her from her seat and she began to relax a bit.

"Good evening, folks," the driver said into the loudspeaker, his voice booming throughout the bus. "Please find your seats and we'll be on our way." Jenny squirmed in her seat and considered getting off the bus to go and find her father, who was probably in the bathroom or, more likely, talking to another woman. Jenny arranged her book bag and her father's duffel carefully across the blue plush seats so as to cause no question that these seats were taken. As she looked out the window she suddenly caught a glimpse of her father, head down, walking quickly around the corner of the bus station and out of sight. Jenny sighed. She had no idea what her father was up to, but it was becoming very clear that they were not going anywhere today. With a huff that blew the bangs off her forehead, Jenny made the decision to get off the bus and rejoin her father.

Jenny stood and hooked her book bag around her shoulder and was halfway bent over to retrieve the duffel when out of the corner of her eye she saw a tall, weedy, ponytailed man turn the corner just behind her father. She straightened and watched in disbelief as her father emerged from behind the other side of the bus station casting furtive glances over his shoulder. Two more men appeared and her father stopped short, hands up in placation as they circled around him, fingers poking at his chest. Jenny's first instinct was to rush off the bus and to her father's side but found that she couldn't move, could barely breathe. The meanest looking of the men, barrel-chested and shaped like a fire hydrant, grabbed her father's face between his thick fingers, causing his lips to pucker as if preparing for a kiss.

Just as the bus rumbled to life, the hum of its engine vibrating in her ears, Jenny tried to call out, "Wait," but words stuck drily in the back of her throat. The bus lurched forward and, off balance, Jenny fell back into her seat just as sirens filled the air. Immediately she slouched low in her seat. Her father hated the police and didn't hesitate to share his distrust with Jenny. "See the cops coming," he would say, "go the other direction."

"Why?" Jenny would probe.

Her father would just shake his head. "Best they don't find you. You don't want to end up in foster care again, do you?"

Jenny most definitely did not want to be sent off to a foster family again. Not that it had anything to do with her father. Her stint in foster care was just before she came to live with her father. No, that was her mother's doing. And the man who stole her mother away from her. Foster care was an experience that she didn't want to relive, though she was only four at the time and had only scant recollections. Snapshots of half-formed memories that she tried to blink away.

Through the rear window, she saw her father lifted roughly to his feet by a police officer. She could see that he was speaking earnestly to the officer, bobbing his head frantically toward the departing bus. She should holler out to the bus driver to stop. That she needed to get off. Instead, Jenny stayed silent, turned her head the other way, just like her father told her to when it came to the police, and hunkered down in her seat, last row, right side. She pulled her book bag onto her lap, leaned forward and pressed her cheek into the seat in front of her, now damp with her tears, and watched as the buildings, the houses, the streets of Benton sped past.

Chapter 5

I awake with a start. The room is too bright, the light streaming across my face much too warm for six in the morning, even though it's the middle of July and the hottest summer on record in more than a decade.

"Adam," I say, looking over at my husband who, jaw slack in sleep, is snoring. I used to, when I had time, in those brief moments when the children were asleep, when work could wait, watch my husband while he slept. The way his brown hair curled around his ears, the dark shadow that magically appeared on his chin during the night. The way, through the years, his face became fuller, more creased, like a love letter folded over and over and opened to be read and reread.

"Adam," I say, leaping from the bed. "It's almost eight o'clock! Get up!" He pops up, eyes wide.

"Jesus, I've got practice in a half an hour!" He is already heading toward the bathroom. "Did you set the alarm?"

"I thought I set it!" I say, trying to recall.

"Remember you're dropping Avery off at the sitter's and I'll take Leah and Lucas with me to practice," Adam says as my cell phone begins to ring. I grab it from my bedside table. Checking the display, I see an unfamiliar number and I ignore it.

"Yeah, okay." I scramble from the bed. The night before is a haze. All I remember is falling into bed exhausted. "I've got a meeting in ten minutes. I can't be late again." But I'm talking to the closed bathroom door, my voice drowned out by the sound of the shower. I rush to the extra bathroom that the kids use and strip off the t-shirt that is still damp with last night's heat. I step beneath the showerhead, letting the cold spray envelope my body. I don't bother to wash my hair but run the bar of soap across my skin, scrubbing the salt of my sweat away. I rinse quickly, avoid looking at my stomach, still slack from giving birth eleven months earlier, and wrap a towel around myself and briefly mourn the loss of my once fit body, uninterrupted sleep, time alone with my husband and evenings out with my friends. "Leah, Lucas, it's time to get up!" I holler as I make my way back to my bedroom.

Adam is sitting on the bed, pulling on his socks. "The kids are up already. I sent them down to grab something to eat before we leave."

"Avery?" I ask, pulling on the first outfit I see in my closet as I step into a pair of sandals.

"Leah changed her diaper and got her dressed. She's in her crib. I'll bring her down," he says, rising from the bed and then hurrying from the room.

"Thanks," I say and run a hand through my cropped hair, once again glad that I keep it short. I finish dressing as my cell phone sitting in its charger on the bedside table begins to vibrate. "Damn," I murmur, and check the display. It's my mother. I meant to call her back last night, but between the baseball game and feeding and bathing the kids, I had forgotten. Again.

I think of the morning after my father had died. My mother rose early, as she normally did, and moved quietly from the bedroom to the kitchen, trying not to awaken me and my brothers ensconced in our childhood bedrooms. She didn't hear me as I followed behind her, silently observing. I watched as she absentmindedly opened the freezer stuffed full of all the things that my father loved best, the foods that he would never be able to eat again. My mother blinked back tears and pulled out the date-nut bread, double wrapped in aluminum foil, the Danish meatballs in Tupperware, and a small container of rice and salmon casserole, and set them on the kitchen counter. Lastly, she pulled out the unopened pint-size container of banana-flavored ice cream dotted with chocolate chunks and walnuts that was my father's favorite.

"Mom," I said, startling her, "what are you doing?"

I looked at the open freezer. "Mom?" I said again, a lilt of fear creeping into my voice. "What's going on?" I heard her stomach rumble in protest, but still she ate, moving on to a Ziplock bag filled with peanut butter crisscross cookies. "Mom!" I shouted, rousing Craig and Danny who by the time they ran down the stairs found me trying to wrestle the plastic bag from my mother, and her dog, Dolly, lapping up the crumbs that tumbled to the floor because of the tussle. We took my mother to the doctor, watched her carefully, encouraged her to get a part-time job, to volunteer. But life goes on. Our own lives resumed, my brothers going back to their own towns and families, me going back to work and my family. She seems better, but I know she is still so lonely and once again I utter a silent vow to spend more time with her.

I ignore the buzz but grab the phone and rush down the stairs, nearly tripping on the pile of folded laundry I had set there the night before to be put away. In the kitchen the TV is blaring, the phone is ringing and the kids are bickering over who gets the last Pop-Tart and who has to have a granola bar with raisins. In exasperation, Adam breaks both the Pop-Tart and the granola bar in halves and gives one each to the Leah and Lucas, who grumble anyway.

"Morning," I say, ignoring the phone and distractedly tucking my blouse into my skirt. Avery is in her high chair, her eyes still heavy with sleep. Leah has dressed her in one of her Sunday dresses and shoved tennis shoes on her feet. She looks beautiful. I bend over and lay a kiss on the top of her head and do the same to Leah and Lucas. "Thanks for helping out this morning, I gotta go," I say, and then stop short. "Damn," Lucas looks at me with reproach. "Sorry. Darn," I amend. "I left my bag upstairs."

I turn on my heel and hurry out of the kitchen. "Ellen," Adam calls after me, "I've got a game in Cherokee tonight, you're going to pick up Avery after work, too, right?" Adam's muffled words continue to follow me to the second floor but are blanketed by the buzz of my phone.

"Okay," I yell from the stairs. Maybe it's my mother again, or maybe Caren, my supervisor, wondering where I am. We have a staff meeting every Tuesday at eight and once again I'm running late. Not recognizing the number, I press the phone to my ear. "Hello," I say breathlessly. Nothing. No one is there. I shake my

head in frustration and grab my bag teeming with notes
and case files.

I skitter down the steps, weighed down by my bag,
and fling open the front door meeting Adam on his way
back in the house.

"Bye, guys!" I shout, blowing kisses in the direction of the kitchen. I am immediately met by the day's
heat; already it must be eighty degrees. As I open the
van door my phone rings again and I fumble for it in
the depths of my purse. Tumbling from my sweaty fingers to the driveway the phone bounces beneath the car.
"Dammit," I mutter, and try to tuck my skirt tightly
around my knees as I lower myself to the ground. The
ringing stops as I snake my hand beneath the van's
carriage, but the phone is not quite within my reach.
Sharp pebbles bite into my knees as I try to angle my
way closer. Again my phone rings. I slip off my sandal
and, using the heel as a hook, I snag the phone, pulling
it within my reach and it falls silent. Sweat has soaked
through my blouse and my skirt is dusty and wrinkled.
I glance at my watch before getting up. I'm late as it is.
The meeting has already started and I will be lucky to
get there before it even adjourns. No time to change my
clothes. I slide into the driver's seat and the heat seeps
through the fabric of my skirt.

Sweetly, Adam has started the van for me and luke-
warm air from the air conditioner strikes ineffectually
at my face. From the front steps Adam is waving. I catch
snippets of what he is saying, *practice, day care, kids.* I
wave back and give him a thumbs-up as my phone trills
once again. "Hello," I say breathlessly into the receiver
as I brush my sweaty bangs from my forehead.

The voice on the other end is young and frantic

sounding, unintelligible. "Slow down," I urge as I put the van into Reverse. "I can't understand you." I back out of my driveway and head toward the office.

I listen for a moment finally realizing that it's Kylie, a seven-year-old client of mine. "Where are they now?" There is no answer. Just heavy, frantic breaths. "Where are you? Are you safe?" I ask. *In the bathroom, I don't know,* she answers uncertainly, more of a whimper actually, and a nugget of fear settles in my chest. Across the phone line I hear a heavy thud. "I'm calling the police and I'll be right over. I promise," I say, but the line is already dead. I stop the van in the middle of the road to dial 911 and I'm vaguely aware of cars honking at me from behind. I give the emergency operator the address, tell her who I am and what little I know about the situation. Cool air is finally puffing through the vents, but I barely notice it as I wrench the steering wheel to the right and pull into the nearest driveway so I can turn around.

Chapter 6

Jenny gradually awoke to the not so unpleasant feeling of being gently swayed back and forth. Disoriented, her mouth sticky and dry, she sat up in her seat, stretched and looked around. With dread she realized that she was not in the musty smelling hotel with her father snoring loudly in the bed across from her, but all by herself on a bus traveling through the countryside.

A few new passengers must have boarded while she was sleeping. In the seat across the aisle was a scraggly man wearing a camouflage jacket, eyes closed, headphones covering his ears; in front of her and to the right was a plump man wearing khaki pants and a striped button-down shirt. The bride and groom had gotten off the bus somewhere along the way as had the businessman. Remaining were the crabby old woman and the lady with the white hair.

Jenny looked out the window where fields painted with gold and green rolled past. She had no idea how much time had gone by, though the sun had risen, and had no inkling as to where she was. A spasm of anxiety filled her chest and tears bunched in the corners of her eyes. The man in the khakis glanced back at her, a look of concern crinkling his friendly face. Jenny bowed her head and she began rummaging through her book bag until she found the bottle of water she had tossed in when she packed her few belongings. The quickest way to find your way into foster care, Jenny knew, was to gain the attention of some well-meaning adult. She blinked back her tears, twisted the lid and tilted the plastic bottle so that the warm water filled her mouth. After replacing the lid and returning it to her bag, Jenny turned her attention to her father's duffel bag, which lay on the floor beneath her feet, and wondered what had happened to him. Remembering the wail of the sirens and the policeman yanking her father to his feet, she figured he was in a jail cell back in Benton. Jenny realized she had abandoned him by remaining on the bus, too scared to move. Jenny's face reddened in shame and she felt the weight of her father's cell phone in her pocket.

She could call the Benton police department and tell them who she was and what she had seen, that it was the three men who had attacked her father. But what would that mean for her? Maybe it would be best if at the next bus station she just hopped on a bus back to Benton. Then she could talk to the police in person, or maybe by then the whole misunderstanding would have been worked out. Jenny had the feeling it wasn't going to be that simple.

She could call her father's former friend-girl. Connie would know what to do. But what could she possibly say to her? Connie and her dad hadn't parted on the best of terms. Her father wasn't mean. He got grouchy once in a while when he got one of his headaches or when his hands started to shake, but he always went right to bed or out for a little while and then he would wake up or come back and be just fine. But Jenny knew that something wasn't quite right about her father. He couldn't keep a job; they never stayed in one place for more than a few months, sleeping on couches and floors of friends, moving in and out of run-down apartments and hotels. Plus he had so many friend-girls that sometimes he would confuse their names.

Even if she could explain to Connie what she had seen, what if her father went to jail for a long time? Then what would happen to her? Why would Connie care? Back to Benton? Back to another foster family. Maybe back to the same foster family she was with when she was little, before she got to live with her father all the time. Never.

She tried to think of who else she could call. Her mother? No. She didn't know where she was, hadn't heard a peep from her since she ran away with Jimmy. When she tried to bring up the topic of her mother with her father, his lips would press into a thin tight line and he would pull Jenny close to him. "You don't want to think about that now. You're safe. No one will hurt you ever again. I promise." Jenny thought about telling him that she wasn't ever really afraid of her mother. Her mother's boyfriend, yes. And even he wasn't always such a bad guy, but when he was mean he was really mean. Besides, she wanted to tell him, there were many kinds of hurt. There was, of course, the pain of being beaten, but there was also the ache that stretched itself across your belly when you realized that your mother was never coming back. Jenny also wanted to tell her father, but wasn't quite sure how to put it into words, that the very worst kind of hurt was the kind that wasn't there yet, but you knew was slowly creeping toward you.

In the seat across the aisle, the rumpled man wearing the camouflage jacket stood, his knees crackling as he rose and stretched his arms above his head. Unsmiling, he nodded at her as he stepped into the aisle and wedged his way through the narrow bathroom door.

Jenny bent over and unzipped her father's duffel bag, hoping to find something, anything that would help her get out of this mess. She riffled past two pairs of jeans, four shirts, underwear, a pair of dress pants that she'd never seen before, a disposable razor, deodorant and a box of condoms. Jenny recoiled. She never actually thought of her father having sex, but of course he did, with all the women who came in and out of their apartment over the years. She learned all about condoms on the school bus while eavesdropping on a conversation between two middle-school girls. "It unrolls right over it," a girl with purple streaks in her hair and a mouth filled with braces explained to her skeptical seatmate with canary-yellow hair and eyes heavily lined with black makeup. The two girls looked up to find Jenny peeking over the seat. The two began giggling, huddled more closely together, lowered their voices and resumed their conversation, but Jenny could still hear.

Jenny pushed the box of condoms to the bottom of the bag and turned her attention to an overstuffed manila envelope that was sealed shut. She pulled it out of the duffel bag and turned it over in her hands. The envelope was wrinkled and battered and there was no writing on the outside to indicate what the contents were. Jenny was picking at the red string that was wound tightly around a small, round metal clasp at the top of the envelope when she felt someone settle in the seat next to her. Startled, Jenny looked up to find the plump man wearing khaki pants in the seat next to her. "You looked lonely back here all by yourself," he said with a wide grin that showed a set of small, straight white teeth. Tic Tacs came to Jenny's mind. "You hungry? I've got trail mix." He produced a baggie filled with nuts, dried fruit and chocolate chips and shook it at her like she could be lured like a hungry puppy.

Jenny shook her head. "Excuse me," she said, "I need to go to the bathroom."

"Someone's already in there," the man said. "He didn't look so good. He might be in there for a while." Jenny looked around the bus, hoping to get someone's attention, but the other passengers were near the front of the bus. She'd have to yell and what did she have to holler about? A man with trail mix? A pink flush had risen up the man's neck and he leaned in closely to Jenny so that she could feel his breath on her cheek. His short, pudgy fingers released the plastic bag and it dropped heavily into her lap. Before the man could retrieve the bag and just as the man in the army jacket emerged from the bathroom Jenny stood up, causing dried cranberries and peanuts to spill to the floor.

"Jeez," she exclaimed. "Took you long enough, Uncle Mike." Jenny squeezed past the surprised man in the seat next to her and quickly stepped into the bathroom, slammed the door and slid the lock into place. Jenny breathed a sigh of relief. If the man in the army coat was surprised at being called uncle, he didn't let on and she hoped that he wouldn't tell the creepy man with the trail mix otherwise. The bathroom was tiny and dimly lit. Realizing she really did have to go to the bathroom, she set the manila envelope she was carrying carefully on the edge of the small sink, spread toilet paper around the rim of the toilet seat as her father had always told her to do. When Jenny was finished and had washed her hands, she found that she was hesitant to open the door and return to her seat, worried that the strange man was still there and that the army jacket man had told him that he wasn't really her uncle. She could stay where she was, ensconced within the stuffy, narrow walls of the bathroom and wait until the bus stopped or return to her seat where her book bag and father's duffel, and possibly the weird man waited for her. There was a sudden knock on the bathroom door, causing Jenny to jump and forcing her decision. Jenny slowly opened the door and found the grouchy old woman in the red-and-pink sundress waiting outside.

"Everything okay?" the woman asked. "I thought you fell in."

"I'm okay," Jenny murmured, ducking past her, relieved to see that the khaki man had returned to his own seat. She avoided eye contact with Uncle Mike, slid into her seat and dropped the manila envelope damp from her sweaty fingers on the chair next to her. Sensing the weight of his stare upon her, Jenny finally looked up to meet his gaze.

He leaned slightly toward her and whispered conspiratorially, "By the way, it's Uncle *Dave*." Jenny responded with a limp smile and returned her attention to the unopened envelope.

She tried to imagine what could be inside. She often played this game with wrapped birthday and Christmas presents, with unopened doors. Maybe there was a treasure map in the envelope with clues to a buried treasure, but the chance of a pirate's booty ending up in Iowa was not a good bet. Maybe there was a wad of money inside, enough for her to buy a bus ticket so that she could get back to Benton and get her father out of jail. Someone was always bailing someone out of jail on television. She could imagine herself walking into the police station, wearing her blue-jean skirt and her best polo shirt. Soft pink and sporting an alligator emblem, she saved this shirt for the most special of occasions: school concerts, holidays, and now for bailing her father out of jail. "Here," she would say importantly as she slapped the money down on the counter. "Billy Briard is coming with me now." The policeman behind the counter would be impressed and quickly bring her father to her.

"If you just open it you'll find out what's inside," the man in camouflage offered. Though Jenny saw the wisdom in this, she was undecided. Inside the envelope could be something awful, the evidence of a terrible crime, some apparently deadly powder that is always being sent in the mail to courthouses and important people. But, even worse, there could be nothing inside. Nothing of value anyway. Receipts or bills or boring clippings from the newspaper. She dared a look at her newly acquired uncle Dave. He was staring expectantly at her as if saying, *Just open it already.* Jenny unwound the red string and pushed back the flap. Peering inside the envelope she could see that she was right on almost all counts. There was no toxic powder, but the envelope held a map, a wad of money and a stack of smaller envelopes held together with a thick rubber band.

"You want me to call someone for you?" Uncle Dave asked, wagging a cell phone toward her.

Jenny shook her head and held up her father's phone. "I'm good. Thanks though." Uncle Dave looked at her thoughtfully for a moment nodded and closed his eyes. Jenny pulled out the folded map of Iowa. It had been folded and unfolded so many times it looked as if it would disintegrate at any moment. "How far are we from Cedar City?" Jenny asked suddenly, struck with a wonderfully, startling idea.

Uncle Dave opened one eye. "It's the next stop, about an hour from here." He sat up, the narrow space between his eyes creased with worry. "You getting off there? You sure you've got someone meeting you? What town are you getting off at?"

"I'm getting off in Cedar City," Jenny answered, hope rising in her chest as the bus lumbered onward.

"Who's meeting you at the station?" Dave asked, his steadfast gaze making Jenny uncomfortable. She didn't like lying, especially to those who were nice to her, but it had never stopped her before.

"My grandma," Jenny said, pinning her eyes to Dave's. The quickest way for someone to figure out you're lying is if you look away when the hard questions are being asked. And, besides, she wasn't really lying, not really, she rationalized, thinking of the letter from her grandmother in the lavender envelope inside her backpack.

Dave didn't look convinced, but Jenny continued looking him in the eye until he sighed and reached for the phone she held in her hand. "Give me your phone and I'll put my number in. If you need something, give me a call and I'll try and help if I can." Jenny reluctantly handed him the phone and he began punching numbers. "Don't try and get so good at it." At Jenny's confused look, he went on. "Lying. Don't get so good at it that you forget what's real." Dave handed Jenny the phone and slumped back in his seat and closed his eyes.

Chapter 7

When I arrive at the familiarly ramshackle neighborhood, I am struck at how depressingly run-down it has gotten through the years. Burnt yellow lawns are edged with rusty metal fences, windows are boarded up and the ones that are intact are covered with grungy sheets or threadbare blankets.

Before I even turn onto Madison Street, I hear the sirens behind me. I pull to the side of the road to let a police car pass. *Please just be precautionary,* I say to myself, hoping that help hasn't arrived too late. I drive the final four blocks as people in the neighboring houses peek out screened windows and step out onto crumbling front steps to see what's happening. I stop three houses away, throw the van into Park and leap out and hit Lock on my key fob. The temperature has risen in just the few minutes I've been driving; the oppressive air crawls heavily into my nostrils and sits like sludge in my chest. Two police cars are idling in front of the house and I rush up to the nearest officer, who has emerged from his squad car and is calmly surveying the house that looks eerily quiet, empty.

Without looking at me, the officer holds up his hand to silence me before I even speak.

"Please stay back," he says.

"I'm Ellen Moore, the social worker. I called 911," I say, as if this explains everything.

He raises his eyebrows, finally looking me in the face. Sweat glistens on his bald forehead, his uniform already darkened with perspiration. "Officer Stamm," he introduces himself. "Then you probably know a lot more about what's going on in there than I do. What's the situation?"

I try to keep my voice composed, level, but it still shakes with fear. "Manda Haskins lives here with her two children, Kylie who is seven and Krissie is four. Kylie called me a few minutes ago and said that her mom's boyfriend, whom Manda has a temporary restraining order against, came over last night. Kylie said that this morning he started beating up their mother, so she and her little sister locked themselves in the bathroom and called me. We got disconnected and then I called you. I'm afraid the boyfriend is done with the mom and now is going after the girls."

I don't have time to go into the entire all-too-familiar story of Manda Haskins's life with Officer Stamm. That Manda is twenty-five years old but still seems to always choose the wrong man. She may have been pretty once, but now Manda looks closer to forty than twenty-five— a meth addiction will do that to you. Her face is set in a permanent scowl. Manda lost custody of Kylie and Krissie two years ago when the police stopped her van and found that she was housing a mobile meth lab inside. She swore that her boyfriend was the one who placed all the drug paraphernalia in the back. In return for testifying against the boyfriend and admitting herself into an inpatient drug treatment center, Manda avoided jail time. In foster care the two children did well and all thought that Manda had done the work. Gotten clean, gotten a job. I'd hoped for so much more for Manda and her girls, but apparently her self-improvement didn't extend to her choice in men.

"Any weapons in the house that you know about?" Officer Stamm asks.

I shake my head. "No. I mean I don't know. Have you been able find out what's going on inside?"

"Not yet. We're going to walk around the house, take a look in the windows, see if we can hear anything. Have you tried to call the kids back?" Stamm asks.

"No," I say. "I was afraid if the phone started ringing it might lead the boyfriend to where Kylie and Krissie are hiding. Should I call now?"

"Yeah, go ahead. We'll walk around the perimeter and see if we can hear a phone ringing. That might give us an idea of where the kids are. If the kids or the mom answer, try to find out the status of the situation and keep them on the line." Stamm and the other officer begin to make their way around the house and I scroll through my received calls to find the number that Kylie called me from, hit Send and the phone goes directly to voice mail. Stamm looks at me over his shoulder and I shake my head in disappointment. He rotates his hand in a keep-trying gesture. I scan my phone looking for Manda's contact information. In the back of my mind I remember that at one time she had a landline number as well as a cell phone. I locate the number, press Send and an instant later I can hear the faint trill of a phone ringing from within the house.

A woman, a neighbor I presume, sidles up next to me. "What's going on?" she asks. I give her a cursory look. She is wearing flip-flops, flannel boxers, a tank top and holds a crusty-nosed toddler on her hip.

"I'm sorry, I can't talk right now," I say to her, and take two steps toward the house. The phone continues to ring and ring. "What's going on?" the woman asks again, this time more insistently. The boy in her arms begins to giggle, a strange sound amid such a tense situation. I turn to face the woman and immediately recognize her as one my former clients, a woman whose son was removed from her home because of severe neglect. "Jade, Anthony," I say. I give the little boy's bare foot a squeeze and he smiles shyly back at me before burying his face in his mother's shoulder. I lower my phone down to my side as it continues to ring, unanswered from within the house. "It's Manda Haskins. The police are afraid that she's got some trouble in there and are worried about her girls."

Jade shakes her head, her dark eyes knowingly serious. "Haven't met her new boyfriend, but I've seen him coming and going. Used to be Manda would be outside all the time in her front yard while the girls played. Her Kylie is real good with Anthony here. They would sit in their little pool." She nods toward the small, round, plastic pool. A yellow duck floats aimlessly and a few Barbie dolls are submerged in the shallow, dirty water. "It's too hot to be inside."

"You don't see them outside much anymore?" I ask.

"No." Jade shifts Anthony to her other hip. "The boyfriend is over all the time and Manda won't let the girls outside by themselves. Haven't seen much of them the past three weeks or so..." Jade trails off and we both watch as Officer Stamm and his partner emerge from the other side of the house and make their way back toward to where we are standing.

"No answer," I say, indicating the still-ringing phone. "Did you see anything?"

"No," the female officer says, running a forearm across her sweaty forehead. "The house is shut down tight. Shades are drawn and the only sound is the phone ringing."

We are silent for a moment, quietly regarding the house. I don't see any sign of activity. "Jesus," Stamm whispers. "It's hotter than hell standing out here. Call for another car," he tells the other officer, "I'm going to go knock on the front door."

I'm vaguely aware of movements behind me. Curious onlookers and neighbors trying to see what is going on.

Jade lays a hand on my arm. "Look," she says, and all our eyes fix upon the front of the house. "Something's happening inside."

There is movement behind the curtains at the front of the house and my attention returns to the Haskinses' home. Abruptly the ringing stops and I quickly raise my cell phone to my ear. "Hello," I say fervently. "Kylie, is that you? Are you okay?"

"Uh-huh," the little girl whispers.

"Where are you?"

"Inside," she whispers.

"Where at inside? Are you in the kitchen, the living room...?"

"The TV room," she answers. Her voice is small and so scared sounding.

"Where's Krissie?" I ask. I tilt the phone away from

my ear so that Officer Stamm can hear what Kylie is saying.

"She's still in the bathroom."

"Good. That's good," I reassure her. "Where's your mommy?"

Kylie's voice quivers. "I don't know. The bedroom door is locked. There was yelling and loud noises and then it stopped. I was afraid to knock. Should I go knock?"

"No, no, Kylie, stay right here with me," I say in a rush, desperate to keep her on the line.

"Tell her we're coming to the door," Officer Stamm instructs.

I cover my hand over the phone. "Can't I go to the door to get them? The kids know me. They won't be afraid of me."

Stamm shakes his head. "No. Too dangerous. Stay down here and you'll be the first person they see when they come out. Tell them that two police officers are coming to the door."

"Kylie, honey," I say. "Two nice police officers are going to come to the door. You open it up for them and then they'll be able to check on your mom, okay?" I nod at Stamm and the two officers move toward the front door.

"Okay," Kylie answers. "Should I go back to the bathroom and get Krissie?"

"No, no. Lay the phone down but don't hang it up. The police officers are almost to the door. Okay, Kylie, go open the door. I'm right outside waiting for you." The front door opens a crack and a short beep indicates that I have another call coming in. I ignore it.

Shouts come from behind me, and when I turn I

find that a handful of people are not watching to see what is happening in the house. They are turned in the opposite direction, their backs to the drama unfolding right in front of them. I face the house again. Stamm and the other officer cautiously enter the home, hands near their weapons. More hollering from behind me, this time urgent, frantic sounding. The commotion behind us has also caught Jade's attention and I can tell she is torn between attending to what is happening in the home and the flurry behind us.

I hang up my phone, confident that the officers are in the house and will bring the girls out safely.

Immediately my phone begins to buzz. I look at the display. Three missed calls, all from Adam. I shove the phone into the pocket of my skirt.

The screen door opens and, to my relief, Kylie and Krissie are being led out of the home. As they exit, I see the fear and uncertainty on Kylie's face and it breaks my heart. I rush forward to meet them, taking comfort in that I will be a familiar face to them and I will whisk them to safety. But I also know that they will hate me. I will be the one who may have to place them in a new foster home, the one who may take them away from their mother whom they love unconditionally, without question, without asking for anything in return. I hope that the entire situation was just an awful misunderstanding. I pray their mother is still alive.

Before I can gather the girls into my arms there is a sharp crack and the sound of broken glass. The crowd behind me has grown and I see that they have gathered around the source of the broken glass. My van. Someone is breaking into my car in broad daylight, a police officer less than a block away. The nerve. But very quickly I realize that these thieves aren't wayward teenage boys with too much time on their hands, but a group of women and a lone man. Mothers and grandmothers by the looks of them, and an old man wielding a crowbar. He steadies himself by placing a hand on the hood of the van, his chest rising and falling heavily. The crowbar slips from his hand, clanking to the ground. A heavyset woman reaches through the broken window and violently flings open the sliding door. She disappears for just a moment and then emerges. It's then that I see what they already know. A flash of pink, a dangling shoelace.

"Oh, my God." A voice I don't recognize as my own erupts from my throat. "Please, no," I whimper. I run toward the van.

It's a terrible thing when you discover your child's life is in danger. God or evolution or whatever you believe in must equip our bodies, our minds, our souls with some sort of talisman. At first I can't believe that it's Avery. She should be at the babysitter's house gnawing on a graham cracker, playing with the other one-year-olds, piling big plastic blocks on top of one another. How did she get in the van? I know I didn't put her there. Did I? No, it was Adam, I think, remembering how I met him coming back into the house just as I was leaving. How could I not even know she was strapped into the seat directly behind me?

The world becomes silent, I see mouths moving but no sound emerges. A numbness has crept into my limbs; a curious heaviness weighs down my extremities. I pray that what I'm witnessing right before me is all a terrible mistake. The bluish tinge that rings Avery's lips is just the slant of light through trees. The way her hands lie limply at her side just means that she is very tired. It is just about time for her morning nap.

Too soon, much too quickly, I realize what I am so desperately trying to deny.

I reach for Avery and the minute she is in my arms I know that nothing will ever be the same, will ever be right again. The heat is rising from her skin searing into my own. There is no flutter beneath her eyelids to let me know she is just sleeping, no discernible rise and fall of her chest. There is nothing. Just as quickly as I have bundled Avery into my arms she is pulled away from me and I am left empty-handed with only the sound of my own cries and the question roiling over and over in my head. *What have you done? What have you done?*

Chapter 8

Jenny was a bit disappointed as the bus made its way into the town of Cedar City. It looked identical to what she knew of Benton. She had been hoping for something new, something greener, maybe. More flowers, more trees, maybe a cornfield or two. Instead, there was just a whole lot of swaying power lines, stores and restaurants with desperate weeds poking up through the cracks of the gray cement.

The bus pulled into the bus station and Jenny hesitated. Should she get off the bus now or continue on to Dubuque, maybe try to find Matthew, her father's friend? With a hiss the bus shuddered to a stop and several passengers stood, gathered their belongings and disembarked. Jenny looked down at her father's overstuffed duffel at her feet and knew she wouldn't be able to drag it very far. Quickly she examined the contents one more time, searching for items of value. In a side pocket she found some loose change and a pack of gum. She shoved these into the front pocket of her jean shorts. Buried beneath a pile of her father's socks and underwear was a charger for the cell phone and as

Jenny slid it into her backpack the driver made one last call for anyone getting off the bus.

With one last swipe, Jenny grabbed her father's favorite t-shirt from the duffel and held it briefly to her nose, inhaling the familiar, slightly smoky scent that was her father. The t-shirt was washed and had been worn so many times that it was faded to a water-washed indigo-blue, and the motorcycle emblem on the back was cracked and peeling. Finding no more room in her backpack, Jenny tied the t-shirt around her narrow waist, wiggled into her backpack and, holding tightly to the envelope, made her way up the aisle toward the exit.

"Hey," Dave called after her, "take care, niece!"

"You, too, Uncle Dave." Jenny smiled in return. She felt slightly better knowing that she had Dave's number in the cell phone, but knew she would never use it. On shaky legs, Jenny descended the bus. The air outside was warm and thick with moisture. Jenny squinted up into the sky where white horsetail clouds filtered the sun. Jenny tried to remember the real name of the clouds, cumulo or nimbus something or other. She couldn't quite recall. But Jenny did remember how her teacher described the wispy clouds as resembling the tail of a horse. Jenny had visions of spectral-like white ponies galloping through the skies.

Jenny tried to push down the anger she felt toward her father for getting her into this mess—allowing her to be swept away all alone on a bus only to land in a strange town, hundreds of miles from anything that was familiar. But she couldn't keep the hot tears from gathering in her eyes or keep the panic from nesting within her rib cage. She didn't know what to do. Immediately get a ticket back to Benton? Call one of her father's old friend-girls to come and get her? Connie came to mind again. She pictured her friendly face. Everything about Connie was big. Big hair, big smile, big chest, big heart. She was the only one Jenny could bear calling. Or maybe she should go to the nearest police station. Jenny knew she needed to make a plan. This was something her special education teacher, Ms. Lugar, always said. *When in doubt, make a list, think it through and make a decision.*

Jenny's stomach rumbled loudly with hunger and she looked around in embarrassment to see if anyone had heard. She made her way around the side of the bus station, the weight of her backpack already causing her shoulders to ache and slump, a small question mark standing on the corner. She decided to start by getting a snack from the vending machine inside the bus station and finding a place to sit down and make her list. Then she saw the most welcoming of sights just across the busy intersection: a slowly rotating yellow-and-blue sign that spelled Happy Pancake Restaurant in large bulbous letters. Jenny scurried across the busy street, not waiting for the flashing green light that signaled that it was safe to cross, ignoring the blare of car horns and shouts of irritated motorists.

Yanking open the heavy glass doors, Jenny inhaled the sweet, buttery scent that greeted her. This was only the second Happy Pancake that Jenny had ever been to, but she was relieved to find that it was exactly the same as the restaurant she and her father had visited the night before in Benton. The same high ceilings, crisply painted white walls punctuated with large framed photos of stacks of steaming pancakes topped with pats of melting butter and dripping with amber maple syrup.

Jenny's stomach grumbled again and she placed a hand over her midsection as if to shush it.

She tentatively looked around for the Happy Pancake mascot named Stack who handed out crayons and children's menus printed with tic-tac-toe grids and word searches and dot-to-dots. Jenny found Stack vaguely disturbing with his oversize pancake-shaped body and oversimplified features: wide staring eyes, a yellow mound of butter for a nose and an upturned strip of bacon for a mouth. Only the mascot's legs and arms sticking out from the vast costume gave any indication that something human resided beneath. Apparently, Stack didn't work the 8:00 a.m. to 4:00 p.m. shift at the Happy Pancake in Cedar City.

A weary waitress with a white ponytail and freckles dotting her nose approached, looking past Jenny's shoulder toward the front entrance as if expecting an accompanying adult would step forward. She was wearing standard Happy Pancake fare, a navy-blue skirt and a blue-and-yellow-checked blouse and a matching scarf tied at a jaunty angle around her neck. Black, thick crepe-soled shoes completed the outfit.

"I'm meeting my big sister here," Jenny lied effortlessly.

"Will it just be the two of you?" the waitress asked, leading Jenny to the table nearest to the door.

"Can we sit in the back there?" Jenny asked, turning slightly so that the waitress could see her backpack hanging from her shoulders. "Homework," she said by way of explanation. If the waitress thought that it was odd that a young girl had homework in the middle of July, she gave no indication. Maybe they had year-round school in this town; maybe the waitress thought that

Jenny was some kind of genius student who took college classes.

"Summer school, eh?" the waitress asked, her voice tinged with sympathy. "That's no fun."

"No," Jenny rushed to explain. "Gifted and talented. I skipped third grade."

"Good for you," the waitress said as she led Jenny to a large booth in the rear of the restaurant. "No one can ever take your education away from you. What are you reading?"

Jenny blinked, drawing a blank. She wasn't much of a reader, though she loved it when her teachers read out loud to her or when her father took the time to read her a book from the small stack of picture books that she brought home each week from the school library.

The waitress was looking at her with interest, waiting for her tell her the name of the genius-level book she was currently reading. Jenny's mind worked furiously trying to recall a title of a book, but all she could think of was *Little Turtle's First Day of School* and she could hardly say that. "The Bible," Jenny finally blurted out. "I go to a very religious school. I've already read half of it."

The waitress looked duly impressed as she set a large, glossy menu on the table. "I'll be back with some water for you. Can I get you anything else to drink?"

Jenny wriggled out of her backpack, slid into the high-backed booth and set the pack next to her on the midnight-blue faux leather seat. The smell of coffee made her think of her father.

She had come to love waking up to the pungent smell of her father's morning coffee. This meant that he was trying, that he was functioning well enough to get out of bed, to face the day, to go to work. The two of them would stand together at the kitchen counter, each sipping the black, caustic liquid. At first Jenny had winced, sticking out her tongue, rolling her eyes back in her head and making a gagging sound in response to the bitter taste, causing her father to laugh. Eventually she grew accustomed to the acrid sensation on her tongue, reveling in the bloom of warmth that flooded her mouth and coated her throat and to the zing of caffeine that nudged her into wakefulness. But most of all she loved the quiet moments with her father, both of them bleary-eyed, crunching on burnt toast and sipping their coffee from mismatched mugs.

"Coffee," Jenny said with confidence. The waitress stood there for a moment, pen poised over her order pad while Jenny busied herself with scanning the menu, trying not to blush beneath the waitress's puzzled gaze and realized her mistake. A waitress would easily remember a ten-year-old who ordered a cup of coffee and read the Bible for summer school. "It's for my sister," Jenny explained. "She'll be here any minute. I'll have milk." The waitress raised an eyebrow at Jenny, her green eyes unwavering. "Please," Jenny added contritely.

Soon the waitress returned, set the glass of milk in front of Jenny and poured a stream of black coffee from a stainless steel carafe into a ceramic white mug that she situated on the place mat across from Jenny. "No sister yet?" the waitress asked, tucking a loose strand of white hair behind her ear.

"Nah," Jenny said casually. "She's always late. I'll just go ahead and order." At the waitress's skeptical look Jenny dug into her backpack. "I've got money. See?" Jenny pulled a wad of cash from the manila envelope.

The waitress's eyes widened. "That's a lot of money, you better put that away," she warned, glancing left and right to see if any unsavory types were lurking around. "What can I get you?" she asked as Jenny shoved the money back into the envelope.

Jenny tapped her finger on her chin as she had seen her father do numerous times when trying to make a decision. "I think I'll have that," she said, poking her finger at a picture of a pile of oddly colored, red-tinted pancakes flanked by fluffy scrambled eggs and two strips of bacon. "Please," Jenny added after a beat.

"Velvety Red Pancake Platter. Good choice," the waitress murmured, writing down the order with a flourish. "I'll get that right in for you."

"Thanks," Jenny told her. "I'm not going anywhere until my sister gets here anyway."

After the waitress retreated, Jenny pulled the coffee cup toward her and breathed in the coil of steam that rose from the thick liquid. She could almost imagine her father sitting across from her in the booth, cracking jokes about the other passengers from the bus. *How 'bout that guy and the girl with the veil. Who would take their new wife on their honeymoon in a bus?* Jenny would have laughed right along with him, but inside she would zing back with, *At least he married her. You couldn't even do that.* Jenny often wondered how her life would be different if her mother and her father ever got married. Maybe her mother would never have run away; maybe her father wouldn't drink so much.

She swallowed hard and bit the insides of her cheeks to stop the tears that threatened to spill. While she waited for her food, Jenny covertly counted her money beneath the table. She lost count three times before determining that she had $633.42. She was rich. She had never seen so much money in her entire life and was a little miffed at her father for holding back on her. She had always thought they were broke. There never seemed to be enough money for new clothes or a trip to the movies; even groceries were iffy. But all along he had all this cash stashed away.

Next, Jenny pulled the photographs from the envelope. There was one of her smiling brightly up at her mother. Her mother looked back down at her, just a whisper of a smile playing at the corner of her mouth. Jenny stared hard at the photo, trying to remember the day the picture was taken. She must have been around three years old, taken before she went to live with her father. She carefully placed the picture back in the envelope when the waitress approached again.

"Here you go, dear," the waitress said, setting the plump stack of deep-red-colored pancakes in front of her. "The Velvety Red Platter." Hands on her hips, the waitress looked around. "No sister yet, huh?"

Jenny rolled her eyes as if this was to be expected. "She's always late—my dad's going to kill her."

"Maybe you should give her a call? Do you need to use a phone?"

Jenny waggled her father's cell phone. "I just called her. She said she's on her way."

"Okay, then. You just let me know if you need anything else. I'll check back with you in a few minutes." Jenny nodded, and was already forking up large pieces of pancake with one hand while pouring maple syrup over the stack already covered with cream-cheese icing and whipped cream when two police officers entered the restaurant and started moving toward her.

Chapter 9

My hands, now empty of my daughter, feel numb and are shaking violently. I paw at Jade, trying to retrieve my daughter's wilted form. "No," Jade says sharply, blocking my efforts. She has Avery lying on her back on the cracked concrete of the sidewalk and for a moment I imagine that it must be so uncomfortable for Avery, lying there, the ground hard and unyielding. Jade leans over, tilts Avery's head back and lifts her chin. *Oh my God, she's not breathing,* I realize as Jade presses her mouth over my daughter's lips and pushes her own air into Avery's lungs.

I notice Anthony standing near his mother, tears running down his cheeks. I have little to offer him. No comfort, no reassuring words, but without thinking, I reach for his hand and he tumbles into me, burying his face in my knees. Jade presses two fingers on Avery's breastbone and pushes down in quick, purposeful thrusts. I should be doing this. Giving my daughter CPR, saving her life. This is something I know how to do automatically, without even thinking. Clear airway. Two breaths. Thirty compressions. Two more breaths. Place your ear against the child's mouth. Listen for breathing. Can you see the rise and fall of the chest? Can you feel the tickle of breath against your cheek? Check for a pulse. Still not breathing? Still no pulse? Repeat. I know how to do this. Every social worker knows how to do this. It's part of our training. But I just stand here, swaying on wobbly legs until a pair of hands steadies me. I do nothing. Nothing. It occurs to me that I am watching my daughter die.

Again and again, Jade breathes, presses, checks, breathes, presses, checks until finally, finally she looks up at me. "I've got a pulse," she says with relief. In the distance I hear more sirens. An ambulance.

Jade must have learned CPR in the parenting class she was required to take by the Department of Human Services, required by *me* to complete in order for her to regain custody of Anthony, and I am so grateful. So indebted to this woman who was unable to care for her own child for a time. That his suffering has become my salvation. I fall to the ground, barely noticing my knees scraping against the jagged concrete. I reach out and lift Avery's tiny hand into my own and whisper a prayer for my daughter, who, to me, remains terrifyingly still.

Again I am nudged aside, this time more gently, by two paramedics. "Tell me what happened," one says, her voice clipped and businesslike. I can't answer her. I have absolutely no idea what has happened here. I close my eyes and run the events of the morning through my head over and over again. Did I put Avery in the car? I would remember, wouldn't I? Such a crazy morning. Overslept, showered, got dressed, kissed the kids good-bye, ran back upstairs to get my bag. No, I definitely did not put Avery in the car. It must have been Adam.

I rarely take the kids to the sitter in the summer; this is one of Adam's tasks because he doesn't teach during the summer months and typically spends his days at home with the kids. If he has baseball practice or another commitment he takes the kids over to the babysitter's house. But still, how could I miss her sitting right behind me in her car seat? She is under a year old —we still have her in a rear-facing car seat, making it harder to see her and know she was behind me, I rationalize. Little consolation. I realize I've hesitated too long.

The paramedic looks to Jade, who quickly explains. "The little girl was in the van. Old John, there—" she nods at the wizened man watching them "—broke the window and they pulled her out." The entirety of what has happened seems to settle on Jade and her voice quivers with emotion. "She stopped breathing for a minute, but I did CPR."

"Heatstroke?" the female paramedic asks aloud, then turns to me. "Are you the girl's mother?" I nod dumbly. "How long was she in the van, ma'am?" I try to shake the confusion and disbelief from my head. I check my watch, the one that Adam and the kids presented to me last Christmas. The watch band, custom-made with each child's name spelled out in in tiny, delicate silver beads, hangs loosely on my wrist.

"See," Adam had said when he placed it around my wrist and lightly kissed the palm of my hand, "there's room to add more names."

"Ma'am," I hear again, this time more incessantly. "How long was she in the car?"

"Forty, forty-five minutes, I think," I say, the words sounding rough and jagged, as if they lost the fight to stay unsaid. Forty-five minutes where no one was watching over my daughter. Forty-five interminable minutes where she sat, ensnared within a rear-facing car seat, unseen and unable to free herself, while the temperature around her climbed.

"Temperature is one hundred and five point six," an EMT says, and they immediately begin to remove Avery's clothes. First the pink dress that Leah had chosen for her this morning, then her tennis shoes and, finally, sliding off her white socks edged with lace trim, revealing her tiny pink toes. I reach out, cupping her bare foot in the palm of my hand. "Ma'am," the paramedic says. "You will need to give us a little room here to work. We need to get her to the hospital as quickly as we can."

"Can I go with you?" I ask, fearful that they are going to tell me no, that I've neglected my child and have lost that right. I am a social worker, I know about these things.

The other paramedic is placing ice packs beneath her neck, beneath each armpit, over her groin. Avery's eyes flutter open briefly and I whimper in thanks. She is still breathing. She is still alive. "Let's go," the paramedic says urgently to the other, and they lift the stretcher and place her in the back of the ambulance followed by two firefighters. *Dear God,* I think. *When did the fire department arrive?* I move to join her but am stopped by an outstretched arm. "We'll have you ride up front with the driver. We need room to work back here."

I rush to the passenger side of the ambulance, climb in and, with trembling fingers, struggle to fasten my seat belt. I look out the window and, as the driver pulls away from the curb, I see Kylie and Krissie sitting in the backseat of a police cruiser, while Officer Stamm and his partner lead a disheveled man wearing only boxer shorts out of the Haskinses' house in handcuffs. Krissie has her thumb in her mouth and is clinging to her big sister whose eyes are shuttered, unreadable. Krissie sees me and a spark of recognition flashes in her eyes. I press my hand to the window and she waggles her fingers in return. The crowd of neighbors still lingers, torn between the unfolding dramas in front of them.

Jade, the old man with the crowbar and the woman who pulled Avery from the van stand side by side, slump shouldered, faces grim. I realize I haven't thanked them. I rap on the window trying to get their attention, but they don't look my way. I roll down my window just as the ambulance gathers speed. "Thank you," I call out the window, but my words are swallowed by a blare of the siren. I raise the window and reach into my purse for my cell phone. I need to call my husband, tell him to meet me at the hospital, but I can't bring myself to do it just yet. I try to listen to what is happening in the rear of the ambulance, but I can't hear anything except the scream of the siren. I want to ask the driver what is happening, what they are doing to my daughter, if she is going to be okay, but I don't want to distract him from his driving. He is expertly moving through streets, slowing only briefly as he crosses intersections, not stopping for red lights, barely pausing for stop signs. This is bad, I think. This is very, very bad.

Within minutes we arrive at the hospital and even before we have come to a complete stop, I've unbuckled myself from the seat belt. I stumble from the cab of the ambulance and already the back doors are open and two doctors and a nurse are there to meet us. I recognize all three from my experiences as a social worker and Dr. Nickerson was the attending physician when Adam and I brought Leah to the emergency room when she fell off a skateboard and broke her wrist.

"Eleven-month female, left unattended in a locked van for approximately forty-five minutes," the paramedic explains. "Temperature currently one hundred and four point nine. Patient was breathing upon our arrival but bystander reported performing CPR. Heart rate is irregular, one hundred and fifty beats per minute, forty breaths per minute. Patient vomited and had a seizure lasting two minutes en route. We administered valium and the seizure activity stopped." I picture Avery in the throes of a grand mal seizure and want to lie down on the floor and weep. I want to stop the throng moving along with my daughter, want to ask questions, but know this would be time wasted.

"Parents?" Dr. Nickerson asks. The EMT nods my way and Dr. Nickerson notices me for the first time. If she is surprised to find that I'm there as a parent rather than an advocate for the child left in the locked van, she doesn't let on. "Ellen…" she begins, searching for my last name.

"Moore," I croak. "Ellen Moore."

"Ellen, we need to take your daughter back now. Someone will be out to keep you updated with what's happening." And before I know it, Avery is being taken away from me. She is very still; her face is covered by an oxygen mask and an IV of some sort coming out of her knee.

I sink down into the nearest chair. "Avery," I call after the doctor's retreating back, my voice breaking. She keeps going, so I yell more loudly, "Avery, her name is Avery." She looks back at me and nods, letting me know that she has heard me. She will call my daughter by her name as she pokes and prods her, trying to undo the damage that I have done.

A heavyset woman with a clipboard hovers nearby. "Hon," she says. "I have some paperwork for you to fill out." With a shaky hand I write down Avery's name and birth date and am struck by the thought that the entirety of my daughter's life only takes up two lines on a medical form. I take the paperwork to the window and hand it to the woman. "When do you think I'll hear something?" I ask, biting the corners of cheeks to stop from crying.

She shakes her head, her jowls bobbing with the movement. "I don't know, hon." I wish she would stop calling me that. "I'll check in with a nurse." She reaches out and touches my hand before I turn to walk away. "Do you have someone to wait with you? Would you like for me to call someone?"

"No, thank you," I say coolly, pulling my hand away. The receptionist looks at me, first with bewilderment and then with suspicion. I know she thinks I'm acting oddly for a parent whose daughter has been brought near death into the emergency room. She thinks that I am acting exactly the way the kind of woman who would leave her daughter in a boiling van would act. Inexplicably, my mind turns to James Olmstead. Did he act so strangely after Madalyn was found on the sidewalk? I brush the thought away—I'm in social worker mode. It's a defense mechanism that I've had to employ often in my line of work. I wouldn't have survived for very long if I didn't become clinical and detached. I want to explain this to the receptionist. I want to tell her that I will not be able to claw my way through this day if I don't hold my emotions at bay.

The emergency waiting room is surprisingly busy for a Tuesday morning. Individuals in various degrees of pain and misery surround me. There is an elderly woman knitting what appears to be a baby's blanket, her knobbed fingers deftly moving, turning out a mosaic of pink, blue, yellow and green. There is a hunched young man carefully cradling his heavily bandaged hand, blood oozing through the gauze. One woman is crying, hiccuping loudly into her phone, pleading with someone on the other side of the line to please not drop her health-care insurance. A small boy of about three toddles over, alternating happily between eating a cracker and sipping juice from a sippy cup. With a smile he holds out a soggy, half-eaten cracker to me as an offering and I take it, pretending to nibble at the edges. His apologetic mother rushes over, sweeps him into her arms and moves to the other side of the waiting room.

A woman and her two children approach the receptionist's window. One of my families. I always make a point to acknowledge my clients, but take their lead as to how much interaction we have when we happen to meet by chance. Today, I hope she doesn't notice me, hope that she doesn't want to talk about her children, the damage that has been inflicted upon them. But she turns, eyes scanning the waiting room, landing where I am sitting. I smile in her direction and she makes her way over to where I am and sits down across from me. "An earache," she explains as she protectively pulls her four-year-old onto her lap and reaches out for her nine-year-old daughter's hand.

"Those are the worst," I reply, but we both know this

is a lie. The worst was when your boyfriend molested your daughter while you were at work or, for me, when you leave your one-year-old to languish in an oven disguised as a minivan. Nine-year-old Destiny, painfully thin, averts her eyes, pulls away from her mother and busies herself with examining the fish tank in the corner of the room.

"Excuse me," I say, standing and holding up my phone to let her know that I am not being rude, that I am not moving to avoid further conversation with her, but that I need to make a call. She nods and her attention returns to her four-year-old son, who is fighting back tears and pulling at his ear. She rubs his back in slow, gentle circles. A good mom with an evil boyfriend.

The phone in my hand pulses like a beating heart and I can't bring myself to answer it just yet. The display reads Love of My Life just as when I call Adam the display pops up as Soul Mate. An inside joke. Early in our marriage, before we had children, we argued over something inconsequential, who forgot to buy the milk or who was supposed to write the check for the cable bill. We didn't talk to each other for three long, excruciating days. I went about my business, stood a little taller, held my chin high and my back straight, as if this would strengthen my resolve in not being the first to speak. We had each tried to fill the silence of the house in our own way. Adam plugged earphones in and listened to music while I talked on the phone with my mother. I tried not to bring my mother into our arguments, but she was an excellent listener and would support me even if I was clearly in the wrong. Not making eye contact, Adam and I would pass each other in our tiny apartment, rap music leaking from his earphones intermingled with my mother's sympathetic chastising of my husband's insensitivity.

Adam broke first, he always did. It was the end of the third day and Adam was standing at the kitchen sink, eating a bowl of cereal. "You're lucky you're my soul mate," he said through a mouthful of Wheat Chex.

"You're lucky you're the love of my life," I countered. And it was over. Like the fight had never happened. From then on whenever we got angry or argued, those words would follow. *You're lucky you're my soul mate. You're lucky you're the love of my life.*

I lift the phone to my ear not to call my husband, not just yet. The phone rings and rings until it goes to voice mail. "Mom," I say, finally surrendering to the tears that have been collecting behind my eyes. "Something happened to Avery."

Chapter 10

As the police officers approached, Jenny froze in fear, a chunk of pancake lodging in her throat midswallow. She reached for her milk, took a swift drink and swallowed hard, willing the mass to slide down her windpipe. Ducking beneath the table, Jenny pretended to search for something on the floor, only raising her head when she was sure the officers had retreated to the far side of the restaurant.

With a sigh of relief, Jenny dug into her breakfast and ten minutes later, the eggs, bacon and four red-tinted, chocolaty pancakes were gone and Jenny was licking syrup from her sticky fingers, her belly uncomfortably full. Jenny fished inside her backpack and pulled out an envelope addressed to Jenny at the apartment where she first came to live with her father. The return address sent a shiver of excitement down her spine. *Margaret Flanagan, 2574 Hickory Street, Cedar City, IA.* It was like discovering an unexpected world, like Narnia and Nimh, the places her teacher read to them about, were real. It was a card for her fifth birthday from her grandmother. Her mother's mother.

The day the letter arrived she watched as her father held the envelope in his callused hands. The letters they usually received were stark white envelopes holding bills that caused Billy to swear beneath his breath. This one he held carefully, staring silently down at the lavender envelope and for a moment Jenny was scared.

"It's for you," he said. Jenny, bouncing in anticipation, squealed in delight when a ten-dollar bill fell out as Billy opened the card. Jenny begged him to read it to her and tell her who it was from. "Your grandma," he said grimly. "It's from your mom's mother." Dutifully, he read the birthday card to Jenny, then retreated silently to his bedroom where he stayed for a very long time. Despite her father's obvious lack of enthusiasm about the letter, Jenny was thrilled and incessantly pestered her father about going to visit her grandmother in Cedar City someday. They never did. Her father lost his job, they moved from their apartment and Jenny never received another letter or card from her grandmother. Eventually, Jenny stopped asking about her.

But now, sitting in a restaurant in Cedar City, in the very town where Jenny's mother grew up, where her grandmother may still live, she slowly, methodically deciphered her grandmother's handwriting. It was written in tiny, cramped cursive and Jenny, on her best days, struggled to read a menu. In the card, her grandmother said she was sorry that her daughter, Jenny's mother, wasn't there for her. That she didn't used to be this way. She was once a caring, loving little girl who spent her days riding her bike around Cedar City and evenings catching fireflies and playing Kick the Can and Boys Chase the Girls. Jenny couldn't imagine her mournful-faced mother ever hollering *Ollie, Ollie oxen free* at the top of her lungs and kicking at an old rusty coffee can with all her might.

Her grandmother wrote that she hoped that Jenny would write back to her, that maybe one day they would meet and she could tell Jenny more about how her mother used to be. She signed the letter Grandma Margie.

Jenny's stomach flipped with excitement. Now all she had to do was find Hickory Street and the house where her grandmother lived. Jenny carefully placed the birthday card back into its purple envelope and returned it to her backpack. She turned her attention to the large manila envelope that held all the important papers in her father's life. "This is it, Jenny," he had said just the night before as they made their way to the bus station, all their worldly possessions in the two bags that they carried with them. "Say goodbye. We're never coming back to Benton."

Jenny slid a sticky finger into the envelope and her touch landed upon three photos. They were the thick kind of old-fashioned pictures that slid out of the bottom of the camera. The kind that you would shake until, slowly, like magic, the picture would emerge. Jenny gasped at the images. She wouldn't have recognized herself if it weren't for the Worlds of Fun t-shirt, once her favorite shirt, that showed a cartoonish map of the amusement park. She never actually had gone to Worlds of Fun, it was just another used article of clothing picked up from Goodwill, but she remembered loving that shirt, wearing it nearly every day. She could imagine herself raising her arms above her head as she rode the mini roller coaster or eating a mound of cotton candy on the carousel. The picture was a close-up of Jenny, both her eyes swollen shut, her upper lip so puffed up that it concealed her nostrils. A large cut slashed across her left cheek and appeared to be oozing, her Worlds of Fun shirt stained with what could only be blood. Jenny felt suddenly dizzy and the pancakes in her stomach churned like stones being skipped across a pond.

"Whoa, you were hungry," the waitress exclaimed, reaching down for the empty plate and gathering wadded-up napkins and syrup-coated utensils. When Jenny didn't respond, she looked down, her forehead pleated with concern. "You, okay?"

"I have to go to the bathroom," Jenny whispered hoarsely, clapping a hand over her mouth, her eyes searching desperately for the restrooms.

"It's thataway." The waitress pointed as Jenny slid out from behind the booth and stumbled away. Biting her cheeks and swallowing hard, she bumped from table to table, not noticing how the other customers recoiled at her approach. Jenny threw open the bathroom door and staggered to an empty stall, fell to her knees and vomited. Drops of perspiration beaded at her hairline and she gasped for breath. Again her stomach seized and she clutched the sides of the toilet trying to steady herself.

Jenny sensed rather than heard the presence behind her, and her face burned with shame at being caught in such a private act in such a public place. One gentle hand pressed against her shoulder and another cupped her forehead as her stomach gave one final violent lurch and the last remnants of her breakfast erupted.

Jenny was unfamiliar with such gentle touches, more accustomed to her father's good-natured nudges and careless ruffling of her hair, but she had vague inklings

of her mother and nestling against her on their old flow-
ered sofa.

"Shh, now," a voice soothed, and Jenny realized that
she was crying. A low, sad moan, thick with mucous
and tears. "It's okay, get it all out." Jenny didn't want to
move her head to see who was standing behind her. She
thought she could fall asleep right there, kneeling on the
floor, next to the toilet, her forehead cradled so carefully
in one cool, capable hand while the other rubbed her
back in slow, rhythmic circles. Jenny looked behind her
and saw the blue hem of a skirt that stopped just above
a thick calf seamed with bulbous purple veins and was
glad to know it was the nice waitress rather than some
stranger. "Are you okay?" the waitress asked. "Do you
think you're all done?"

Jenny closed her eyes; the sweat had cooled on her
skin, causing her to shiver and the fine hair on her
goose-pimpled arms to stand at attention. Her stomach
burned slightly, felt hollowed out, empty. An ulcer, the
doctor had warned last year when her father had taken
her to the community health center after weeks of com-
plaining about stomachaches. Jenny had a vision of her
stomach with one perfectly round circle carved out, the
red velvet pancakes she just ate wandering out of the
hole and flowing into other parts of her body, floating
aimlessly through her bloodstream.

"You think you can stand up?" the waitress asked,
and Jenny reluctantly nodded. She pushed herself up
from the grimy linoleum and stood on shaky legs. The
waitress made sure Jenny wasn't going to fall over and
then turned to the sink, wet a dishrag that she pulled
from an apron pocket and handed it to her. "Wash your
face with this," she urged, and stepped around Jenny to

flush the toilet. Jenny was impressed. The last time she had the flu, her father had gagged right along with her, tossed her bedding into the Dumpster behind the apartment building and spent the rest of the evening lying on the couch with a cold washcloth covering his eyes.

"You want it back?" Jenny asked after she wiped her mouth with the rag. The waitress didn't even hesitate or wrinkle her nose as she plucked the towel from Jenny's hand and stuffed it back into her apron pocket.

Jenny faltered as the waitress opened the door that led back into the restaurant's dining area. "Do you want me to call your sister for you?" the waitress offered. "You can wait in here until she comes."

Jenny shook her head. "Nah, that's okay. I'll just call my mom, she's going to be so mad at my sister," Jenny lied. She bit her lip and looked up at the waitress apologetically. It was too much to ask for this nice lady to go and gather all of her things and bring them back to her hideout in the bathroom just because she ate too much and dreaded the long walk past the other diners back to the booth where her book bag rested.

"You wait right here and get your bearings and I'll grab your bag for you," the waitress said, reading her thoughts. "I'll be right back." Jenny watched the woman push through the door, the sunny fabric of her uniform stretching tightly across her swaying rear end like a waving flag. It was funny, Jenny thought, how different people could look in the front compared to the back. The waitress had an old, tired face and a young rear view. She remembered once, when she was little, she had gotten separated from her mother at Walmart. Jenny had looked anxiously around at all the knees that surrounded her until she found a set of tennis shoes and faded jeans that resembled her mother's. She'd wrapped her arms around the familiar legs in relief until she was shaken gently off. Her heart had skipped in her chest when she looked up into the eyes of a bemused stranger who handed her off to a blue-smocked greeter who gave her jelly beans until her mother, out of breath and teary-eyed, rushed up to claim her. Her mother had swept her into her arms and covered her face with kisses, Jenny remembered, as she looked at her own pale-faced, red-eyed reflection in the mirror.

Jenny turned on the water faucet and held her hands beneath the tap and ran her wet fingers through her long tangled hair, trying to force it flat. *Like trying to tame a rabid squirrel with its tail caught in a light socket,* her father laughed about Jenny's unruly hair and Jenny had laughed halfheartedly right along with him.

Jenny miserably waited until the waitress returned to the restroom with her backpack. When the door finally opened, Jenny snatched at the bag, set it on the sink and quickly inventoried the contents. Envelope, cell phone and clothes, all accounted for. Jenny slid her hand into the envelope, felt past the photos and letters to the cash and pulled out a twenty-dollar bill. "Here," Jenny said, and thrust the money toward the waitress, who looked down at her with an expression that she couldn't quite read.

"No, no," the waitress answered, gently pushing Jenny's hand away. "It's on the house. We don't make customers who get sick from our food pay for it."

Jenny wanted to tell her that it wasn't the food, that the red pancakes were actually very good, that it was this day, her father's fight and getting separated from him, the strange man on the bus, the letter, the pictures,

that made her throw up. Instead she shoved the bill back
into the envelope, stepped past the waitress, out of the
bathroom, into the restaurant and out the main doors
into the parking lot, fleeing the Happy Pancake without even a backward glance.

The morning air was scorching but Jenny welcomed
the relief from the frigid restaurant air. Traffic was still
busy along the street and Jenny measured her options.
There was a hotel just down the block and she knew
how to reserve a room. She had done it several times
when she was with her father and found that she needed
to do the talking. It was easy, just tell the clerk that
your father was getting the bags and your mother was
changing your little brother's diaper in the car. Look
the clerk straight in the eyes and push the thirty dollars across the counter and wait for him to push back
the key. It always worked.

The problem was this hotel looked much nicer than
the ones she and her father ever stayed in. It looked like
it probably even had a pool. Jenny would have liked
that, a hotel with a pool. She imagined luxurious fluffy
white towels and a heated whirlpool.

Her other option was to cross the street to the bus
station and purchase a ticket back to Nebraska. She
wondered if her father was in a hospital or maybe even
in jail. When she returned she could use the cell phone
to call one of her father's friend-girls, one who hadn't
figured out that her father would never have just one
friend-girl, and see if she could stay with her for a day
or two. The thought of climbing back on the bus and the
eight-hour ride back to Benton in the dark with a bus-
ful of strangers made Jenny's stomach wobble again.
She knew what she needed to do next. She would check

around, find out where Hickory Street was. Take a bus or a cab there. Certainly her grandmother would be glad to see her, to actually meet her. And maybe, just maybe, her mother would be there, too.

Chapter 11

I check in one more time with the receptionist, hoping there is some kind of update on Avery. She shakes her head. "I know it's hard to wait," she says kindly. My red eyes and mascara-stained cheeks must have convinced her that I do have a soul.

"I'm going to go outside and make a phone call. Could you…" I begin.

"I will come out and find you the second the doctor comes out," she assures me.

I step through the automatic doors and a surge of heat washes over me and I immediately begin to sweat. I don't think, I just press the button that connects me to Adam.

"Ellen!" he says by way of greeting. "I've been trying to get a hold of you for two hours!"

"Adam," I interrupt. "I'm at the emergency room with Avery." My social worker persona is trying to take over, but I don't want it to. This is about Avery. This is my husband. "Please come. Please hurry," I choke. "Please."

"I'll be right there," he says, and hangs up. I wonder if Leah and Lucas are with him or at the babysitter's house. I hope they are with the sitter. I don't want them to be afraid; I don't want them to see me explain to their father what has happened to Avery.

I try to call my mother one more time, but again there is no answer. Next, I dial Joe, knowing that he's at the police station. Ever since the first day we met, amid the tragedy that was the Twin Case, we've been good friends. Joe is now a detective with the Cedar City Police Department, and I wonder if he has heard about what has happened to Avery. As soon as he picks up his phone, I know that he hasn't. "Hey, stranger!" he exclaims. "How're you?" There is a happy lilt in his voice that he unknowingly reserves just for me. Sometimes I think Joe might be a little bit in love with me, but I choose to ignore it. I don't want to lose our friendship.

"Joe," I begin, "I left Avery in the car. I didn't know. I didn't know!" I am quickly losing the fight to keep my emotions under control. I do my best to explain the events of the morning, but even to my own ears, it sounds unbelievable.

"Hang on," Joe finally interrupts. "Where are you right now?"

"At the hospital. They aren't telling me anything. I don't know what's happening."

Joe is quiet for a moment and I know his detective mind is itching to ask me a thousand more questions. To his credit, he doesn't. "I can be there in ten minutes," he finally says.

"No, no." I shake my head. "Don't do that. Adam is on his way." Even across the telephone line I can almost feel Joe bristle. "Thank you, though. I just wanted…" What do I want, I wonder. "I just wanted to let you know," I finish lamely.

"She'll be okay," Joe offers kindly. We both know that this is not an absolute. In our lines of work we have seen way too much to ever believe that things always turn out just fine. Still, my heart lifts for a moment. There are successes: the father who goes to anger management classes, the mother who regularly attends AA, the families reunited. "Give me a call when you can," Joe says, "and I'll do some checking around here."

I thank him and hang up the phone, wondering, after the fact, what he would need to check on at the police station.

With shaking hands I call Kelly, my best friend since third grade. Kelly lives in Cedar City and stays home with her four boys, all under the age of six. There was a time when Kelly and I would talk nearly every single day, no matter how busy our lives got. This isn't the case any longer. Kids, work, laundry, our husbands always seem to come first. Still, we make a point to get together once a month for breakfast at a local bakery. Some months we only have half an hour to spare, but still we meet, exchange the high and low points of what is happening in our lives, hug and then go back to our insane lives.

"Kelly!" I exclaim as soon as she answers, but that is all I can say. I find it impossible to once again put into words what has happened. But Kelly is a master at prying information out of people, a remnant of our high school days when Kelly was the editor of the school newspaper.

Who, what, where, when, how? Kelly asks, listening carefully as I respond in equally short, staccato answers. *Avery, heat stroke, van, this morning, I don't know,* I say between sobs.

"I'm calling Nick to come home to be with the kids," she says. "I'll be there as soon as I can," she assures me.

Then it hits me, a quick strike to my solar plexus. Leaving a child locked in a hot car is neglectful, abusive, criminal. I could be charged and arrested for child endangerment and if the unthinkable happens, if Avery dies, I could be charged with worse. I could lose my entire life, my family, my career. "I didn't know," I whisper. Then again more loudly, "I didn't know." Passersby give me curious glances but keep moving. "I didn't know she was there!" I plead to no one in particular, my breath coming now in ragged gulps. I feel light-headed, dizzy, and clutch at the wall to keep from falling.

"Shh, now," the receptionist from the emergency room is at my side, trying to hold me up, keep me from collapsing to the floor. "Dr. Nickerson is ready to speak to you. She has word about your daughter. Come quickly."

Chapter 12

Jenny spied a small convenience store and stepped inside to ask the woman behind the counter where Hickory Street was located. "It's not too far from here, just about two miles," she explained, pulling out a small map of the city and highlighting the route that Jenny would need to take. "Do you have someone here with you?" the woman asked, worry lacing her voice.

"My grandma," Jenny said with confidence. "She's waiting for me in the car."

Jenny didn't know what she was going to do if she couldn't find her grandmother and didn't really want to spend the money she knew it would cost to stay in a nice hotel. She was suddenly very tired and the later she checked in at a hotel the more questions about where her parents were could come up.

Jenny referred to the map the woman had given her and started walking, deciding that she would keep an eye out for an inexpensive motel just in case her grandmother had moved. Very quickly the straps on her too-small flip-flops began rubbing the skin between her toes until she finally decided to take them off. The sidewalk was rough and hot from the day's heat and Jenny carefully scanned the ground in front of her for bits of broken glass and sharp-edged pebbles.

She heard the beep of a car horn, not as insistent as the bleat of the car that almost smushed her earlier in the day, but still… Jenny looked up and whirled around ready to spew forth a few of the choice words that her father often muttered and then quickly apologized for when she saw the familiar face peering at her through the driver's-side window of a small, yellow car with rounded edges that she and her friends at school called slug bugs.

It was the nice waitress from the Happy Pancake and Jenny couldn't help but smile, and then stopped herself, suddenly suspicious. Maybe the waitress had changed her mind and was coming to collect the money for her red velvet pancakes, even though she told her that she didn't have to pay. Maybe the restaurant manager told her to get the money or call the police. Jenny thought quickly. She could make a run for it and dart down a side street. She was a fast runner, even without wearing any shoes, and was confident she could ditch the old lady and her yellow car. Jenny glanced around at her surroundings. The busy main street seemed to go on forever and the nearest intersection was almost a football field away. Plenty of time for the lady to call the police if Jenny started to run. Her other option was to just pay her the money for the pancakes and hope that the waitress would be on her way. Once again Jenny slid the backpack from her shoulders and reached into the envelope, peeling off a twenty from the wad of bills.

"Hey, there," the lady called through the car window. "You okay?"

Jenny nodded and shoved the money into the open window of the car, releasing it so that the bill fluttered down onto the woman's lap and, without a word, continued marching down the street, her flip-flops hanging loosely from each thumb. "Oh, no," the waitress called after her, "that's not why I came to find you." Jenny didn't slow her stride, hoping the woman would get the hint and just drive away. Instead, the yellow car crept along slowly, keeping pace with her steps. "I was worried about you. Can I call someone for you?"

"No, thanks," Jenny said as breezily as possible, "I'm meeting my sister just down the street here."

Jenny could feel the woman's gaze upon her and knew that she didn't believe her. While Jenny knew she was a pretty good liar, she also had a good sense of who truly believed what she was saying. The bullshit-o-meter, her father called it. *Dust off that bullshit-o-meter,* her father would whisper to her when a landlord or the guy at the pawnshop was trying to pull something over on them. Jenny walked more quickly; she was now only a short distance to the corner.

"Hey, wait a minute," the woman called. "I just want to talk to you."

Jenny slowed her steps, but not to make it easier to have a conversation with the lady. If she timed it just right she could reach the corner as the light was turning and dash across the street, leaving the woman and her yellow car stuck at the red light.

"What's your sister's name?" the waitress asked. "I could call her for you or your mother if you'd like." Jenny, despite herself, warmed at the thought of the woman thinking that Jenny actually had a mother to call. A mother who would be worried when she didn't come home on time, who kept her dinner warm in the oven, covered lightly with tin foil. Her friends and teachers back in Benton knew that her mom wasn't around, some even knew why. A lot of kids didn't live with their dads or even see their dads, but at least they all had a mom, even stepmoms. She was the girl without a mother.

"Nah, I'm good," Jenny answered, looking intently up at the traffic light, resting stubbornly on green.

"Can I at least drive you somewhere? I don't like leaving you out here by yourself on the street," the woman pleaded.

"No, thanks," Jenny said offhandedly as the light jumped to yellow and she bent her knees slightly, looking to the left and right, getting ready to run.

"Hey," the woman said loudly, causing Jenny to hesitate and look over. The woman's face was taut with concern, her eyes filled with something that Jenny couldn't name. "I saw the pictures." Jenny's heart stopped. "Please," the woman implored, "let me help."

Jenny's stomach gave a sudden heave and she vomited into the street.

The woman hopped from the car and hurried to Jenny's side. "Please, let me take you home or at the very least call someone for you." Miserably, Jenny clutched at her stomach and began to cry. "What's your name?" she asked gently.

"Jenny," she wept.

"Jenny, just tell me who I can call and I will." The woman reached out and placed the back of her hand against Jenny's forehead. "You're sick. I can't just leave you here." The woman looked around helplessly. "Maybe I should call the police?"

"No!" Jenny said emphatically. "Don't call the police," she begged. Jenny found herself actually considering getting into the yellow car, the entire time hearing her father screaming in her head, *Don't you dare get in that car, Jennifer Briard!* Jenny ignored her father's voice and dizzily climbed into the passenger seat.

The woman drove slowly through the unfamiliar streets and Jenny sneaked sidelong glances at the waitress who introduced herself as Maudene Sifkus. It was so different than the rides with her father, who was always in a hurry, impatient to get to wherever they were going. He barely braked at stop signs and was known to shout out the window in frustration at nimrods, as he called the drivers who, in his opinion, nearly killed them both.

"I live just a few blocks from here," Maudene told her, hunched over and hands gripping clawlike to the steering wheel. They crept along slowly, pausing for what felt like an eternity at stop signs, though Jenny didn't mind all that much. Initially, once Jenny had climbed cautiously into the car and got over the shock of learning that Maudene had seen the pictures from her backpack, Maudene mentioned that perhaps she should take Jenny to the police station. Jenny threatened to leap from the moving car—perhaps this was why she was driving so slowly—and Maudene promised to take her to her house. "My daughter has kids around your age." Maudene didn't take her eyes off the road as she spoke. "Eleven, right?"

"Ten," Jenny said automatically, and then mentally kicked herself. The less information she shared, the better.

"Ten?" Maudene said in surprise. "You seem so much older. Very mature for your age."

"I guess," Jenny said nonchalantly, but swelled a bit with pride at the compliment. "You got a husband?" Jenny asked before she could stop herself.

Maudene was silent for so long that Jenny thought she must not have heard her. Jenny knew that old people could be a bit hard of hearing, so she sat up straighter in her seat and turned to face Maudene. "You got a husband?" she said loudly, enunciating each word very carefully, then saw the stricken look on Maudene's face and closed her mouth. They drove along in silence until Maudene slowed the car and turned on the blinker as she pulled into a driveway.

Jenny gaped at the sight. It was the sweetest house that Jenny had ever seen. It wasn't big, but cozy looking with the welcoming glow of the sun shining through the thick trees. The steps leading up to the porch and the front door held pots teeming with flowers that were so bright they hurt her eyes. A flicker of movement from behind the curtains of the front window made Jenny's heart catch in fear. Maudene never answered her question about a husband. Maybe he wouldn't like the idea of Maudene bringing a little girl to their home. Maybe he was just plain mean. Jenny felt her stomach, sore from vomiting, clench again.

"Come on in, and I'll introduce you to my dog." Jenny followed Maudene up the front walkway to the house, dropping her shoulders to avoid the low-hanging branches of an elm tree, its long, fingerlike limbs nearly brushing against her neck.

"Watch your head there," Maudene said, putting a protective arm around Jenny. "I need to get that tree trimmed. Someone is going to get their eye poked out."

"We have one of those in front of our school. No one

is supposed to climb it, but they do. One kid fell out and landed on his head." Jenny picked a leaf and rubbed it between her fingers, wishing that she had climbed the tree in front of the school. There were no trees to speak of near the places where she and her father lived. Narrow, weedy things that wilted beneath the weight of their own leaves. Maybe Maudene would let her climb this tree later, before she asked her to take her to look for her grandmother.

They ascended the creaky wooden steps that led to the front door, Jenny hanging back a little. Maudene noticed the hesitancy and stopped. "You don't have to come inside," she said gently. "I can call someone for you, take you somewhere if you want." Jenny didn't answer, just looked uncertainly at the wooden front door inlaid with a rectangle of stained glass illuminated by a dim light from within the house.

Jenny didn't want to tell Maudene that she really had nowhere to go, no one to call, that the reason she got off in Cedar City was because there was a tiny chance that a grandmother that she had never met, had never even spoken with, lived in this town. "Is your dog nice?" she finally asked.

"Dolly is very nice," Maudene assured her. "I promise she won't hurt you. She'll probably come up and sniff you because she's curious, but then she'll go back and lay down." Jenny nodded but didn't move. "Do you want me to go in first and put Dolly in the bedroom?" Jenny thought about standing outside on the porch all by herself surrounded by the talonlike branches and low whispers from the swaying trees and shook her head no.

"It's okay. I'll come in," Jenny answered, pulling her

backpack from her shoulders and holding it in front of her like a shield.

Maudene slid a key into the lock and nudged the door open with her shoulder. "Dolly," she called. "I have someone special for you to meet." Dolly, from her post by the front window, eyed Jenny sleepily and Jenny responded with her own wary gaze. "Come here, girl," Maudene cooed, and Dolly stiffly obeyed. Jenny tensed and instinctively stepped behind Maudene as the large dog approached. "Hold your hand out like this." Maudene held out her arm, palm down, toward Dolly's nose and Jenny reluctantly did the same, her hand shaking slightly. "She's a German shorthaired pointer. Best dog ever," Maudene said as Dolly sniffed the air around Jenny's fingers and, as if sensing her trepidation, ducked and raised her head beneath Jenny's hand. Jenny flinched and pulled her hand back as if burned. Dolly, wounded by the rebuff, skulked from the room. "Are you hungry or thirsty?" Maudene asked. "Can I get you something to eat?"

"No," Jenny said, cradling her stomach, still sore from earlier.

Jenny knew she should thank Maudene for being so nice to her. It wasn't that Jenny wasn't thankful for the offer; it was just that there were so many things to look at in Maudene's home that she got distracted. Jenny had never seen so much wood in one room. The walls were paneled halfway up the wall in coffee-colored wood. There were built-in shelves filled with books and knick-knacks; there was a fireplace and columns that led to another room all made out of the same dark rich wood. Even the ceiling was lined with thick beams. Jenny had never seen anything like it.

The telephone rang and Jenny watched as Maudene looked at it in surprise. "Aren't you going to get that?" Jenny asked.

"No one ever calls me at this time of the day," Maudene responded as she glanced at the wooden clock hanging on the wall. "Probably just a telemarketer."

"Does that have a cuckoo in it?" Jenny asked, nodding toward the clock.

"A cuckoo?" Maudene asked distractedly, looking at the telephone that had finally fallen silent.

"Is that a cuckoo clock? Does a little bird come out every hour?"

"No, dancers," Maudene said, turning back to Jenny. "It was a wedding present from my parents. It's over forty years old."

"It's pretty," Jenny said, scrutinizing more closely the intricately carved clock in the shape of a peaked house. "When do they dance?"

"Every hour. Come on, I'll show you where you can put your things and where the bathroom is. And when you're ready we can talk about what you want to do next." Maudene led Jenny up the wooden steps that were intersected with a narrow, worn strip of carpet and once again the telephone began to trill.

"Maybe you better get that," Jenny, who found in her short life that phone calls most often meant bad news or a new friend-girl for her father on the other end, said nervously.

"It can wait," Maudene assured her as they continued up the steps. "You can put your things in the room that used to belong to my daughter." Maudene opened the door and flipped a light switch, revealing an oddly shaped room painted pale pink. The ceiling was low, the walls were angled haphazardly and the headboards of two twin beds were situated into a narrow nook beneath a small bank of windows covered in white, lacy curtains. Jenny realized they were at the tippy-top of the house. "It's so pretty," Jenny breathed, running her hand over the pink coverlets that lay across the beds.

"I like it, too," Maudene said with a smile. "Would you like to rest for a little bit?"

"I'm kind of tired," Jenny said, unable to stifle a yawn.

"Well, you are welcome to take a nap."

Jenny slowly spun in a circle, taking in the crisp cleanliness of the room.

"You make yourself at home and I'll be right downstairs." Maudene turned to leave but hesitated. "We'll have to talk, you know, when you're ready." Jenny remained silent. "I know someone we can call and talk to about your situation. A social worker."

Jenny froze. An icy claw of fear scraped against the back of her neck.

"But not until you're ready," Maudene said and quietly closed the bedroom door behind her.

Jenny untied her father's t-shirt that was wrapped around her waist, neatly folded it and set it on the bedside table. Wearily, Jenny sat down on the very edge of the bed, being careful to not let her grubby fingers touch the petal-pink blanket. Her eyes scanned the beautiful room and exhaustion and disappointment pricked at the tender spot behind her eyes causing tears to puddle. Social workers meant trouble and she knew that it was already time to move on, to try and find her grandmother on her own, but fatigue pinned her to her spot and she closed her eyes. *Just for a minute,* Jenny thought. *Then I'll go.*

When Jenny awoke, she felt a warm, moist breeze on her neck and pulled the sheet up to her nose. She wondered if someone had come into the room and opened the window. Jenny did not like to sleep with the windows open. Images of rabid dogs and free-floating vampires climbing through her window made her heart hammer in terror. She blamed her father. One weekend he insisted on watching a marathon of horror movies based on the novels of some writer who he said made a bazillion dollars scaring the shit out of people. Jenny tried not to watch. Turned her back to the television and busied herself with painting her toenails with the bright pink polish that she picked from the prize box in her classroom. It didn't matter, though; cemeteries for pets and men with axes kept crowding into her brain.

She looked toward the windows and found the curtains lying still against the panes. Then her bleary eyes fell to the side of the bed, where Dolly, breathing heavily, stood looking hopefully up at her. She sat up with a start, realizing where she was and a renewed sense of urgency to leave pawed at her chest and she swept her legs over the side of the bed. At least there wasn't any white foam dripping from the corners of the dog's mouth, Jenny thought to herself. "Go away," she whispered at the dog, whose mournful eyes regarded her solemnly. Despite herself, she reached out and patted Dolly's head, so dark brown it was nearly black. She ran her fingers beneath Dolly's chin where a crop of white whiskers framed the old dog's muzzle, and the dog raised her chin and closed her eyes in bliss.

"Ah," came Maudene's voice from the open doorway. "I see that Dolly found you. You've been asleep for a few hours. You must have been tired." Jenny wiggled her toes and closed her eyes, suddenly shy in the older woman's presence. "When you're ready to get up, come on downstairs and I'll fix you something to eat. A sandwich, or I have some leftover meat loaf in the refrigerator."

Jenny, not used to being given any options for meals, except when they went to the Happy Pancake, where she swore she would never, ever eat again, usually could only find cereal or peanut butter and crackers, the meager provisions her father scraped together. Maudene, to Jenny's surprise, was not wearing her blue-and-yellow waitress uniform, but was dressed in a pair of jeans and a short-sleeved t-shirt. "Thanks," she said shyly.

Maudene smiled. "You're welcome. I'll see you downstairs."

Jenny rummaged through her backpack hoping to find, by some miracle, a brand-new outfit inside. She didn't want to go and meet her grandmother for the first time wearing her denim shorts with the hole in the pocket, and her favorite pink polo and skirt now looked faded and frayed. She thought of the envelope filled with money—maybe Maudene would take her to Walmart for new clothes for the occasion—but then she thought twice. Maudene said she was going to call a social worker and the last thing Jenny wanted was to find herself in some office with a stack of drawing paper and markers in front of her with a strange lady asking her about how she felt and if anyone had hurt her lately. Instead, she would use the money to take a bus or a cab to Hickory Street where her grandmother hopefully still lived.

She changed quickly, turning her back to Dolly who was watching her intently, and ran her father's comb through her matted hair. She padded through the hallway to the bathroom with Dolly close at her heels and brushed her teeth, being careful to rinse out the sink. She had never seen such a clean bathroom, and Jenny had to wonder if anyone actually ever used it. She returned to the bedroom, made the bed, folded her dirty clothes and returned them to her backpack. Jenny wanted to bring her backpack downstairs with her but thought that Maudene might think it was weird that she carried it around with her everywhere. She looked around the room trying to decide where she could hide it. She couldn't bring herself to look beneath the bed and the closet was too obvious, so in the end she decided to bring it downstairs with her.

The walls that led down the stairs were filled with framed photos that Jenny hadn't noticed earlier. There were dozens of them in various sizes. School pictures and family portraits, team pictures and wedding photos. Jenny thought back to the few pictures hidden in her backpack. Her father never had enough money to buy any of her school photos. Not even the package that had the words *Best Buy!* written next to it.

As she came down the steps she heard the murmur of a television. A slightly sweet smell greeted her when she entered the kitchen and Jenny was surprised to find that she was hungry. After being so sick a few hours before, she thought she would never want to eat again. A small portable television was positioned beneath a set of kitchen cabinets made of the same dark wood that was found throughout the rest of the house and was set to a news channel. "I made corn muffins—how does that sound?" Maudene asked.

"I've never had them," Jenny said honestly. "They sound gross." And after a beat she added, "But they smell good." Jenny looked at the table, set just as it was at the restaurant with plates and napkin-wrapped silverware and small glasses filled with milk. She and her father usually ate standing up or sitting on the edge of the bed while they watched television. Maudene set the golden muffins, steam rising in curls from the basket that held them, on the table.

"They're delicious with butter and strawberry preserves, if I do say so myself," Maudene said, nodding toward a small covered dish and a bowl of quivering red jelly. "Help yourself."

Jenny sat down at the table and reached for a muffin, singeing her fingers and hastily dropping it to her plate where it bounced and tumbled to the floor. Jenny quickly bent over and retrieved it before an ever-present Dolly could snatch it away. "Sorry," she said, righting herself and carefully setting the muffin on her plate. Maudene hadn't even noticed. She was staring intently at the television, where a woman reporter was standing in front of a hospital saying something about the heat and a baby. Maudene stood, walked toward the television and bent down close until her nose almost touched the screen.

"Oh, no," Maudene murmured. "Oh, dear God, no."

Chapter 13

Adam rushes into the emergency room just as Dr. Nickerson steps into the waiting area. She reaches out to shake Adam's hand and introduces herself. "We have Avery stabilized and her core temperature is down to one hundred and two degrees. We will have to watch her very carefully. More seizures are a real possibility. We are moving her to the pediatric intensive care unit. The biggest concern now is if any organ damage occurred. Being subjected to such intense temperatures can be especially dangerous for the kidneys. We'll do further blood tests as well as check Avery's urine to look for muscle breakdown, infection and electrolyte abnormalities. Avery is in and out of consciousness right now and when she opens her eyes she appears to be quite confused."

Adam looks bewildered and keeps looking back and forth between Dr. Nickerson and me. I squeeze his hand trying to convey through my touch to be patient, that I will explain everything after Dr. Nickerson leaves. "This is a critical time for your daughter right now. We have her on an IV of cool liquids and oxygen as a precaution in case she stops breathing again." I bite back a gasp and Adam lightly shakes his hand from mine. "We don't know the long-term effects, if any, that this will have on her. Time will tell." Adam has stopped looking at Dr. Nickerson and his gaze remains fixed on me. "Dr. Campbell is the nephrologist who will be monitoring Avery's kidney function. She's the best in the state," Dr. Nickerson continues. The weight of Adam's stare lies heavily on me and if I look at him I'm afraid of what I'll find in his face. "Perhaps," Dr. Nickerson says, looking back and forth between Adam and me, "you'd like a quiet place to talk?"

"Yes, please," I say as Adam scrubs a hand over his face as if trying to rub away the visions of Avery hooked up to an IV, an oxygen mask covering her heart-shaped face.

Dr. Nickerson leads us to a small room labeled Family Consultation. "Take your time. It will take a few minutes to move Avery to the sixth floor. We've already contacted your general practitioner and he'll stop by on his rounds, as well." She shakes both our hands and says her goodbyes, leaving Adam and me alone.

"Adam," I begin.

"What happened, Ellen?" he asks, not angrily, not accusatorily, but in disbelief.

"I don't know. I don't know," I say in a rush. "I didn't know she was in the van. Did you put her in there?"

Adam looks taken aback. "Yes, I put her in the van. I told you, don't you remember? You were upstairs getting your bag. You yelled, 'Okay.'"

I shake my head. "I don't, Adam. I swear to God I don't remember." My voice is shaking and I swallow hard.

"I had early baseball practice because of the heat.

Leah and Lucas were going with me to help. You were going to take Avery to Linda's. I *told* you." I'm still shaking my head back and forth as Adam's voice rises. "I called to you before you got in the van. I said, 'Avery's all set.'"

"No." I cover my face with my hands, trying to remember. "No, I didn't hear you. It was such a crazy morning."

"Ellen, you gave me a thumbs-up!" Adam voice echoes through the tiny room. "A thumbs-up means you heard me!"

I feel as if I've been punched. I stumble backward, bumping into the wall. Adam's face is twisted in grief, not anger, which is worse. "I'm so sorry, Adam. I'm so sorry," I whisper, taking a tentative step toward him. There is a light knock on the door and I stop short. Through the narrow window of the consultation room, a sturdy, white-haired figure stands. My mother. I fling open the door and fall into her arms. She clutches on to me like I had hoped my husband would have. She strokes my hair and rubs my back, whispering, "It's going to be okay," over and over again into my ear. She releases me and envelopes my husband, who is twelve inches taller than she is but still he collapses into her capable arms. I watch as my husband dissolves into helpless tears and my mother comforts him.

It's then when I see the little girl standing nearby, her long hair falling messily into her face. At first I think she is lost and I scan the hallway for an adult she might belong to. Her face is strikingly familiar to me. A former client, maybe. My mind scrolls through the endless list of children that I've worked with over the years. Then I think she is just a nosey, curious girl gawking at our display of human heartache, and I move to shut the door, but my mother, still clutching one of Adam's hands, puts her other hand on the door. Tears glisten in my mother's eyes and the tip of her nose is bright red. "This is Jenny." I wait for further introduction, but none comes. "Jenny," she continues, "this is my daughter, Ellen, and her husband, Adam."

"Hi," we all offer awkwardly, and I look at my mother questioningly. She responds with an *I will tell you later* raise of the eyebrow.

"How is she?" my mother asks, pulling a tissue from the box that sits on a small table in the corner of the room.

"We don't know." My voice breaks. "They're moving her up to the pediatric intensive care unit. We need to go and meet her up there." I reach for Adam's hand and am relieved when he doesn't pull away. Together, we make our way to the elevator and the little girl named Jenny looks up at us. "Sixth floor," I tell her, and she dutifully pushes the button.

"Whoop," she says, and giggles as the elevator rises quickly, causing my own stomach to flip. I figure that my mother is taking care of a granddaughter of one of her friends or the daughter of one of her co-workers at the restaurant, but it still puzzles me.

"Where are Lucas and Leah?" I ask Adam as the doors open to the sixth floor.

"They're over at the Arwoods'."

I nod. This is good, the kids spending the afternoon at the Arwoods' home, our neighbors who have two children just the same age as Leah and Lucas.

"You got my message?" I ask my mother and I find myself carefully watching Jenny, who seems transfixed by the artwork that lines the pediatric hallway: bright watercolors of elephants and lions, whimsical prints from the story of Peter Pan, and handcrafted kites with delicate tails affixed to the walls. Again, I feel as if I know this little girl. Did she go to school with Leah? Did I visit her home? Place her in foster care at one point?

My mother shakes her head. "No, I saw the television."

"The television?" I ask in surprise.

"I saw the reporter and the camera when I came into the emergency room," Adam confirms.

"And I saw you on TV going into the emergency room," my mother says to Adam. "The reporter was talking about a little girl left in a car—" she glances carefully in my direction "—and then I saw Adam rushing into the hospital. I knew something was terribly wrong and came right here."

"Oh, my God." My knees feel weak and my stomach sick. "Why were they talking about it on the news? It was an accident." But I know why this has caught the attention of the media and the dizzying sensation that things are unraveling, that all control is being lost, presses upon me.

"Never mind that now," my mother soothes. "You just need to worry about Avery. Everything will get sorted out soon enough."

The corridor is bustling with foot traffic. Doctors, nurses and other hospital personnel walk purposefully, hands wrapped around paper cups filled with coffee. Families move more slowly, pushing wheelchairs or gingerly guiding a loved one connected to an IV pole through the hallways. Jenny halts in the middle of the walkway, her eyes pinned to a small boy slowly pedaling a Hot Wheels tricycle. His head is smooth and hairless, the tender skin beneath his eyes bruised-looking, his face a pale full moon covered by a yellow mask. He is tethered to an IV that drips an innocuous-looking clear liquid into his veins and is rolled along by his mother, who follows close behind. At first I think it is the little boy with whom Jenny is fascinated, but it's the mother she can't pull her gaze from. She is mesmerized. With rapt attention she scans the woman up and down as if memorizing her tightly drawn, exhausted face, the hunch of her shoulders, each leaden step. I see it, too. The way the mother looks at her ill son. It hurts to watch. But there is something in Jenny's own face, and in the children I work with, that I've seen before too many times to count. A longing, a deep-seated need. I wish I had something to offer Jenny, some words, a hug, a pat on the shoulder. But I've got nothing. All I can think about is Avery.

Chapter 14

Jenny looked carefully over at Maudene as they made their way through the hospital parking lot toward the car. Maudene's steps were slow as if she were hesitant to leave. The day had grown hotter somehow and Jenny felt the rubber bottoms of her flip-flops soften as heat rose from the asphalt. Jenny knew that Maudene wanted to stay with her daughter, but they wouldn't let Jenny anywhere near the pediatric intensive care unit and Ellen wanted Maudene to go and get her other children. "I could sit in the waiting room," Jenny offered once again. Jenny was good at waiting patiently. She waited whenever they visited one of his father's friend-girls, whenever the truck broke down and whenever she had to wait for her father to come home after a night out with his friends. Jenny was the queen of waiting.

"That's okay, Jenny," Maudene assured her, unlocking the car door though her gaze returned to the hospital. "Besides, I can help by going and getting Lucas and Leah."

"I really don't mind," Jenny said sunnily. "I won't bug anyone. You could even just drop me off at your house if you want to come back. I won't steal anything."

Maudene gave a little chuckle and Jenny wasn't sure why but was glad for it. "I'm not worried a bit about that." They both slid into the car, the temperature of the vinyl seats causing them both to fidget uncomfortably. Jenny moved to roll down her window and Maudene put up a hand to stop her. "Wait just a minute," she ordered, and Jenny's finger froze on the button. The air in the small car was sodden and heavy. Immediately a thin layer of perspiration appeared above Maudene's lip.

Jenny watched Maudene out of the corner of her eye as the older woman propped her hands firmly on the steering wheel and closed her eyes. Jenny liked to watch people when they didn't know she was looking. She gathered faces like people gathered pretty stones or shells on the beach. Maudene had an interesting face, Jenny decided. Not beautiful, but maybe it was at one time. The skin beneath her chin sagged, and deep wrinkles had settled into the corners of her eyes and around her lips. She had a narrow, straight nose with faint freckles scattered across the bridge. Jenny had always wanted freckles, but to her dismay her skin was, in her opinion, colorless and boring like a cheap piece of manila drawing paper they had to use in art class. Maudene's cloud-white hair was pulled back in a neat ponytail and Jenny peered more closely to see if she could get a hint as to what color it used to be. The heat within the confines of the car was becoming stifling and Jenny felt the tickle of droplets of sweat skimming down her back. Maudene remained still, eyes closed, chin tucked into her chest.

Jenny wondered if she could be sleeping but didn't know how that could be possible in the rain forest that was overtaking the yellow VW. Jenny felt suddenly,

overwhelmingly thirsty. Her tongue felt heavy and dry,
her stomach vaguely sick. Slightly panicked, Jenny had
reached over to shake Maudene out of whatever trance
she was in when Maudene's eyes opened. With a quick
swipe of her fingers Maudene swept away the moisture
on her cheeks that Jenny, uncomfortably, realized were
probably tears.

"My daughter is a good mother," Maudene said, eyes
fixed on the windshield, and with an angry flick of her
wrist she started the car and Jenny took this as permission to roll down her window. Even the hot air outside
the windows was a welcome relief from the stagnant
sauna of the car and Jenny gulped great breaths of air.

"I can sit in the waiting room," Jenny said again. "I
don't mind."

Maudene reached over and patted Jenny's hand and
smiled sadly. "No, no. We are going to go to the grocery store and pick up a few things. I've got company
coming." At Jenny's confused look, she continued. "My
grandchildren. They are going to stay with me for a few
days so Ellen and Adam can be with Avery at the hospital as much as possible."

"Boys or girls?" Jenny asked.

"One of each," Maudene answered as she pulled out
of the hospital parking lot. Jenny liked Maudene just
fine, but the thought of meeting her grandchildren made
her stomach bubble nervously.

"You know, I haven't forgotten about you and your...
situation," Maudene added after a slight hesitation.
Jenny busied herself by looking at her fingernails. She
had always wanted long, pretty nails, but hers were
short and stubby and ragged from constant gnawing.
"If I'm going to help you, you're going to have to give

me some more information." Jenny fiddled with the radio, trying to find a station that played something besides talking. "It's just that there is so much happening," Maudene continued, "with my granddaughter. Later, after we go and get Leah and Lucas, we have to talk. Decide what to do next. That social worker I told you about—" Maudene looked over as Jenny leaned her head slightly out the passenger-side window hoping for a slightly cooler slice of air. "It's my daughter." Jenny closed her eyes trying to calm her stomach, which was starting to feel wobbly again. "Jenny," Maudene said more firmly. "Look at me." Jenny swung her eyes toward the older woman in tired resignation and prepared herself for the word that she was soon to be dropped off at the police station or in front of the Department of Human Services. "It's going to be okay," Maudene said with finality. "I promise."

They drove in silence through the streets of Cedar City. Jenny's initial appraisal of the town as being somewhat dumpy was quickly changing. They wound through neighborhoods where the trees along the streets yawned over them in a great green canopy and where houses stood solid and upright. Nothing like the sagging structures in her neighborhood back home.

They pulled into the parking lot of a large, newly constructed grocery store.

"Hey, we have one of these," Jenny exclaimed. "It's just not so big."

Together the two wound their way across the gleaming floors and aisles brimming with food, and when they were through, Jenny helpfully set the groceries on the conveyor belt. She loved to hear the rhythmic beep of each item being passed over the scanner. *Mine,* each beep seemed to say and her stomach began to grumble.

Jenny and Maudene loaded the groceries into the narrow, shallow storage space in the hood of the VW. "Can I have these?" Jenny asked, holding up the Bugles. "I can pay you for them," she added.

"Help yourself." Maudene waved her hand dismissively. "I think it's gotten even hotter, if that's possible." She squinted up at the sun, which seemed too far away, too pale, to be emitting such heat.

Jenny tore open the bag of Bugles, sending a rainfall of chips into the air.

"Whoops." Jenny automatically bent over to retrieve them and popped one in her mouth. She caught Maudene's observant eye and let them fall to the concrete.

"I bet the birds will eat them," Maudene said, climbing into the car.

Jenny settled into the passenger seat, arranged five of the cone-shaped Bugles onto each finger of her right hand and waggled them at Maudene. "This is the best way to eat them," Jenny explained. She plucked each off with her lips, noisily chewed, and then replaced each Bugle. "What are you going to tell them?" Jenny asked, tilting the bag toward Maudene, who shook her head.

"Tell whom?" Maudene asked as she drove from the parking lot.

"Tell your grandkids. Who I am?" Jenny asked. "We could say I'm your neighbor's grandkid or maybe someone from work needed you to babysit me. You could say someone's mother died and they couldn't afford two plane tickets and she asked if you could watch me for a little while." Jenny sat back with a satisfied smile. "That will work."

"I'm not going to lie to my grandchildren," Maudene said firmly. "What I mean is, I don't think we need to make up a story," Maudene amended gently after seeing Jenny's stung expression.

"Okay," Jenny said, blushing furiously and sliding down in her seat.

They continued on in silence, Jenny staring out the window until a green street sign caught her attention. *Hickory,* it said. She sat up tall in her seat and began counting the number of streets they passed until Maudene signaled a right turn. Seven streets. She was only seven streets away from her grandmother's street. She wanted out of the car but didn't know how to get Maudene to stop. Three blocks later they turned into an older but well-tended neighborhood, with small houses, neatly mowed lawns littered with bicycles, baseball gloves and other detritus of childhood. Maudene pulled up to a tidy two-story where a young boy stood at the front door, hands pressed against the glass. When he spied Maudene's yellow car he disappeared briefly and returned with a woman and three other children. Three blocks back that way and then seven more blocks to Hickory. Jenny had walked to places much farther away than that.

Maudene put the car into Park and stepped from the car, signaling Jenny to join her. "Nah," Jenny said, opening the passenger-side door. "I'll just wait here."

Jenny watched as Maudene made her way up the front steps and as a heavily pregnant woman answered the door, followed closely by a boy and a girl just around Jenny's age. Jenny waited until Maudene stepped into the house and then eased herself from the car, closing the door quietly behind her. First slowly and then more quickly she began walking. Three blocks back that way and then seven more to Hickory Street and her grandmother.

Chapter 15

After saying goodbye to my mother and Jenny, Adam and I move quickly down the quiet corridor toward the pediatric intensive care unit past the nurses in brightly colored scrubs and doctors in white coats. We check in at the nurses' desk and we are directed to Avery's room.

As much as I want to get to Avery, I'm afraid of what I will find and I let Adam step into the room first. A small cry escapes from his lips and I force myself to look. Avery looks so small lying on her back in the center of the high-railed crib; the strange IV still snakes from her knee, which is taped securely in place to a padded board.

"What is that?" I ask the nurse who has followed us into the room.

"It's called an Intraosseous IV. It's a device used to puncture an IV line directly into the bone marrow of the child. It's important to get fluids right into her," says the young nurse in pale blue scrubs dotted with grinning frogs and dragonflies. "We'll have to watch her carefully to make sure she doesn't pull out her IV. I'm Meredith—I'll be taking care of Avery tonight."

"I'm Avery's mother, Ellen. And this is Adam, Avery's father." I nod toward my husband. I can see the fear on his face.

"Can we touch her?" I ask.

"Yes, please do."

I reach through the crib bar for Avery's hand. It is cool to the touch. "Can we stay with her tonight? Do we have to leave at a certain time?"

"One parent is welcome to stay the night in the room. Any siblings?" Meredith asks.

"Two," I say. "An older brother and sister. Nine and seven."

"Kids under twelve aren't normally allowed on the PICU. Hopefully Avery will be here just a short while and we can get her to the general pediatric floor. Brothers and sisters can visit down on that floor."

I lightly press my thumb into Avery's palm. It is soft and cool. "She's just sleeping?" I ask.

"Yes, she's just resting right now." Meredith lowers one side of the crib, leans over, checks the IV site and takes Avery's temperature. "One hundred and one," Meredith reports, writing it down on Avery's chart. "Down another half a degree. That's good."

Adam stands close behind me, looking down at Avery from over my shoulder. "Is she in pain?" he asks, his voice shaking with emotion.

"She's resting comfortably. We'll watch her carefully. The doctor will be in a little bit later to check on her again and will talk to you." She smiles encouragingly at us and leaves the room.

Stroking Avery's hand, I marvel at her tiny fingernails. Her face looks thinner somehow, more gaunt. How can a one-year-old be gaunt? I wonder. "I wish

I could hold her," I say. "Do you think they'll let me hold her?"

"Ellen," Adam says softly.

"I mean, I think if they would just let me hold her for a few minutes…"

"Ellen," Adam says again, setting his hands on my shoulders and turning me around. "We need to talk about what happened."

I step backward, lightly bumping into the crib; a faint squawk comes from my child, a brief, pained protest. We both watch, holding our breath as she settles back into sleep. "It was an accident. A stupid accident, Adam. I didn't hear you, I didn't know." I struggle to keep my voice low. "I promise you, I had no idea that Avery was in the van."

Adam holds his hand out trying to placate me, his eyes darting back and forth from me, to Avery, to the doorway, back to me. "I know. I know it was an accident, Ellen. But it was a bad accident."

"Not now, Adam," I plead with him. "Please do not do this now. We do need to talk about this, but not right now." I am crying openly now. I can't stand to see him look at me the way he is, with disbelief, disappointment.

A retching sound comes from the crib and instantly we are both at Avery's side. Her eyes are woeful slits, sunken into her head, trying to open but keep falling closed. Heaves wrack her little body and a surprisingly small amount of liquid spews from her mouth. Adam hurries out into the hall to summon help, while with one hand I use a tissue to wipe away the spittle that remains on Avery's lips and the other to try to comfort her. She is shivering; goose bumps erupt beneath my fingers and her lower lip trembles in pain or fright. Probably both.

A doctor and Meredith, with Adam close behind, come into the room. "Vomiting is common with heatstroke. So is diarrhea," the doctor explains. She is fit and wiry, somewhere in her late fifties, with ash-colored hair cut into a razor-sharp bob. "That's one of the reasons we need to keep hydrating Avery." We all look down at Avery, who has settled back into a fitful sleep, a wet thumb sliding from her slack mouth then being replaced. "I'm Dr. Grant, one of the pediatric physicians on staff. Dr. Campbell, the nephrologist who is overseeing Avery's case, will stop by shortly." I am chilled by this statement. Avery has been reduced to a case that must be overseen. "Dr. Campbell specializes in kidney function. In assessing someone who comes to us with heatstroke we watch for kidney problems, rapid heartbeat, hyperventilation and seizures. All of which Avery has displayed."

Next to me, Adam is swallowing hard and breathing deeply and I'm worried that he might start hyperventilating. I reach for his hand, but he shoves them in his pockets, his face to the ceiling, eyes closed. The doctor must be worried, as well. "Let's sit down for a minute and talk more," she suggests. In the small room, even though it is set up to house two patients, Adam sits in a recliner covered in green, faux-leather material while Dr. Grant and I each pull up an institutional plastic chair. Once Adam's breathing has calmed, Dr. Grant continues. "We've also ordered several tests—a chest X-ray to check for edema and acute respiratory distress, an electrocardiogram and an echocardiogram and a CT of the head to look for any brain swelling. We've already started running several lab tests. Organ failure, renal failure, especially, is often found in heatstroke patients.

"I also need to tell you that as a medical professional,

I'm a mandatory reporter…" Dr. Grant says as Meredith busies herself with Avery's IV tubing, avoiding eye contact with us. I know exactly what a mandatory reporter is. I'm one myself. Iowa law defines classes of people who must make a report of child abuse within twenty-four hours when they believe a child is a victim of abuse. These mandatory reporters are professionals who have frequent contact with children, including those in medicine, education, child care, law enforcement and, of course, social work.

"I understand," I interrupt, holding up my hand to stop her. "I'm a social worker. I will call my supervisor right now. It was an accident, just an awful accident."

The doctor nods. "I'm sure everything will get sorted out." Dr. Grant stands and Adam and I do the same. "In the meantime, we will continue to watch Avery very closely. Do you have any questions?"

"Will she be okay?" Adam asks. "She's not going to die, is she?" Each word is brittle, in danger of breaking. Without even looking at him, I know that Adam is trying to be strong, trying not to cry.

"Avery's condition is very serious. The very young and the very old are much more susceptible to heatstroke and its lingering effects. The next several hours are critical, but she's right where she needs to be."

Dr. Grant exits and Adam and I watch silently as Meredith exchanges Avery's empty IV bag with a full one. When she leaves, I step closely behind Adam, press my face to his back, encircling my arms around his midsection, inhaling his smell, a mixture of fresh-cut grass and sunshine. And something else, something unpleasant. Fear, I think. "I'm so sorry," I whisper into the fabric of his t-shirt. He doesn't answer, but carefully untangles himself from my grasp and walks out of the room, only pausing to touch Avery's little hand as he leaves.

I pull up a chair as close as possible to Avery's crib. I try to keep my hands on my lap, but they keep straying to stroke her forehead, now smooth in sleep, or to squeeze her hand. I know she needs to rest so that her little body will heal, so that her heart will return beating to its regular, strong cadence and her kidneys will resume carrying waste and water away from her blood, so that her temperature will fall to a tepid ninety-eight point six degrees. I can't stop the tears—they fall freely down my face, rolling down my neck, dampening the collar of my blouse.

I don't want to leave Avery's side, will not leave her side. Adam's disappointment in me is a physical ache and I wonder where he has run off to. I don't know what I can say or do to convince him that I had no idea that Avery was in the car. That I am so sorry. I blow my nose and wash my hands vigorously in the small bathroom connected to Avery's room.

I need to call Caren, my supervisor, right away, inform her about what has happened. My mind flashes to what my mother has said about the television reports. In a matter of hours, if it hasn't happened already, the entire state is going to know that a social worker has left her child in a van, unattended, on the hottest day of the year. I will be crucified. Surprisingly, this doesn't terrify me the way it should. I would offer out my palms to be nailed to a tree, gladly, if I could undo what I have done.

The door opens and I expect the nurse, but it is my husband. His face is gray, his eyes frantic. In two large steps he is in front of me and I quickly rise to my feet. "Did something happen?" I ask, fearfully looking down at Avery. She is sleeping so peacefully. Her chest is rising and falling. "Did the doctors find something out?"

Adam grabs my hands in his, holds them tightly, almost painfully. "I should have made sure that you heard me." His voice is barely a whisper. I have to lean in more closely to hear him. "I should have come out to the van to tell you that I put Avery in the backseat. I'm sorry."

My shoulders sag in relief. "We'll get through this, okay?" he assures me. I nod, my face pressed against his chest, and I begin to cry. Great, heaving sobs that I try to bite back so that I don't disturb Avery, but I can't. I hold on to Adam for a moment longer and then extract myself from his arms and escape to the tiny bathroom in the corner of Avery's hospital room. I turn on the faucet to try and drown out the sound of my weeping. Adam's words are a gift that I am at once grateful for and undeserving of. When I look up into the mirror over the sink I look wretched. My hair is standing on end, my eyes are puffy and bloodshot, my skin blotchy and the tip of my nose bright red. I look down and my knees are skinned and dotted with dried blood from where I had knelt down next to Avery after she was pulled from the van. The hem of my dress is edged with dirt and grass stains, and dry earth has wedged beneath my fingernails. I look back into the mirror and try to see what I've seen in the eyes of countless other mothers I have met over the years. The ones who have dipped their children into scalding hot water, knocked them to the ground, beaten them with belts. I lean in more closely to the mirror until my nose is nearly touching the glass. I search for the manic glint or the deadened gaze in the green depths of my eyes. But it's just me. I can't be like them, those women.

There's a rap at the door. "You, okay?" Adam asks.

"Fine," I answer. My voice shrill and high. Not my voice at all. "I'm fine." I wash my face and scrub the dirt from beneath my nails. My dress is hopeless and a sweaty, acrid odor rises from me. I need a shower but don't want to leave Avery to go home to retrieve a change of clothes.

I step from the bathroom and see that another doctor has come into Avery's room. He is a tall, slope-shouldered man of about sixty. Reading glasses sit atop his gray head.

"Mr. and Mrs. Moore," the doctor greets us with a nod. "I'm Dr. Campbell, the nephrologist. I'd like to update you on Avery's condition."

Once again we take a seat and anxiously look at the expert who can save our child. "We have Avery's core temperature normalized. We continue to watch her closely for delayed end-organ dysfunction. This means that even though her temperature is normal and she is stabilized, she remains at high risk for multiple organ failure, the breakdown of muscles, high potassium levels, low calcium levels and abnormally elevated phosphorus levels, all which can lead to kidney injury and renal failure."

Dr. Campbell scans our faces as if trying to glean whether or not we understood what he was saying. We both nod. "We will monitor Avery until we are sure these levels are within normal ranges and she is seizure-free."

"How long do you think that will be?" Adam asks.

Dr. Campbell shakes his head. "It could take twenty-four hours or weeks. It just depends on how quickly Avery responds to treatment."

Before leaving us, head bowed, Dr. Campbell rests one capable hand on each of our shoulders and I'm reminded of the faith healers who, just by touch, supposedly can send currents of curative volts of electricity through your system. I feel nothing. Adam and I sit next to Avery in her hospital room for the next four hours, speaking only out of necessity. He flicks through a stack of old newspapers, periodically sending text updates to well-wishers. Waves of tears come and go. I try to cry soundlessly, keeping my eyes on my daughter who is sleeping fitfully. Every squawk she makes sends me to my feet.

I hear a small commotion outside the room and look up to find Caren Regis, my supervisor at DHS, as well as Richard Prieto, the county attorney that I've worked with many times. I am relieved to see Caren, but I'm puzzled about Prieto's presence. I'm not here today to visit a neglected, abused child or here to chronicle the many indignities they have endured. The sight of Richard Prieto is alarming.

I put a finger to my lips to signal that Avery is sleeping and lead them to the hallway just outside the PICU entrance. "Hi, Caren, Richard." I nod briefly at each of them. "What's going on?" I ask, panic clawing at my chest. Wordlessly, Prieto hands me a piece of paper. A piece of paper that I have handed to parents countless number of times. A piece of paper that has the power to snap a mother's heart into two jagged pieces. "Caren?" I say, looking at her in disbelief. Her gaze remains steady, unemotional, just as mine would have been if we had reversed roles.

Prieto clears his throat. "I wanted to inform you in person. We're discussing the possibility of assembling a grand jury to determine if we will move forward with formal charges."

I'm still looking at Caren, waiting for an explanation, the words on the piece of paper ordering me to stay more than five hundred feet away from my daughter at all times blurring. "Charges?" I finally whisper, my throat suddenly dry.

"Child endangerment with serious bodily injury. Iowa Code Section 726.6," Prieto says.

"I know the code," I say sharply to Prieto. Iowa Code Section 726.6 is the child endangerment section. If the child suffered death, it would be a Class B felony, with a maximum of twenty-five years in prison. I turn back to Caren and lower my voice. "Caren, is this necessary? You know me..." I try to hand back the piece of paper. Prieto pushes it back at me.

Caren straightens her spine and her face resumes the professional mask I am used to seeing. "You know how it works, Ellen. We're going to pass the DHS investigation to Peosta County to insure an unbiased examination of the facts."

I scan the piece of paper that Prieto has pressed into my fingers. "Oh, no, no, no," I cry in disbelief. "A protective order? Are you telling me I can't see Avery?" My voice cracks. By the look on Caren's face she understands that this is killing me. I wonder where the assertive, decisive woman I was just a few hours ago has gone. I should be demanding to see my daughter, but I feel unworthy, so afraid. "What about Leah and Lucas? Can I still see them? You can't keep me away from them, can you?" Of course I know they can keep

me away from my other children if they think that they
will be endangered in my care. For the first time the
implications of what I've done and how it could impact
Leah and Lucas hits me. How will they look at me, what
will they think of me once they learn the details of what
happened to their sister?

I want to scream at Prieto and Caren. I want to ask
them how they can live with themselves knowing that
they are keeping a very sick little girl away from her
mother.

"Richard, can you give us a second?" Caren asks
Prieto, who looks suspicious but pulls out his phone
and walks away. "Ellen…" The impassive expression
remains on her face but her voice softens. "We have to
go by the book on this one. I know it was a terrible accident. Richard knows that it was a terrible accident,
but we have to investigate carefully and thoroughly just
as we would if it was anyone else. In fact, we have to
be more thorough."

"Caren, what's going on? Avery could die and you're
telling me I can't be there with her. What if Avery is
crying for me? I can't go to her? What about Lucas and
Leah? Are you keeping them away from me, too? You
can't think I'm a danger to them?" I'm so afraid of the
answer. I know the process very well.

"You will get an FSRP just like anyone else in this
situation," Caren explains.

I shake my head unable to believe what I'm hearing.
We will be assigned a Family Safety, Risk and Per-
manency caseworker or a FRSP. An in-home provider
whose job it is to make our lives very uncomfortable.
FRSPs are young, overworked and underpaid. Most
have an undergraduate degree in some kind of human

services field, but they are not experts. They are not counselors and they get sent out into homes to be the eyes and ears of the department. The FRSP assigned to us can drop in at any time of the day or night. She can enter our home, ask to see any part of the house. She can come to see what we are making for dinner, come to see if the house is clean, if the beds are made. She can talk to Lucas and Leah without us being present. Most importantly she checks to see if the children are safe. It can be excruciating for families, but there is a reason for it. I just can't believe it's needed in my case, for my family.

As if reading my mind, like she has always been able to do, Caren tosses me a scrap of hope, lowers her voice to a low whisper. "I know this was an accident, Ellen. I will do anything in my power to help get you through this. They have twenty days to investigate this and I'm positive they will find in your favor."

"Caren," I plead, reaching for her hand. "I need to be with Avery. She could die."

"Twenty days," she says, gently pulling away from me.

"What if we don't have twenty days?" I say again, more desperately. "I need to see her. Please," I beg.

Caren lowers her eyes and takes a short, harsh breath and raises her hands helplessly. "I don't know what else to tell you. For now the right thing is for us to follow procedure."

"The right thing is to let me see Avery. I'm her mother—she needs me!" I am crying openly now. No one walking down the busy hallways of the hospital even slows down or casts a sympathetic eye toward me. Everyone is either immersed in their own personal medical hell or so used to the daily dramas played out within these corridors they don't even notice the sobbing woman begging for permission to see her children.

Prieto is walking back toward us. "You need to leave right now," he says sternly, looking around to see if anyone is listening. "You need to stay away from your daughter and the PICU until the investigation is complete." He sighs. "And get a lawyer, Ellen," Prieto advises. "You're going to need a good one."

They leave me standing there by myself and I sink onto a padded bench beneath a window that looks out over the hospital parking lot and cry.

Chapter 16

Jenny counted blocks as she walked. One. What would her grandmother say when she opened the door and saw her on the front step? She would be surprised, that was for sure. But would she be happy? Jenny thought of the birthday card nestled in her backpack. Yes, Jenny was certain. Her grandma would be happy.

Two, three blocks. Seven more to go. Jenny picked up her pace, anticipation propelling her forward. Four, five, six. What if her grandmother had moved away? What if no one answered the door? What would Jenny do then? She wasn't sure if she could find her way back to Maudene's house or if she even wanted to. The threat of calling a social worker scared Jenny more than wandering the streets of Cedar City. There was no way she was going to go into foster care.

Seven, eight blocks. Only two more. Despite the heat, Jenny started to run. Two more blocks and she could be at her grandmother's house. Someone who had to love her because they were related. Jenny quickly pushed away the thought of her mother. Being related hadn't mattered much to her. Breathing heavily, Jenny slowed as the green street sign announcing Hickory Street came into view. Jenny wasn't sure which way to turn. Left or right. She pulled the lavender envelope from her bag, now smudged with sweat and dirt, and committed the address to memory—2574 Hickory Street. Left, she decided. One-thirteen, was scrolled in black letters on the first house she passed, then 111, 109, 107.

With a sinking heart Jenny realized that she was moving in the wrong direction. And even though she wasn't very good at math, Jenny understood that it would take a long time to walk from 107 Hickory all the way to 2574. With sagging shoulders, Jenny turned and started walking in the opposite direction.

Twenty minutes later, Jenny could feel her scalp burning as the afternoon sun beat down relentlessly on top of her head. Knowing that she was already sunburned, Jenny stepped into the slightly cooler shade beneath an enormous oak tree and pulled out a plastic bottle half-filled with tepid water and restrained herself by taking just one drink. Jenny gnawed on her thumbnail as, once again, doubts began to swirl around her head. What would happen if her grandmother no longer lived on Hickory Street? With a sniffle, Jenny hoisted her backpack onto her shoulders and stepped out from the leafy branches, squinting into the unyielding sunshine as a familiar round car pulled up next to the curb. Three faces stared out at her from inside the car.

Maudene rolled down her window and Jenny cringed slightly, awaiting the angry admonishment she expected to follow. Maudene looked kindly at her as her two grandchildren eyed her suspiciously. "At least let me take you to wherever you're going."

"My grandma's," Jenny said in a tremulous voice.

Saying it out loud to Maudene made it seem even more real, even more possible. Through the window, Jenny handed Maudene the envelope with her grandmother's address.

"It's going to be a tight fit," Maudene told Jenny as she squeezed into the back of the car with a boy who looked a few years younger than she.

"This is Jenny," Maudene said simply. Jenny cut her eyes toward Maudene, waiting to see what she would say next. "Jenny, these are my grandchildren, Leah and Lucas."

"Hi," Jenny said shyly.

"I want to go see Avery." Leah barely glanced Jenny's way. "When can we see her?"

"Soon," Maudene promised. "We have one stop to make and then we'll head over to my house and call your mom and dad to see how Avery's doing."

They drove in silence. Jenny noticed this about Maudene. She didn't talk much while she drove. Not like her father who talked the entire time, commenting on everything from how the guy in front of them was driving to the number of potholes that pocked the road. Jenny figured this was Maudene's thinking time. Connie, her father's old friend-girl, said that everyone needed time to think. Connie said she liked to think in the shower and that Jenny's dad preferred to act first, think later. Jenny didn't think this was a compliment, but Connie smiled when she said it and had kissed her father on the cheek. Jenny didn't have a special thinking place, but thought it could probably be in a cozy bedroom like Maudene had in her house.

Jenny's heart knocked uncomfortably within her rib cage. "Maybe you could go to the door first," Jenny proposed, her voice shaking, "just to make sure it's the right house."

"I can do that," Maudene answered, surprising Jenny with a quiver in her own voice. Maudene drove slowly down the busy street and peered at each house number before announcing, "This is 2574, the address on the envelope." The four of them sat and stared across the street at the house where Jenny's mother grew up. The yellowed lawn was choked by weeds and was dotted with sprightly lawn decorations: plump garden gnomes, a small family of rabbits, an angel knelt in prayer. Jenny's shoulders dropped slightly in relief. A person who had an angel outside their home couldn't be all that bad. The small house was painted white but had grown dingy with age and with the extremes of Iowa weather. The two front windows were girded with green shutters and the window boxes were filled with what appeared to be cheap, brightly colored plastic flowers.

"Can I come with you?" Lucas asked, reaching for the door handle.

"You three stay here and wait for me to come and get you, okay?" Maudene said as she reached back and retrieved her large, black leather purse from the floor next to Jenny. Seeing Jenny's wounded expression, Maudene shook her head and smiled wearily. "I don't think you are going to steal anything from my purse, Jenny. I might need to show your grandmother some identification so she doesn't think I'm a crazy lady and call the police."

"Oh," Jenny said, taken aback. She hadn't thought of that. Maudene took a steadying breath and, with purse in hand, pushed open the car door and tripped to the curb to avoid the traffic whizzing past. Maudene looked

left and right, then left and right again, until it was safe
to cross the street. Jenny mulled over climbing out of
the car and joining Maudene on the curb and grabbing
her hand so they could cross safely together. Maudene
was still looking from left to right, and just as Jenny
was reaching for the door handle to go and cross the
street with her, Maudene saw a break in the traffic and
scurried across the street. Once safely across, Maudene
smiled and waved at Jenny, who waved back. Maudene
stood for a moment, staring up at the house then pulled
herself up to her full height, shoulders back, and carefully picked her way up the crumbling cement steps that
led to the front door. She watched, holding her breath as
Maudene raised her fist and rapped on the front door.
Finally the door opened and a figure stepped into sight.
Jenny shielded her eyes, but the sun was so bright she
couldn't tell if the person who answered the door was
male or female, young or old. Maudene, with her back
to Jenny, appeared to be talking with the figure, but
Jenny was much too far away and the traffic was too
noisy to hear over.

Though the car windows were down, the heat was
suffocating and Jenny thought about Maudene's granddaughter who nearly died while sitting in a car. She tried
to imagine what that would feel like, closed her eyes,
held her breath for as long as she could. She lasted about
twenty seconds and then gulped in the hot air greedily.
When she opened her eyes, both Leah and Lucas were
staring at her as if she was crazy.

Maudene's conversation seemed to be taking forever
and Jenny thought about climbing out to get a better
look at the person standing in the doorway. Maybe it
was her grandmother. Maybe she was a grandma who

baked cookies and knitted scarves. But maybe she was one of those grandmas who smoked long, thin cigarettes, swore and liked to watch TV all day long. And worst of all, maybe she didn't want anything to do with a granddaughter who unexpectedly showed up at her house. Before Jenny could make up her mind, Maudene turned and quickly made her way back down the steps. Jenny peered between the fast-moving traffic to try and get a glimpse of the shadow that still stood in the doorway watching Maudene's retreating back, but with no luck. Had she found her grandmother? Jenny scrutinized Maudene's face, which wore the same look that her father's did when he realized there was no beer in the fridge or the look that Connie had on her face when she received the phone call saying that her mother had a heart attack. Suddenly Jenny realized that while she couldn't see the person in the house, maybe he or she could see her and hastily slid down in the seat so that her head was hidden just below the window.

Jenny didn't sit up in her seat until Maudene got back into the car, fastened her seat belt, started the car and pulled into traffic. "Well?" Jenny finally asked. "What did they say? Does my grandma still live there?"

Maudene continued to drive in silence, her face a mask of worry. Once they arrived at Maudene's home, Leah and Lucas leaped from the car and ran into the house. Maudene and Jenny followed slowly behind and, once on the porch, Maudene took Jenny's hand in her own. "I'm sorry, Jenny," she finally said. "Your grandmother passed away last year." Maudene pulled her into a hug. "But don't worry, we'll figure something out," Maudene assured her. "I promise."

"Oh," Jenny whispered. "It doesn't really matter."

And, staring down at the wooden planks of the porch, she blinked back tears, surprised that she really did think it mattered. It mattered more than anything.

Chapter 17

I have seen the damage that parents can inflict upon their children. In my nearly indecipherable scrawl I have documented the atrocities I've seen in what my husband has named *The Notebook of Seven Sorrows*: addicted infants, convulsing, their hearts, no bigger than their tiny trembling fists, pounding in their chests. Three-year-olds who never learned to walk, the whole of their world a three-by-five crib snowing down lead-infused paint flakes. Five-year-olds whose X-rays are an atlas of human suffering. Broken bones, skull fractures, the fissures healed but the beatings not forgotten. The eleven-year-old girl whose nightmares begin when the sun sets, when her mother closes the bedroom door for the night and when her father or stepfather or mother's boyfriend silently opens her bedroom door and crawls beneath her comforter covered with dancing ballerinas. Cigarette burns, hot water burns, curling iron burns. Black eyes, busted lips, broken ribs, broken hearts. Little girls who supposedly try to fly out of their third-floor window. I have seen these firsthand. But nothing, nothing, can prepare me for the damage my carelessness has inflicted upon my own daughter.

I am not one of those parents.

Suddenly, Adam is sitting by my side, his arms around me. I am shaking with fear and rage recalling every word of my conversation with Prieto and Caren. "What's happening, Ellen?" he asks helplessly. "Did something happen to Avery?"

I force myself to stop crying. The hallway, for the moment, is empty. "I don't believe it," I say, panic flooding my chest.

"What? What?" Adam says insistently. "What's going on?"

"They said that I can't see Avery until they finish their investigation." I swallow hard; I'm having trouble forming the words.

Adam blinks and jerks his head back. "Investigation? What's to investigate? You told them what happened, right?"

"It doesn't matter what I tell them," I say bitterly. "They are going strictly by the book."

"Why would they want to do this?" Adam asks. "You've given every spare minute to taking care of the kids you work with. You protect them, for God's sake! They know what kind of person you are. It doesn't make sense."

"I know," I cry. A low growl of frustration emits from my throat and a hospital worker pushing a large cart of dirty laundry eyes us curiously as he passes by. I wait until he is out of earshot before continuing. "If Prieto or Caren treat me differently than anyone else in the same situation, their credibility would be ruined. Every decision they make will be questioned."

"But they have some discretion with these things. I know they do."

I raise my hands helplessly. "It looks like they've already made up their minds."

"How long can they keep you away from Avery?" Adam asks in defeat. His face is pinched with fatigue and worry.

"They have twenty days. They have to finish their investigation in twenty days unless they need more time and request a waiver for more time." Twenty days seems like an eternity, I can't imagine having to be away from Avery for more than a few minutes let alone twenty days.

"It doesn't seem fair," Adam says, leaning wearily against a wall. "Avery needs you right now. What happens if you just ignore Prieto and still come up to see Avery?"

"I could get arrested for violating the order of protection. This is serious," I say more to myself than to Adam. "They're looking at convening a grand jury to see if there's enough evidence to charge me with child endangerment."

If possible, Adam's face becomes even paler. "You could go to jail? Oh, my God, Ellen. What are we going to do?"

I shake my head. "I don't know," I cry, "I just don't know." I step close to him and lay my head against his chest.

"The grand jury will indict you, you know," Adam says quietly. "They always do."

I know this is true, but I don't want to believe it. Parents are on grand juries. Grandparents, too. They know the exact same thing could happen to them at any minute. Or, I think, the mothers and fathers on the grand jury will say to themselves, *How could she? How could she be so careless with something so precious? She never deserved this gift of being a parent. Send her to prison, prohibit her from seeing her children. She had her chance.*

"I'll tell them it was my fault," he says with more confidence than I know he really feels.

I rotate my head from side to side, still enveloped in his embrace. "No, don't do that. They'll know that you're just trying to protect me. No sense in you losing your job, too."

"They won't fire you," he says firmly. "They'll do their investigation and it will all be over soon." I lift my chin to look into his eyes, red with exhaustion. I don't have the heart to tell him. It doesn't matter what Caren's investigation unearths or whether Prieto's grand jury decides that there is enough evidence to send me to jail. My life as I know it is over.

Hand in hand we slowly make our way back to Avery's hospital room. I'll be damned if I don't at least get to say goodbye to my daughter. I sniffle and move purposefully toward where Avery's doctor and an unfamiliar nurse are clustered over a clipboard. "Excuse me," I say. They both look up at me. "With your permission—" I clear my throat "—I'd like to say goodbye to my daughter. It might take a few days for everything to be cleared up." They both nod, Dr. Campbell with practiced coolness, the nurse with discomfort.

Dr. Campbell scans the hallway, tilts his head toward Avery's room and I take that as an invitation to follow him. Once inside the room, Dr. Campbell closes the door behind us. Avery is lying on her back, thumb in her mouth, eyes half-open, but when she sees me they widen. She reaches for me, her arms extended her fingers opening and closing. Her way of saying *gimme*. I look back at Dr. Campbell for permission and again I am struck by how my life suddenly mirrors those of my clients. They would give me the same looks. *Can I go to my son? Can I hold my daughter? Am I worthy?* Now it's Dr. Campbell who wields the power. "Take your time," he says. "I'll just sit over here." He indicates a hard-backed chair in the corner of the tiny room. It's the farthest away he can go in order to give us privacy, but his message is clear. He can defy the protection order just this once, allowing me to say goodbye to Avery, but he won't, under any circumstances, allow me to be alone with her.

"Avery," I whisper, tears streaming unstaunched down my cheeks. A wisp of a smile greets me. Weakly, Avery raises her arms to me and I look at Dr. Campbell, hoping for his permission to take her into my arms.

He shakes his head apologetically. "Her condition isn't stable enough for you to hold her just yet." Tearfully, I take her little hand in mine and brush my thumb across her dimpled knuckles trying to memorize the way she looks in this exact moment. I brush her wispy hair away from her forehead. There are dark circles beneath her eyes, her skin is pale, but at least it's cool to the touch. I will never forget the intensity of heat that rose from my daughter's pores when she was pulled from the van.

She makes no sound and I wonder if the trauma of the whole event has caused her to regress in regard to some of her milestones or, worse, if some irreversible cognitive damage has been done. I push those terrible thoughts away and focus on the daughter I have right here. Avery is struggling to keep her eyes open, but when she does her gaze goes right to my face as if making sure I'm still standing over her. I know my time with Avery is short and that I need to say what must be said, understanding that it could be days before I'm allowed to see her, speak to her again, but I am conscious of Dr. Campbell sitting nearby so I lean down into the hospital crib and whisper into her ear. "I'm so sorry about what happened," I say.

Avery's eyelids surrender to exhaustion, her thumb poked securely into her mouth, her chest rising and falling steadily.

"I'm so sorry." I beg my daughter for forgiveness. "Mommy didn't mean for it to happen. I didn't know you were in the car." I go on, knowing that Avery doesn't care about intentions or accidents, just knows that her mother had left her tethered into the back of a van whose interior reached one hundred and nine degrees in a matter of minutes. Will she remember this forever? An indelible imprint that travels with her the rest of her life? Maybe not the event itself, but the feeling of being abandoned, forgotten? Would she grow up unable to trust, or have post-traumatic stress disorder? A fear of small, enclosed spaces, of hospitals? Of me?

"Mommy has to go and take care of Lucas and Leah right now, so Daddy is going to stay with you. You'll see me in a few days… I promise," I add after a slight hesitation. "I love you, Avery," I sob, and Avery sleepily reaches up to touch my face. "I love you so, so much," I say fiercely, and kiss her four times—forehead, left cheek, right cheek, lips. Just like we do every night before bed.

Behind me I hear the scrape of chair legs against the floor and understand that Dr. Campbell has gotten to his feet, signaling that my time with Avery has come to an end. I don't move until Dr. Campbell clears his throat and Adam places a gentle hand on my elbow. I nearly double over from the pain of stepping away from Avery, like a piece of my soul has been ripped from within me.

A birdlike scream emerges from the crib and I turn back to see Avery's eyelids flutter violently.

"What's happening?" I ask desperately as Dr. Campbell brushes past me.

"Seizure," he says shortly.

Avery's hands clench into tight fists and her little body begins to rhythmically spasm, the IV in her knee swaying with each shudder. "Do something," I beg as Dr. Campbell calmly looks at his watch. Saliva bubbles at Avery's lips and trickles down her chin. "Please," I say, but the doctor remains maddeningly still, clinically looking down at my daughter.

"Please," I plead again, this time to Adam, who steps forward and reaches into the crib to lift Avery into his arms.

"No!" Dr. Campbell says sharply. "That could do more harm." Adam freezes, then brings his hands up to his face, covering his eyes. Though I want to do the same, I am transfixed, can't pull my gaze away from the unmistakable fear in Avery's glassy stare until her taut muscles seem to relax.

"Seventy-three seconds," Dr. Campbell announces. "This one didn't last as long as the ones in the ambulance and in the E.R." Avery begins to cry, great gasping breaths, and I have to ball my hands together to keep from snatching her up.

"Is she going to be okay? Is she in pain?" I ask, my own breath coming out in sharp, hitching gulps.

"It's concerning, but not uncommon," Dr. Campbell answers. "We'll watch her closely, adjust her medication. It can take some time to get it just right. Seizures can be exhausting. She will most likely sleep now." He gestures toward the door and looks expectantly at me.

"What?" I squawk in disbelief. "I can't leave her like this." I am vaguely aware that Adam has backed up against the far wall of the hospital room and that I am crying again.

"I'm sorry," Dr. Campbell says. The clinical tone of his voice has fallen away and all I hear is sympathy. "We have to follow the court order."

"Please," I cry. "I can't leave. Please don't make me leave," I am begging now, tugging on the sleeve of Dr. Campbell's lab coat.

Hearing the desperation in my voice, Adam comes to me, enclosing his arms around me. "It's okay, El," he says, trying to reassure me, but I hear the tremor in his voice. "I'll call you if anything happens," Adam promises, trying to hold back his own tears. "I love you." He leans over and kisses me.

"Love you," I manage to say. I nod at Dr. Campbell in gratitude for this time with my daughter. He nods back and I think I see tears glistening in his own eyes.

I step out of Avery's room, dazed, not sure what to do next. The PICU is a buzz of activity. Doctors and nurses move in purposeful strides, parents in various stages of disbelief and grief are trying to hold back their own tears. I need to go to Leah and Lucas but feel incapable of offering them one single thing. Blindly I make my way out of the unit and wander the halls until I find a public bathroom. I go inside, lock the door behind me, sit on the floor and cry. I do my best to keep my sobs quiet, but they come from a place that I didn't know existed and I'm sure the sounds of my cries slip out beneath the door and into the hallway. I cry until there are no more tears, vomit into the toilet, stand on shaky legs, wash my hands and face, step out into the hall.

I know I need to go to my other children, but I find I can't leave the hospital. I need to at least be in the same building as Avery. I walk back toward the PICU, stop outside the entrance and then turn back around. Taking a deep breath, I begin walking, counting each step on the way to five hundred. Five hundred feet, the protective order says. The distance of one-and-a-half football fields, the height of a five-story building, one tenth of a mile. Five hundred feet will keep my child safe. Four hundred ninety-seven, ninety-eight, ninety-nine, five hundred. I find myself next to a sunny bank of windows near some elevators. There are no chairs or couches, but it doesn't matter. I find a corner away from foot traffic and slide to the floor, my back resting against the wall, and wait. Five hundred feet and no more.

Chapter 18

Jenny lagged behind as she helped Maudene, Leah and Lucas begin to unload the bags of groceries, some of the frozen items already a melted mess.

"Whew," Jenny exclaimed with false cheer as she set the bags on the table in the breakfast nook, trying to mask the disappointment of believing that she had a grandmother only to learn that she had died before she ever got the chance to meet her. "These are heavy!" Dolly approached on arthritic knees and sniffed at the bags curiously. "No, no!" Jenny scolded. "You get!"

"She's not hurting anything," Leah said hotly, settling her parcels next to Jenny's.

Jenny looked skeptically down at the dog.

"Dolly's a good dog." Lucas came to the dog's defense. "Right, Grandma?"

"Wes trained Dolly very well," Maudene agreed. "She'd no sooner eat something off a counter than bite someone."

"Who's Wes?" asked Jenny, digging through the plastic bags, pulling out the frozen items and placing them in a neat pile.

"Our grandpa," Leah said derisively.

Jenny felt her face burn. "Well, how would I know *that?* I just got here."

"Now, now," Maudene said soothingly. "Jenny, why don't you help me unpack the groceries, and Leah and Lucas, you go get settled in."

"Where are we going to sleep?" Leah asked, casting a disdainful look at Jenny.

"Well, there are a few options," Maudene said as she opened the refrigerator and stowed away the gallon of milk and a carton of orange juice. "If Jenny ends up staying the night, you and Jenny could share your mom's old room and Lucas can have the boys' old room. There's just one bed in there. Or Leah and Lucas can have your mom's old room and Jenny can go into the boys' room. Whatever you decide."

"Lucas and me get the pink room," Leah said with finality. She hoisted her bag on her shoulder and moved toward the stairs. "Come on, Lucas."

"Hey," Jenny said, worriedly thinking of her father's t-shirt that she left behind on the bed upstairs in the pink bedroom. "My stuff is already up there!" She dropped the loaf of bread she was holding and scrambled after Leah and Lucas, who had started running up the steps. Bolstered by the excitement, Dolly gave a low-throated bark and joined the fracas, her nails clacking against the hardwood floors. Hearing the dog's approach, Jenny shrieked in fear, overtook and squeezed past Leah and Lucas on the stairs. Jenny bolted down the hallway, up the two flights of stairs and reached the pink bedroom first, flung open the door, stepped inside and slammed the door shut. She searched wildly for a lock and, after finding none, slid down to the floor with her back pressed against the door.

She heard the footfalls of Leah and Lucas, but it was the clicking of Dolly's paws scrabbling hurriedly through the hallway that brought the tears.

"Open up!" Leah called through the doorway and turned the knob. Jenny could feel Leah and Lucas knocking and pushing against the wooden door, forcing it open an inch. Jenny pushed back, pressing her feet into the floor trying to maintain her footing. "Open up!" Leah shouted again. "This is where Lucas and I are staying! It's not your house!" In the small opening that Leah and Lucas had established, Dolly inserted her snout, her nose brushing against Jenny's elbow. Jenny fell away from the door as if bitten, clutched her arm and scuttled on her knees across the bedroom floor. With mouths agape, Leah and Lucas watched the unkempt girl cowering in fear beneath the whitewashed desk where their mother, as a child, did her homework. Dolly, exhausted by the to-do, climbed creakily up onto the bed, curled up into a small ball and closed her eyes. In shame, Jenny laid her head against her knees and covered her head with her hands and tried to calm her breathing.

"What in the world?" Maudene exclaimed as she stepped into the room and surveyed the scene. "What happened?"

"She's crazy," Leah said just loud enough for Jenny to hear her.

"I am not!" Jenny protested. "That dog bit me!"

"Oh my goodness," Maudene said, rushing over to Jenny. "Let me see." Jenny gingerly showed Maudene her arm, offering it with marked difficulty so that Maudene could inspect the injury.

"Dolly didn't bite her," Lucas said, sitting down on the bed next to an oblivious Dolly. "She's making that up."

"I am not," Jenny said woefully. "She attacked me."

"Now, now," Maudene said, gently examining Jenny's elbow. "Leah and Lucas, you take Dolly on downstairs and finish putting the groceries away. We'll be down in a little bit." With a sniff, Leah eased Dolly down off the bed by her collar and the three exited the room, letting the door shut behind them with a satisfying slam. "Let's get you out from there and I can take a better look at your arm," Maudene urged.

After making sure all was safe, Jenny unfolded herself from her crouched position and emerged from beneath the desk. "I'm sorry I made a mess," Jenny said contritely, taking in the knocked-over desk lamp and scattered pencils and markers that were stored in a whimsically decorated coffee can.

"Nothing that can't be set right," Maudene assured her. "Now sit down right here and let me take a look at your arm. I just can't believe that Dolly would bite you. She doesn't have a mean bone in her body."

Jenny's face fell. "See, it's all red." Jenny rubbed the afflicted area.

"It is that," Maudene agreed. "Do you think it might have been an accident? Maybe Dolly thought you were playing a game and she just got a little too excited?"

Jenny considered this. "Maybe."

"Well, at least the skin isn't broken," Maudene noted. "No rabies shots for you." Jenny's eyes widened in alarm. "I'm just teasing. Dolly definitely doesn't have rabies. How about I bring you up an ice pack? I bet that will make your arm feel better." Jenny nodded, wiped at her eyes and sniffled for good measure. "Were you bitten by a dog once?" Maudene asked as they moved from the room. Jenny grabbed her backpack and her father's t-shirt and glanced back for one last look.

"No, I just don't trust them," Jenny said simply, and Maudene realized that Jenny wasn't just talking about dogs anymore.

"Lucas and Leah are nice kids," Maudene assured her. "They are going through a very difficult time right now, not knowing if their little sister is going to be okay. Try and be patient with them, okay?"

Jenny didn't answer but nodded reluctantly. Maudene sighed as they slowly descended the stairs, Jenny's eyes darting around nervously for any sign of Dolly. "This room is where my sons slept when they were young. My room is right next door if you need anything during the night." Maudene pushed open the door and Jenny was pleasantly surprised. She didn't think that a room could be more wonderful than the one at the top of the house, but this one was beautiful. Jenny's bare feet, flip-flops discarded in the Dolly fiasco, sank into the thick cream-colored carpet that ran the full expanse of the room. Through the dim coolness, Jenny could see a large double bed that she figured she would need a chair to climb into. The snow-white comforter hung nearly to the floor and pillows of varying sizes, shapes, textures and shades of white formed an inviting hillock. Folded neatly at the base of the bed was a thick quilt, each patch a different square of white. Some with an intricate swirl of stitched flowers, others as simple as a dish towel. The walls were painted the color of fog.

"This ain't a boys' room." Jenny whispered because such a room called for hushed tones.

"No, I guess it isn't," Maudene chuckled. "But it sure used to be. Painted blue with posters of football players and filled with baseball cards and smelly socks."

"Don't your boys come home anymore?" Jenny asked, lightly gliding a hand across the quilt.

"Oh, once in a while. They live in Minnesota." Jenny's ears perked up with this information. She had been born in Minnesota, in a town called Blue Earth. Such a pretty name for a town, she thought, like a smooth, bright marble. "They have their own families and work. Busy." Maudene flipped on a switch and bare branches arranged in a cast-iron vase were draped with fairy lights and twinkled from the corner of the room. "When my husband got sick, he didn't sleep very well, so I slept in here a lot so he could rest. I got tired of tripping over Craig and Alan's old LEGO so I decided to redo the room."

Jenny nodded. This made sense. "Why was he sick?" Jenny asked, looking around for a place to set down her backpack, which seemed much too grimy for this room.

"Sometimes people just get sick. We don't always know why." Maudene glanced at a framed photo sitting on the bedside table of a young woman dressed in a white wedding gown standing with a man wearing a suit and tie. He had the kind of haircut that looked like you could set a plate on it and it wouldn't fall off, and he wore black, thick-framed eyeglasses. "Why don't you get settled in here and I'll go downstairs and talk to Leah and Lucas. Don't be too hard on them. They're just worried about their little sister and their mom and dad. Okay?" Jenny nodded. She certainly understood what it felt like to worry about her parents. She didn't have a brother or a sister, but she imagined it would feel much the same. Worry was an aching loneliness that you went to bed with each night and woke up with each morning. Maudene turned to leave but stopped short. "Can I call anyone for you, Jenny? I'm sure people are looking for you. Did you run away from home?"

Jenny shook her head in the negative. Maudene stood there for a moment waiting for Jenny to answer. Jenny offered nothing, just quietly began unpacking her bag, setting each item lovingly on the long low dresser that was set against one wall.

"Jenny," Maudene said and Jenny glanced up to see Maudene's face furrowed with concern. "We really need to talk."

Jenny remained silent, feeling the weight of Maudene's skeptical gaze as she continued to unpack her things, laying out a small black comb, a cell phone and several small plastic Stack figurines, the Happy Pancake mascot toy they gave out free with the purchase of a children's meal. Jenny reached back into the bag one last time, pulled out the tattered manila envelope, hesitated, changed her mind and placed it back into the bag, added her father's t-shirt and zipped it shut.

Jenny heard the quiet click of Maudene shutting the door behind her and waited until she could no longer hear her footsteps in the hallway. She regarded her father's cell phone sitting on the dresser. It wasn't a fancy phone. It flipped open and didn't have a texting keyboard like some of the kids at school had, but her father hadn't minded. She pressed the power button and the phone came to life with a brief shiver. The display read seven missed calls, one voice mail, and ten missed text messages. Someone was always texting her father. Jenny scrolled through them but found nothing of interest, just the random ramblings of her father's friends. There was one from Matthew from Dubuque saying he would meet up with them later tonight. She thought about texting him back and saying that there was a change of plans, but felt tears well in her eyes at the thought so she kept on scrolling through the list.

Her fingers hovered over the call button. Should she call Connie? What if Connie called the police and they showed up at Maudene's house? Would they think that Maudene had kidnapped Jenny? She envisioned the cops tackling Maudene the way they jumped on her father at the bus station.

"Coming down, Jenny?" Maudene called from the bottom of the steps.

"In a minute," she hollered back.

Jenny hoped that the voice message was from her father, saying that he was out of jail, that it was all just a terrible misunderstanding, that he was on his way to come and get her. In disappointment, Jenny listened to the voice mail from some credit card company saying that legal action would be taken if her father didn't send in a payment. Jenny wanted to climb onto the downy bedding but knew she was much too grimy, so she sat down on the floor, her back resting against the bed frame. Jenny reviewed her options one more time: Call Connie and ask for her help or tell Maudene what really happened to cause her to end up in Cedar City. With her stomach fluttering nervously, Jenny pressed the send button that would connect her with Connie.

Chapter 19

Minutes seem like hours and hours seem like days, but still I sit, five hundred feet from my daughter, waiting. For what, I'm not sure. The protective order to be lifted? For Avery to miraculously get better and be released from the hospital? For my husband to truly forgive me for what has happened?

In a matter of minutes my life has been completely altered. The way people look at me has changed. All I've ever wanted was to be a mother and to help other children.

It's difficult for me to imagine staying away from my workplace, my second home. The Department of Human Services building is housed in the old Williams Elementary School building located in an older residential part of Cedar City. The children of the neighborhood, who once spent hours playing kickball in the street, hide-and-seek behind the wispy branches of weeping willows, and tag on the school playground, eventually grew up and moved away, leaving their elderly parents behind. The school census fell drastically, causing the system to redistrict, bussing the remaining children from the neighborhood to a brand-new school five miles south. It seemed such a waste, leaving a perfectly good building to sit empty, so the powers that be arranged for the department to move in about ten years ago. My office, one I share with my co-worker, Ruth Johnson, is in what was once the gym teacher's office. It is small, still smells vaguely of sweat despite the plug-in air fresheners that I replace twice a month, high ceilinged, with tall shuttered shelves painted an institutional green popular in the 1970s. It once held a wide array of PE equipment: jump ropes, tennis rackets, bowling pins, baseball bats, mesh bags filled with red rubber playground balls, soccer balls and basketballs. There is even an old portable tetherball pole that I've begged the maintenance man to leave in place. A few times a year, when I have to bring Leah and Lucas with me on a weekend so I can catch up on paper work, I will roll the pole into the hallway outside my office door and they will swing and smack at the dingy white ball hanging from the rope while I work.

The injustice of it all brings angry tears to my eyes. What kind of society lets the James Olmsteads of the world get away with pushing his four-year-old daughter out of a window and punishes someone like me, someone who has spent countless late nights reading through children's files, sleepless nights thinking about the ignoble acts forced upon them, because of one mistake? I think about all that I have missed with my own children because I was looking after children whose own caretakers had been negligent, abusive, cruel. I think about how after Avery was born I returned from my maternity leave two days early so I could follow up with a case that I thought could be handled by no one else but me.

I will never get back those two days with my daughter.

Suddenly, someone is crouching down next to me and for a moment I think I'm being ousted from my corner of the hospital by a security guard. Startled, I look over to see Kelly, my childhood friend. Her dark brown eyes are filled with worry and sympathy. "Ellen" is all she has to say and I know in that one utterance, she doesn't judge or blame me. And somehow this means the world to me. I am glad for my mother's unwavering support and greedily accept anything offered by my husband, who I know is struggling to understand what has happened. With Kelly it's different—we're not related in any way, but we have a history together. Growing up, we rode bikes all around Cedar City, we spent the night at one another's homes. When we were ten we ran away together, angry at our parents for not letting us do something or other. When we were sixteen we did the same. We could talk about anything and everything.

Kelly settles in next to me, sits cross-legged, opens a paper bag and offers me a croissant from my favorite bakery. I reach in and take one, but know that I will not be able to eat. "Thanks," I say, bringing the pastry up to my nose and inhaling its almond scent.

"How are you?" she asks, sliding an arm around my shoulder. I lean into her and shake my head, unable to answer. "How's Avery?" she asks after a moment.

"Holding her own," I say as I place the croissant back into the paper bag and set it on the floor next to me. Then in between hiccupping cries I tell her about Caren, Prieto and the protective order.

"Who's your attorney?" she asks in her no-nonsense manner that I'm so accustomed to.

"I haven't gotten that far," I say miserably, glancing at my watch. It's approaching five o'clock.

"Ellen," Kelly says levelly. "You need to get a lawyer."

This is exactly what Prieto advised and I know they are both right. As a social worker, I know a lot of lawyers, have testified against their clients in countless family court and criminal cases. Never once in my life did I think that I would have the need for a defense attorney. "You're right. I will call someone tomorrow."

"No," my Kelly interrupts. "You will call someone today."

"Okay," I acquiesce. "Today."

"Right now," she says with a finality that I know I can't argue with. "Think," she orders. "Who is the best attorney you know?"

Immediately a name comes to my mind, but it sickens me, too. Ted Vitolo is an excellent criminal defense attorney with an impressive acquittal record. In fact, I've been cross-examined by Ted many times during court cases involving his clients, mothers and fathers accused of abusing their children. He is smart, always prepared and likable. A great combination. James Olmstead knew that, too. Ted Vitolo was the attorney who, to my shock, got James acquitted in the death of Madalyn.

Over and over Vitolo brought up the claim that Madalyn thought she could fly, even digging up obscure witnesses who swore they heard the little girl say just that. He brought in experts who said that the screen on the window was improperly secured, brought in medical experts who explained and diagrammed how Madalyn's fall was consistent with a little girl standing on a window ledge, her hands pressed against a faulty screen window. Vitolo kept me from testifying about the alleged abuse to Madalyn and her mother, saying it would be prejudicial to the jury. He somehow made James Olmstead the victim, the poor brokenhearted father and T-ball coach who lost his daughter.

Kelly is staring at me, waiting for me to give her the name so she can look up the number on her phone. "Ellen," she prompts.

"Okay," I say taking a deep breath. "Ted Vitolo at Vitolo and Cooke. If anyone can help me, he can."

Kelly searches for Vitolo's contact information on her phone, presses a few buttons and in seconds is connected with Vitolo and Cooke. "He'll see you right now," Kelly says after she hangs up.

"What?" I say, surprised. "How can he get me in so fast?" Vitolo has to be one of the busiest defense attorneys in Cedar City.

"He's seen the news," Kelly says in an apologetic voice.

I lower my face into my hands. "Great," I say through my fingers. "He's going to represent me for my notoriety and the free press I'll get him."

Kelly pulls my hands away from my face and forces me to look at her. "You said he's the best, right?" I nod in agreement. "Good. Let's go."

"You're coming with me?" I ask. "Really?"

"Of course, I am. Remember in college when you kept running out buying me pregnancy tests because even though tests kept coming up negative I was sure I was pregnant? And when I finally believed that I wasn't pregnant you told me someday I would be a great mom."

I smile at the memory. "You are a great mom."

"And so are you," Kelly reminds me as she pulls me to my feet. "Come on, let's go meet this lawyer. He's got some ass-kicking to do."

Chapter 20

The phone rang four times before Jenny heard Connie's familiar voice, filled with caution, answer. "Hello?"

"Connie?" Jenny squeaked, angry with herself that once again she felt like crying.

"Jenny? Jenny is that you?" Connie asked, and Jenny thought she might have heard a smile in her words.

"Yes," was all Jenny could think to say.

"How are you?" Connie asked over a chatter of voices and the echo of someone being paged over an intercom system.

"Okay," Jenny answered, stalling for time, not wanting to tell the one nice lady her father knew that he was jumped in a bus station and got hauled off by the cops.

"I'm at work right now, but I can talk for a minute," Connie said. "Just let me go somewhere quiet." The din from the other side of the phone faded away and Connie, sounding a little out of breath, spoke. "I'm so glad you called! How are you?"

It started as a burning in the back of her throat, which she thought was odd because she always thought crying started in the eyes. But when she tried to swallow, the tears, too big, too thick maybe, wouldn't stay down. "Jenny," Connie asked in alarm, "are you hurt? Are you okay?" It took several moments for Jenny to be able to form the words, but she finally blurted out the entire story beginning with the Happy Pancake in Benton and ending with the Happy Pancake in a town called Cedar City. Jenny skimmed lightly over her father's fight and the police cars. Surprisingly, Connie wasn't all that concerned about Billy, but wanted to know more about her bus trip and where in the world Cedar City was located. "Who are you with right now?" Connie asked, her voice threaded with panic. "Are you safe?"

Jenny snuffled wetly and rubbed her eyes with the heel of her hand. "I'm fine," she replied tremulously. "I'm staying with a really nice lady named Maudene. Her granddaughter is in the hospital because someone left her in a hot car. Her other grandkids are kind of mean, but she bought Bugles and fruit snacks and I get to sleep in a pretty white room. She has a dog named Dolly who chased me but Maudene swears she doesn't have rabies." Jenny took a long shuddering breath.

"Jenny, listen to me. You need to tell me exactly where you are. Let me talk to this Maudene person?" Connie demanded.

Jenny almost smiled at the concern in Connie's voice. It felt so good to be fussed over. She shook her head. "I'm okay. I'm just really, really tired. Maudene is downstairs with Leah and Lucas. She tried to help me find my grandma."

Connie was silent for so long Jenny wondered if they had gotten disconnected, but when she finally spoke, her voice was calm. "Jenny, are you talking about your dad's mom? She passed away a long time ago. You knew that, didn't you?"

"It's my mom's mom. But she died, too."

"Do you think that's a good idea, trying to find your mother's family?" Connie asked guardedly. This was when Jenny knew that her father had talked to Connie about what her mother's boyfriend had done to her. Maybe had even shown Connie the pictures of her damaged face. Jenny felt a sizzle of anger at her father for telling Connie all of her personal, private business even if Connie was the only friend-girl that she would ever dream of telling. Jenny fought the urge to hang up on her, but if truth be told, Connie was the only friend-girl she ever imagined her father marrying, so instead she asked her own question.

"Could you maybe call someone and check and see if my dad is okay?" she asked hopefully.

"Of course I will. But, Jenny, you need to tell me exactly where you are. Put Maudene on right now."

"She's busy right now." Jenny eyed the closed bedroom door. She wasn't sure if she wanted Connie and Maudene to talk just yet, at least not until Connie could find out about her father. "Can she call you back?"

"Jenny," Connie warned. "Tell her it's important that I talk to her."

Jenny had a nebulous feeling that maybe she could get Maudene into some kind of trouble. "You'll see if you can find my dad?" she asked hopefully. "Please?"

"Of course," Connie said with exasperation. "Have Maudene give me a call as soon as she can. And, Jenny, call me if you need anything."

"I will," Jenny promised. She set the phone on the dresser and watched it for a moment, almost wishing that Connie would call right back. Her stomach felt empty and a little wobbly.

She crept to the bedroom door, opened it a sliver, peeked out for any sign of Dolly, saw none and stepped out into the hallway. At the top of the stairs she bent over, trying to see if Dolly was lurking at the bottom of the stairs. "I'm coming down," she called out. She was met by silence. "I'm coming down!" she hollered more loudly. "Is that dog put away?"

Maudene came to the foot of the stairs, wiping her hands on a dish towel. "It's okay, you can come on down. Dolly is in the family room." She saw Jenny's hesitation and waved her forward. "The door's shut, she won't bother you." Maudene waited until Jenny made her way down the steps and put a protective arm around her shoulder. "You okay, honey?" she asked. Usually, when people called her hon, or sweetie or dear, Jenny just got irritated. Store clerks, waitresses, friend-girls didn't know her well enough to call her such endearments. Only her father. But *honey* sounded right coming from Maudene. Jenny couldn't quite name it but knew it didn't come from a place of wanting a bigger tip, her father's phone number or her father's love, and that was exactly what Jenny needed just that minute. She leaned into Maudene's embrace, breathing in the older woman's powdery, dry scent.

"I'm kind of hungry," Jenny admitted. "Can I have something to eat?"

"Sure. What'll it be? Cheese Puffs, Snack 'em Cakes?" Maudene asked with mock haughtiness. "Perhaps a nice bowl of Sugar Jingles?"

"Hmm," Jenny said, matching Maudene's aggrandizing tone, her nose in the air, "I think a few Pizza Rolls will do nicely."

"Then Pizza Rolls it is," Maudene said with a firm nod, leading her to the kitchen. While Maudene preheated the oven and retrieved a pan from a cupboard, Jenny opened up the freezer and shuffled through the contents until she found the Pizza Rolls. "I've been thinking," Maudene said casually as she carefully arranged the frozen cheese-stuffed pillows on the baking sheet, "that maybe you really weren't waiting for your sister to come and pick you up from the restaurant." Jenny pointedly avoided Maudene's eyes, went back to the refrigerator and scanned the contents until she found what she was looking for. "And that backpack of yours," Maudene went on, as Jenny peeled the cellophane from a wilted piece of American cheese, "the way you won't let it out of your sight. Makes me think that all your worldly possessions are stuffed inside."

Jenny methodically began tearing the cheese into small pieces, laying each fragment on her tongue like a communion wafer. Maudene slid the pan into the oven, looked at the directions on the bag and set the timer for twelve minutes. "I'm worried that maybe you ran away from home, Jenny. I'm worried that your parents are out there terrified about what has happened to you." Jenny went back to the refrigerator, opened the door, pulled out the gallon of milk, opened and closed four cupboard doors until she found the one filled with drinking glasses. She stood on her tiptoes and pulled down a glass etched with a large letter *S*. "And I'm even more worried as to *why* you ran away. Or who you ran away from." Jenny picked at the milk lid until the small plastic tag that sealed the jug pulled loose. With shaky arms she lifted the large container and tried to pour the milk into the glass, sloshing the contents across the countertop. Without comment, Maudene wiped away the spill and refilled Jenny's glass. "I want to help you, Jenny. But if I'm going to, you need to tell me what's going on. I saw the pictures. Who did that to you? Is that who you're running from?"

Jenny took a long drink, ran her arm across her frothy upper lip and weighed her options. "My dad didn't do that to me," Jenny said with such ferocity that Maudene didn't doubt her. "I didn't run away from home." Jenny deliberated whether or not to tell Maudene about her father, the fight, and the police, but couldn't stand to besmirch her father's name to a stranger, even if it was Maudene. "I think my dad got in some trouble and I thought maybe my grandma could help."

"Are we having pizza?" Lucas asked as he rushed excitedly into the kitchen, making a beeline to the oven.

"I'm not hungry," Leah said sadly when she came into the kitchen. "Can we go to the hospital?"

"I'm sorry, Leah," Maudene answered. "Your mom and dad don't think it's a good idea for you to go to the hospital tonight. Children under fourteen aren't allowed into the intensive care unit." Leah looked crestfallen. "But…" Maudene continued "…your mom is going to stop by first thing tomorrow morning and they'll call in a little bit to talk to you."

"Oh," Leah said in nearly a soundless whisper. Jenny had never heard such a little word uttered so sadly and she felt sorry for her.

"I'm not hungry," Leah repeated, this time near tears. "I'm just going to go watch TV for a little while."

"Me, too," Lucas added in a show of solidarity with his sister.

"Okay." Maudene sighed. "You can always come grab something to eat if you get hungry. Do you want to try and call your mom and dad right now?" Both Leah and Lucas nodded. "All right then, let me find my phone." As Maudene checked her purse and the various countertops and kitchen drawers, Leah gave Jenny a pointed look. Jenny knew that Leah wanted her to leave the kitchen so that they could talk to their parents in private, and slowly she began making her way out of the room.

"Ah, here it is," Maudene said triumphantly, holding the phone above her head. "Let's give them a call and see how Avery's doing." The three moved into the living room, leaving Jenny in the kitchen to finish eating by herself, which suited her just fine. She used the opportunity to investigate her surroundings. Maudene's kitchen was small and cluttered. The refrigerator was covered with pictures of Leah and Lucas and some other kids that Jenny figured were the other grandkids that lived out of town. Voices drifted in from the other room.

"Hi, Mom!" Leah exclaimed happily before dissolving into noisy sobs. Jenny held her breath, trying to harden her heart to her new enemy's cries. Jenny didn't know if it was Leah's tears, the word *mom* or the combination of the two that got to her, but she couldn't bear to listen anymore. She slid open the pocket door of the large pantry and stepped inside, pulling the light cord that dangled above her head so she could see. Quietly sliding the door shut, Jenny took in all the shelves and shelves of food in front of her. Cans of soup, boxes of crackers, tins of exotic-looking teas, bags of white sugar and flour, as well as many of the snacks they had purchased that afternoon.

Jenny reached for a box of snack cakes, a package of chocolate chip cookies and a bag of potato chips, inched open the door, peeked out and, still hearing the muffled phone conversation from the other room, tiptoed out into the kitchen, through the living room and up the stairs to the white room. She shoved the treats under the bed, thought a moment, pulled them out and set them in the bedside table drawer, but it was too small. Pressing the chips and cookies firmly into the drawer she managed to get the drawer shut. She looked around the beautiful room, searching for another hiding spot and finally lifted the feather pillow, set the box of snack cakes into the space where the headboard met the mattress and returned the pillow to its rightful spot.

Her father's cell phone began to vibrate and dance across the dresser and Jenny hesitated before reaching for it, afraid that it was Connie calling her back. The number on the display was unfamiliar to Jenny and, hoping that it was her father, she answered. "Hello," she said tentatively.

"Hello? Who am I talking to?" a strange voice asked. Jenny remained silent. "This is Officer McAdam from the Benton Police Department. Who am I speaking with?" Jenny's heart slammed against her chest. Her father must be in jail in Benton. Why else would the police be calling her on her father's phone? "Who am I speaking to?" the man said again. "Is this Jenny Briard?" Jenny dropped the phone as if it burned her fingers, scrambled to pick it up and stabbed at buttons until the call ended.

On shaky legs she crawled into the bed and pulled the covers over her head. The police had her father and now they were looking for her.

Chapter 21

As I open my eyes it takes me a few moments to figure out where I am and what day it is. I look around and see the familiar artwork on the walls and hear the hum of an industrial-sized vacuum cleaner. Last night, after Kelly and I visited the law offices of Vitolo and Cooke I returned to the hospital. After checking in with Adam and saying good-night to Avery via cell phone, I found a waiting area with a television set and just sat, trying not to think. I must have fallen asleep. I check my watch, it's six in the morning. Wednesday. Yesterday at this time, we were fast asleep in our own beds, oblivious to the nightmare that was to come. I text Adam, letting him know where I am and asking how Avery's night went.

Five minutes later, Adam steps into the waiting area. He looks as tired as I feel, but he seems happy to see me and pulls me into a hug. "Did you stay here all night?" he asks, taking in my messy hair and day-old clothes.

I nod. "I just couldn't leave," I try to explain.

"Are Lucas and Leah with your mom?"

"Yeah, I'll go see them in a bit. How was Avery's night?" I ask.

"Fine, she slept pretty well. Probably better than I did." Adam runs his hands across his eyes.

"I met with a lawyer last night," I blurt out. I didn't have the heart to tell him when we spoke in the night. He sounded so tired on the phone.

"That's good, El," he says. "I'm sorry that I wasn't able to go with you." He takes my hand in his.

"Kelly went with me. I think he'll be good." Kelly and I had spent thirty minutes with Ted Vitolo, and after only three minutes I was certain that he was just the right attorney to represent me. His expression didn't falter once as I told my story.

"Clearly an accident," he'd said. "Don't talk to the press, don't talk to the cops," he'd advised.

"He's the lawyer who got James Olmstead acquitted," I confess, afraid to know what Adam will think of this.

"Good," he says with vehemence. "He must be good if he got Olmstead off." I look at my husband warily, trying to determine if there is any hidden animosity behind his words. But all I see is hope. "You hungry?" he asks.

I shake my head. "No, I'm okay. Did you get something to eat?"

"I will in a minute. Why don't you go to your mom's house, shower and change and check on the kids. We'll be okay here for a little while."

I shake my head. "I wish I didn't have to leave," I say.

"No offense, El," my husband says with a teasing smile. "You are kind of a mess. Anyway, Lucas and Leah are probably dying to see you." He winces slightly at his choice of words but goes on. "You can get Avery's yellow blanket and her Bunny Bear."

Bunny Bear is Avery's favorite toy. A plush stuffed
bear dressed in bunny pajamas. Lucas dubbed him
Bunny Bear and the name stuck. Avery drags him
everywhere with her and, with a stomach-churning
thought, I wonder if Bunny Bear is sitting in the back
of the abandoned van amid shards of broken glass. I had
forgotten about the van. "Okay," I acquiesce reluctantly.
I look at the clock on the wall. It's still too early to go
and see Lucas and Leah. I scan Adam's face looking
for any hint of worry.

"She really is doing okay right now. The doctor won't
be here for rounds for a few hours yet," Adam assures
me.

"I'll run home first and get Avery's things. Do you
need anything?" I ask, and Adam shakes his head no.
"Then I'll go check on Leah and Lucas. You'll call me
if anything comes up?"

"Yep, we'll be fine," Adam says confidently. I lean
into him and he hugs me tightly, kisses me on the cheek
and pulls the set of keys for the truck from his pocket
and hands them to me.

"Give Avery a kiss for me," I tell him and, unsteadily,
from exhaustion I imagine, I move through the quiet
corridors of the hospital and make my way to the emergency room parking lot where Adam has parked the
truck. The exit doors open and while the early morning air has cooled during the night, it is still heavy and
hot. As I hoist myself up into the truck I try to decide
whether to go back to the van to see if Bunny Bear is
there or to go home first to shower and change. Bunny
Bear wins. I can't bear the thought of Avery's favorite
toy sitting abandoned on the floor of the van.

I slowly travel the same streets that the ambulance

flew through to carry Avery to the hospital. The eastern sky is pearled pink and I pass a few early-morning joggers and pet owners walking their dogs before the heat of the day descends. As I once again enter Manda's downtrodden neighborhood I can't help wondering if she is okay. If the domestic drama that brought me to their doorstep ended not only with my daughter in the hospital but Manda, as well.

I turn onto Madison Street and can see that my van remains in the place where I parked it the day before. I move slowly past the van to assess the damage. The side door is windowless and there is a large dent in the door, but someone has taken the time to sweep the glass from the street. I pull in front of the van, put the truck into Park and step out onto the still-sleeping street. I pull open the door and I can already see that the entire van has been picked clean. No Bunny Bear on the floor and someone has taken Avery's car seat. I move to the front of the van and open the passenger-side door. The CD player has been ripped from the dash and the stack of CDs that we stored in the center console is gone as is my stainless steel travel mug. I open the glove box and the maps, pens and pencils and the various odds and ends that find their way into the compartment are gone. Someone has even removed our insurance and registration information that we stored in a small envelope. But it's Bunny Bear that I'm most concerned about. I don't want to go back into that hospital without Avery's stuffed bear. I return to the rear of the van and on hands and knees reach beneath the seats in hope that the toy was pushed aside during the upheaval. Nothing.

"Got your stuff right here," a voice says from behind me, causing me to jump. I extract myself from the van to find Jade standing there holding a bulging plastic bag, Avery's car seat sitting at her feet. "After the ambulance left, I took everything to my house for safekeeping. All your stuff would've all been stolen if we let it be overnight. Couldn't do nothing about your CD player or hubcaps. Sorry."

"Oh, Jade." The words snag in my throat and tears spring to my eyes. I've been crying nonstop for the past twenty-four hours, but these at least are tears of gratitude. "I can't thank you enough for what you did for Avery."

Jade briefly stiffens in my embrace. I am, after all, the social worker who took her son away from her, but almost immediately she relaxes and returns my hug. What a sight we must make: the social worker and the young woman who drank so much alcohol that she nearly died and in her inebriated state forgot that she had a two-week-old son, who nearly died in his crib from dehydration.

"Well," Jade says, releasing me, crossing her arms and self-consciously looking down at her feet. "Anyone would have done the same. I just hope she's going to be okay."

"She's in intensive care. I don't think she would have made it if your neighbors didn't get her out or if you weren't there to do CPR." I find myself getting choked up again, thinking about how Jade, once so lost and misguided, saved Avery's life, pushed her own breath into my daughter's lungs. I clear my throat and reach more deeply into the bag for Bunny Bear, find a long ear and tug.

Jade shifts uncomfortably from foot to foot and looks

nervously up and down the street. I can tell she wants to say more.

"I'll make sure someone comes to move the van," I assure her. "I'm sorry. In all that's been going on, I forgot about it."

She shakes her head. "That's not it." Her face is grave. "You should know that some people are talking." I nod. This is to be expected. "You know Lucy Pike?" Again I nod. I was the caseworker who recommended that Lucy's children be removed from her care. "Lucy's pissed. She's telling anyone who will listen that you took her kids away from her when you should have been watching out for your own baby."

"Oh," is all I can eke out, but I feel my face redden with anger and embarrassment.

"I just thought you should know," Jade says apologetically. "I know what happened with your daughter is…different."

"Thanks," I say and, wanting to change the subject, ask, "How are Krissie and Kylie. Is Manda okay?"

"The girls are okay. Manda was bust up pretty good. After you left, another ambulance came to take her to the hospital. It was crazy," Jade exclaims, shaking her head at yesterday's commotion. "Police hauled her boyfriend away and then that bitchy social worker came and took the girls away. You know the one I'm talking about?"

I do know who Jade is talking about. Ruth Johnson isn't as bad as Jade makes her sound, but I understand why people might think she is cranky and difficult. She has been a social worker for over thirty years and has seen everything that can possibly be done to another human being. She is tough, she is hardened, but she is conscientious and possibly the best advocate a child in need could have. We are not exactly friends, do not converse beyond the scope of our professional life, but we share an office and, over the years, I have developed a respect for Ruth, though grudgingly. I've learned from her meticulousness and attention to detail. I know that Krissie and Kylie will be well taken care of.

"Thank you, again," I say to Jade, and reach out for her hand. She takes mine and pulls me into a firm, brief hug.

"You take care of yourself," she says. "And I'll tell Lucy to mind her own business." Jade's dark brown eyes are filled with empathy.

"Thank you." I am both grateful and humbled by Jade's kindness. I haul Avery's car seat and the bag filled with the contents of the van over to the truck. Once inside, my mind begins to whir with all that Jade has told me. I could lose my job, my social worker license. I could go to jail. But most of all I'm worried about losing my daughter. Nothing compares to the terror of knowing that Avery could die, could be permanently damaged.

Chapter 22

Morning sun peeked from behind the bedroom window's heavy blinds and, buried beneath piles of cotton sheets, blankets and a down comforter that felt like heaven against her skin, Jenny stretched her arms and legs luxuriously. She could lay here forever, she thought to herself. Back in Benton, in the places she and her father stayed, climate control was always a problem. In the winter, weak, ineffectual wafts or inconsistent blasts of hot or cold air would make the motel rooms unbearably cold or miserably hot.

This bedroom was perfect, Jenny decided. The temperature outside the confines of the blankets was cool, almost cold; the constant whir of the air conditioner had lulled her to sleep, despite nagging worries about the phone call from the police last night. For the moment she felt snug and safe beneath the weight of the fluffy, white comforter, and when she was reunited with her father and they were settled into their new home, she would ask him for a blanket just like this one. She wondered if the jail cell her father was in was like the ones she'd seen on television. Small and grim looking with bunk beds and a filthy toilet right out in the open. Her face burned with the injustice of someone having to actually pee, or worse, in front of complete strangers. She thought of her father, waking up on a narrow bunk bed, high above the ground, covered in a thin, smelly blanket. Her father did not like heights, often telling his friends that the pharmaceutical airline was the only way to fly. Jenny wasn't exactly sure what he meant by this, but by the way they had laughed, casting shifty-eyed looks at one another, she figured it wasn't necessarily a good thing.

She tried to imagine who his cell mate might be and hoped that he would have given her dad the lower bunk. Surely it wouldn't be one of the men who had attacked him at the bus station. But they did that all the time on the cop show she and her father watched on the Friday nights they stayed at home. The police were forever putting suspects into cells with hulking men with dead eyes and tattoos of skulls, scorpions and spiderwebs crawling up their arms, in hopes of getting the guy to confess. But everyone liked her father. You just couldn't help it. Even the men who had jumped him would like her dad if they took two minutes to talk to him. Maybe it was a case of mistaken identity, also a common theme on the police shows they watched. A big mistake, Jenny realized, and exhaled in relief.

From the edges of the drawn window shades, Jenny could see that the sun had risen, but she was reluctant to leave the cozy nest of a bed, despite the rumbling of her stomach. She thought of the grandmother she almost met, could almost picture her in her mind. She snaked a hand from beneath the covers, tugged open the drawer next to the bed and pulled out the bag of chocolate chip cookies. Carefully, Jenny nibbled on a cookie, cupping her hand beneath her mouth, so as not to get crumbs or chocolate on the pristine sheets. There was a tap at the door and Jenny shoved the rest of the cookie into her mouth.

Maudene opened the door, poked her head in and called, "Good morning, Jenny."

"Morning," Jenny mumbled sleepily as if just waking.

"Come on downstairs when you are ready. You can eat breakfast and then we need to make a plan for the day." Jenny's stomach twisted nervously. Plans were not always a good thing.

After Maudene retreated, Jenny reluctantly slid from beneath the covers. She had taken a bath the night before in Maudene's spotless tub. The bathtubs in the apartments and motels where she and her father lived were always grimy and had jagged cracks and suspicious stains, causing Jenny to speedily use the shower instead. She wanted to return to the tub, fill it with warm water and bubbles up to her ears, but figured Maudene would say that there was no way that Jenny could have gotten that dirty during the night to need another bath so soon.

She ran her father's comb through her snarled hair, slipped on a change of clothes she had in her backpack, rechecked the contents of the manila envelope and counted her money. It was all still there, not that she thought that Maudene would have come in during the night to rob her, but she wouldn't put anything past Leah or Lucas.

As she padded down the steps, she was welcomed by the smell of bacon frying and again her stomach grumbled loudly. She couldn't understand why she was so hungry all the time now. It wasn't like she was starving before, though she and her father could go for days eating ramen noodles and macaroni and cheese and there were times when the only real meal she got was at school during lunch. The table was filled with food: freshly cut melon, a plate filled with toasted bread, jars of peanut butter and jelly, cartons of milk and orange juice. Lucas and Leah were already sitting in the breakfast nook eating scrambled eggs and bacon. Jenny couldn't help but compare Leah's sharply pressed shorts and bright white t-shirt to her own rumpled outfit. "Grab a plate, Jenny," Maudene said cheerfully, and Jenny complied, bringing it to the stove where Maudene filled it with eggs and crisp bacon. "That enough for you?"

"Yeah, thanks," Jenny said, surveying the kitchen for somewhere else to eat besides next to Leah and Lucas. She settled for standing at the counter next to Maudene as she cracked more eggs into the cast-iron skillet.

"Can we go call Mom and Dad now?" Leah asked. "I want to see Avery today."

Maudene glanced at the clock on the microwave. "It's a little early, but it should be okay." Maudene turned off the stove and moved the egg-filled skillet from the hot burner. "Let's go in the other room and give them a call. Jenny, you go ahead and finish eating and we'll be right back."

"Mom?" came Leah's voice from the living room. Jenny didn't think she had ever heard one single word sound so sad and lonely and she tried to block out the conversation by crunching loudly on a piece of toast. "When can we see Avery?" Leah was crying now, her words barely discernible between sobs. "Are you coming to get us?" The response on the other side of the phone must have been what Leah wanted to hear because her cries gradually tapered away. The conversation continued for a few more minutes with Lucas and Maudene both speaking in muted tones.

"The good news is that Avery had a good night and Ellen is on her way over right now," Maudene said in a cheery, overbright voice as she came back into the kitchen. Leah scowled at Jenny as she ran through the kitchen and out the back door with Lucas close at her heels. Maudene began scooping eggs and bacon onto a clean plate she pulled from the cupboard. "For Ellen when she gets here," she explained, seeing Jenny's quizzical look. "I wish you and Leah got along a little better." Maudene shook her head. "You both are going through a hard time right now. I was hoping maybe you could be friends." Handing Jenny the plate, she added, "Put this in the microwave, would you? I want to keep it warm for Ellen." Jenny took the plate and with a twinge of guilt placed it in the microwave. She didn't care much about Leah, but she didn't want Maudene feeling bad, especially after how nice she had been to her, giving her food and that beautiful bedroom to sleep in. Jenny vowed to try harder with Leah if only because it would make Maudene happy.

Together, Maudene and Jenny scraped and rinsed the dirty breakfast dishes and frying pans and placed them in the dishwasher. Jenny knew she should tell Maudene about the phone call from the police in Benton last night but couldn't quite bring herself to, worried that Maudene would immediately call them back. Jenny watched Maudene carefully from the corner of her eye. Her face was pale and the corners of her mouth were pulled down with worry. In that moment Jenny realized that Maudene could have easily let Jenny leave the Happy Pancake without a second thought, could have just let her keep going when they had stopped to pick up Lucas and Leah. But she didn't. She came after Jenny. Twice. Maudene clearly had plenty of other things to worry about: Avery, Ellen, Lucas and Leah, but still she found time for Jenny.

On impulse, Jenny stood and threw her arms around Maudene. "Thank you!" she whispered into the old woman's ear. Just as quickly she released her, grabbed her backpack and sat back down, leaving them both a bit stunned at her impulsive display of affection.

"Mom!" came a shout from the backyard.

"Ellen's here." Maudene stood, a wide smile spreading across her face, making her appear years younger.

"I'll get her plate," Jenny said, already moving toward the microwave while Maudene rushed to the back door.

Chapter 23

Leah and Lucas leap into my arms before I even step into the house. "Mommy!" Leah yells, something she hasn't called me in three years.

"I'm so glad to see you two," I say, trying to squeeze back tears. Leah grabs my hand and tries to lead me out the doorway.

"Can we go see Dad and Avery now?" she asks hopefully. "When does she get to come home? Let's go to the hospital right now!" Futilely, Lucas is also trying to chime in with his own questions that I can't hear over Leah's pleading.

"Hold on, now," I say with a smile. "I know that Dad and Avery can't wait to see you two, either, but kids aren't allowed in the intensive care unit. You'll have to wait to see Avery when she's moved to a regular room. We'll leave for the hospital in a little bit. Let me talk to Grandma for a few minutes, okay?" Leah and Lucas nod their heads, but Leah refuses to let go of my hand, as if she's afraid that I will suddenly flee. "Hi, Mom," I say to my mother as I give her a one-armed hug. "Thanks for watching the kids. Were they good for you?"

"Oh, they were wonderful," my mother says, waving away my concern, but Leah looks away guiltily. "Do you realize this was the first time they spent the night here in almost a year? We'll have to have a lot more overnights."

"With Avery," Lucas says firmly.

"Of course," my mother says as if that is a given, which I pray to God will be the truth.

"Are you supposed to go into work today?" I ask her. Her job at the restaurant has been a nice distraction for my mother since my father died.

"Don't worry about that. I called in and am taking some vacation days," she assures me. "I have as much time off as I need."

I notice the rumpled girl hanging back near the kitchen entryway. She has long, messy brown hair and is wearing a wrinkled t-shirt and shorts. Her feet are bare. In one hand she is holding tightly to the same backpack she carried at the hospital last night and in the other is a plate heaped with bacon and eggs. "Ellen, you remember Jenny, don't you?"

"Hi, Jenny," I say politely. I am curious about the story behind Jenny's sudden appearance into my mother's life, but I'm eager to talk to my mother about the protective order, about witnessing Avery's seizure yesterday, about my visit with the attorney. But most of all I want to hug Lucas and Leah and get back to the hospital.

"Hi," she says shyly, stepping forward and handing me the plate of food.

"Thanks," I say, realizing for the first time that I hadn't eaten anything since my quick breakfast the day before. I'm famished.

"You go on and sit down and eat," my mother orders.

"Lucas and Leah, why don't you two go and brush your teeth and find the get-well cards you made for Avery last night." Lucas immediately rushes up the steps and Leah reluctantly drops my hand before following her brother. I glance around the kitchen. Growing up, this was my favorite room in the house. My parents hadn't changed a thing over the years except for the addition of a dishwasher and a new refrigerator, an anniversary gift from my father to my mother just before he died. He never even got to see them once they were installed.

I settle into the same breakfast nook that I sat in every single morning that I lived in this house and it is like I never left. The warm summer sun is beating through the windows that surround the nook, making me sleepy. What I wouldn't give to trudge up the steps to my old bedroom and crawl beneath the sheets of my childhood bed. "What are the doctors saying?" my mother asks as she pours me a cup of coffee. Jenny is at the sink rinsing out a dishrag and wipes it across the kitchen counter.

"She's stable, thank goodness." I breathe in the rich aroma of the coffee. "I haven't even been able to hold her yet," I say, emotion thickening my voice. "They're worried about her kidneys and the seizures she's been having."

"Doctors can do just about anything these days," my mother says, patting me on the hand. I smile up at her. With the busyness of our lives, I haven't seen much of my mom lately. There is always work and the kids' activities to keep us running. And when we aren't doing that we are at home trying to catch up on laundry and yard work. It is never ending. I try to remember the last time we had spent time with her. Three months ago, I

realize with dismay, at Leah's birthday. We had gone
to a pizza place that specialized in birthday parties and
inflatable bouncy houses for the kids to exhaust themselves jumping around in. I was so busy attending to
the seven nine-year-olds Leah had invited that I had
barely spoken to my mother that night. I remember her
appearing particularly thin. She obviously hadn't been
eating much since my father's death last year, and, despite the smile she kept on her face the entire night, she
didn't seem happy. I remember thinking to myself that
I needed to call her, to take her out for lunch, just the
two of us spending time together. But I didn't.

"Thanks for watching the kids," I tell her again. "It
means a lot to Adam and me that they're here with you.
I still can't believe they won't let me see Avery. This
is a nightmare." My mother comes over and hugs me.
I lay my head on her shoulder and inhale her familiar
scent, lily of the valley.

"You know, when your brother was a year old, he
very nearly died and it was all my fault." I raise my head
and look at her questioningly. "It's true," she says. "I
was young and overwhelmed with two boys under the
age of three. Plus, I was pregnant with you. I put Craig
in one of those baby walkers with the wheels on the
bottom and accidently left the basement door open."
I wince at what I know is coming next. "From across
the room I saw him scooting along right toward the
steps. I couldn't get to him fast enough and he flipped
head over toes down the steps." My mother frowns at
the memory. "It was a miracle, but he landed, still in
the walker, upright on his feet. Not a scratch on him."

"But Avery isn't fine," I say. "I don't think anything
will ever be fine again. She could have died, could still

die. I think I've lost my job for good and I could go to jail."

Tears well in my mother's eyes and she grasps both of my hands in hers. "I guess what I'm trying to say is that we all have our moments. We all have those times when we turn our backs, close our eyes, become unguarded. I don't know why Craig ended up being okay and other children don't, but I know that no matter what happens you'll get through this. *We'll* get through this. You have to look for the little mercies, the small kindnesses and good that come from the terrible."

I want to argue with her, that there could be no good that comes from any of this but we hear the squeak of a screen door and a thunk before it slams shut again.

"Newspaper's here," my mother says. "Can you run and get it?" she asks Jenny, who trots off to the front door. Once she is out of earshot, she says, "I just can't believe they won't let you see Avery."

I shake my head helplessly and put a finger to my lips. I don't want Lucas and Leah to know I've been banned from seeing their sister.

"Mom, who in the world is that little girl? Where did she come from?" I ask, taking Jenny's leave as an opportunity to find out what is going on.

"She's just staying with me for a bit. I don't want you to worry about her, you've got too much going on already. I'll fill you in on everything tonight."

"No, I want you to tell me right now. Who is she?" I insist.

"I'm not exactly sure, but…"

I exhale loudly. "Mom, I'm on leave from the Department of Human Services. Please call Ruth Johnson, my co-worker at DHS. She'll be able to help you. Promise me you'll call her." I imagine the press getting wind of this and the headline that would follow: Negligent Social Worker Harbors Runaway. And if Caren learned of this, my already tenuous career will be irreparably damaged. "Mom, you need to call the police or DHS today, do you understand?" My mother nods silently.

"Hey," Jenny says, coming back into the room, an impressed look on her face. "Your picture is in the paper." She holds up the newspaper and sure enough my picture is on the front page. It's an old photo that was taken several years ago when I had been interviewed for a story about our local Department of Human Services. My heart tumbles. I reach for the newspaper with shaking hands.

Lucas and Leah come into the kitchen and, seeing my stricken face, Leah begins to cry and Lucas quickly follows suit. "No, no," I soothe her. "Avery is fine. Everything is okay. I didn't mean to scare you, honey." I hand the newspaper to my mother, who bites back a gasp. I pull Leah and Lucas into a hug. "Let's go to the hospital. I'll even ask the nurse if you two can peek in on Avery." I turn to my mother, who is still reading the front page, her face drawn with worry. "Do you and Jenny want to come with us?"

She bites her lip and I know she wants to ask me about the article but won't in front of the kids. "You go on and then call me when you want me to come and pick up Lucas and Leah. They can stay here as long as you need them to." Next to me Leah begins to protest, but I silence her with a stern look.

"Thanks, Mom," I say, and give her another hug. I realize I've hugged her more times in the past twenty-four hours than I have in the past two years. "Let's go, kiddos," I say. Together we get into the truck. I see the paper carrier plodding up my mother's street, tossing newspapers onto front steps, sliding them into mailboxes, all with the same terrible headline: Local Social Worker in the Hot Seat.

For Lucas and Leah, I try to disguise my worry for Avery and the implications of the newspaper article by peppering them with questions about the time they've spent with their grandmother and Jenny.

"She's weird," Leah says with disgust. "She acts like she's lived in Grandma's house forever, but she's been there for one day."

"Does she live in town?" I ask. "Do you know her from school?"

"She doesn't go to my school," Leah says with a shake of her head. "I'd remember her if she did."

"I don't think she lives here," Lucas pipes up from the backseat. In the rearview mirror I can see that he is rubbing the strap that holds Avery in her car seat between his fingers like a worry stone.

"What makes you think that?"

"She didn't know where her grandma lived," Lucas explains.

"How did she end up here then?" I wonder out loud.

"I just wish she'd go back to wherever she came from," Leah says, and scowls.

"Well, hopefully everything will get settled and back to normal soon in a few days," I say, knowing that it could take much longer than just a day or two.

Leah squawks in dismay, "I thought you said that Avery was getting better! I'm not staying with Grandma if *she* is there. I won't. I'll stay at the Arwoods' house."

Lucas's eyes flick between me and his sister as if trying to gauge how upset he should be.

"I'm not staying there," Leah says again with a finality that I've come to dread. I think Leah would rather sleep in a tree then have to spend another night under the same roof as her grandmother's houseguest. I decide not to argue the point. Maybe Avery will be stable enough so that one of us can go home to be with the kids. My hopes rise at the thought as we turn into the hospital parking lot and then quickly disappear. There is a news van with Eyewitness News Eleven emblazoned in large blue letters across its body and a reporter and a woman with a camera are leaning against a stone pillar near the front entrance. Based on the headline in the newspaper, I have a sick feeling that they are here for me and I know I can't take my children through these doors. I've had several high-profile cases in my work and have learned how to dodge a reporter or two even in this very hospital. I take a quick right and turn into a smaller lot on the west side of the hospital whose entrance leads to an outpatient physical therapy facility. We have to travel across the skywalk and maneuver through a maze of intricate hallways, but anything would be better than having to face those reporters.

Once again we walk through the glass doors of Cedar City Hospital, a hospital I've been in countless times in my role as a social worker for the Department of Human Services.

Sometimes, more times than not, I'm the one seen as the villain, the monster who takes these children from what they know, no matter how awful. But my hope has always been that over time, even if it's years

later, the children that I remove from their homes come
to understand why I've done the things I have. I can't
erase their horrible memories, I can't renew their trust
in the world, but I can give them one thing—a chance
at a less broken life.

I see Adam before he sees me. Again I'm reminded
why I fell in love with him. There is something absolutely innocent and unguarded about my husband. Every
emotion he is feeling can be found on his face, in the tilt
of his head, in the slope of his shoulders. He is sitting on
a bench in the lobby, his cell phone pressed against his
ear. Lucas and Leah have run ahead of me and Adam
immediately hangs up the phone and pulls them into
his arms. They are leaning so tightly into him they
look like they are one entity. I want to go to him, kneel
down before him and lay my head in his lap. But I can
see how grief and exhaustion are pressing down upon
him and wait patiently until he looks up and notices me.

I take a tentative step backward, bumping into a
group of young residents moving en masse through the
hallway. My startled yelp causes Adam to drag his attention away from the kids and toward me. Immediately his smile widens and I breathe out a sigh of relief.
"Hi," I say once the sea of white coats moves past me.

"Hi." Adam draws me toward him, closing his arms
protectively around my shoulders.

"How's Avery?" I ask, already knowing the answer.
No change. I can see it in his eyes.

"The same. No more seizures since yesterday. It's
her kidneys they are still most worried about." I nod
silently because there are no words. "The nephrologist
hasn't stopped by yet this morning, but is supposed to."

We sit down on the bench next to each other and

Lucas and Leah wander a few feet away to look out the window that overlooks a garden landscaped with brightly colored flowers and whimsical sculptures. "How do the kids seem to you?" he asks. We both worry about Lucas. He is such a particular little boy, lost without his routine.

I shrug. "They're worried about Avery. They miss her, they miss you. They want to go home. They want us all to go home.

"Will you give this to her?" I hand Adam Avery's stuffed animal and my voice breaks. "Tell her it's from me?" I am so afraid that Avery will think that I don't care, that I am choosing to stay away from her.

"Of course," Adam assures me. His eyes are red and bruised-looking from fatigue.

"Were you able to get hold of your mom and dad?" I ask.

"Yeah, I just got off the phone with my mom. They're flying in from Arizona tomorrow afternoon. They'll get in around four."

"That's good," I say. Adam's parents are nice people and they will be a great help to Adam since I can't stay with Avery. He'll be able to come home, shower, get some good rest.

But I do worry about what Adam's parents think of me now, what Adam has told them about what happened to Avery. Will they look at me differently now? Look at me as the woman who nearly killed their grandchild?

"Did Joe get a hold of you?" Adam asks suddenly.

"No, why?" I ask. I hadn't talked to him since the day before when I gave him an update on Avery. "He stopped here looking for you a little while ago. I told him you were at your mother's house. He's probably on his way over there now."

I check my phone. I've had no missed calls from Joe and I wonder what is so urgent that he feels he needs to see me in person rather than just call me. By the look on Adam's face I can tell he is wondering, too. Ever since Joe's divorce, Adam is sure that Joe has a thing for me. I assure him that's definitely not the case even though secretly I think Joe would have liked for us to be more than friends. "It can't be the grand jury already," I say, more to myself than to Adam. "The lawyer said it would be at least three weeks before they decide to indict or not." I think of the grand jury that will decide if I'm a monster. Are they in their cars right now, driving to the courthouse to begin to hear the evidence that will decide another stranger's fate? Are they wondering about whose life they have in their hands today? Three weeks seems so far away, but in some ways too soon. For the first time I really think about the possibility that I could be arrested for what happened to Avery, what I did to Avery, no matter the intention. I hear it all the time from mothers and fathers that I work with. *I didn't mean to, it just happened, it was an accident, you have to believe me.*

"What do you think he wants then?" Adam asks, and I see the fear in his eyes. "He wouldn't tell me. Just said that he needed to talk to you."

I shake my head. "I don't know." But I'm afraid I do. The newspaper article, the determination of Prieto and Caren to follow procedure to the letter. Joe isn't just looking for me to see how I'm faring.

Adam blanches as if reading my mind. "No," he says. "They can't do this."

"It will be okay," I say with more confidence than I feel. "I don't want it to happen here, at the hospital." I pause, a terrible thought striking me. "I don't want it to happen in front of the kids. Oh, my God, Adam. What if they arrest me in front of Leah and Lucas?" I've seen it happen before with parents accused of abusing their children. I've even had to peel a bruised child's fingers from her mother's arms as a police officer informs her of her rights.

Adam shakes his head from side to side. "They wouldn't arrest you in front of the kids. No one can be that cruel."

Chapter 24

After Ellen left to take Leah and Lucas to the hospital, Jenny stood in front of the bathroom mirror and ran a wet comb through her hair, trying, with little luck, to get it to lie smoothly against her head. She wondered if Maudene knew how to French braid. There were girls at school whose mothers carefully braided their hair. Jenny had checked out a book from the school library once that gave directions on how to braid hair in different ways. There were pictures of girls with pigtail braids and tiny microbraids lined with beads and long horsetail braids that lay against your back, but her favorite was the French braid. Jenny had taken the book home and tried to decipher the words and the directions, her fingers clumsily trying to twist her hair into smooth plaits. In frustration, she'd handed the book to her father, who tried valiantly for a few minutes, but kept getting distracted by the basketball game on television, accidently pulling her hair when someone made a shot.

"You need some help there?" Maudene asked as she paused in the bathroom doorway to see if Jenny was ready for the day.

"It's my hair," Jenny said with disappointment. "It just lays there. Do you know how to French braid?"

Maudene's eyes lit up. "I used to braid Ellen's hair all the time when she was little. She used to have hair all the way down to her behind. When she was about four years old she took a pair of scissors and cut it all off. Oh, how I cried when I saw her. All that beautiful black hair on the bathroom floor." Maudene shook her head at the memory and laughed to herself. "Anyway, I will be happy to braid your hair for you. It's been years since I've done it, but I imagine it will come back to me. Come on over and sit down and I'll see what I can do." Maudene led Jenny to the kitchen, pulled a chair out from the table. Jenny settled into the chair, sat up straight and folded her hands in her lap as Maudene began to run a soft-bristled brush through her hair.

"Jenny, I have someone coming over to talk with you," Maudene said, gently gathering Jenny's hair at the crown of her head and separating it into three sections.

Jenny froze. "Who?"

"It's a social worker that Ellen works with. Her name is Ruth Johnson." Through the mirror, Maudene saw the panicked look on Jenny's face and dropped the braid. She gently turned Jenny around by her shoulders. "Jenny, you've got to trust me," Maudene said plaintively. "Ruth did some checking. Your father has been going crazy with worry about you and the police from your hometown have been looking for you."

Jenny couldn't respond.

"I promise I will not let anything bad happen to you. Ruth is coming over just to talk to you." Jenny's shoulders relaxed a bit and Maudene once again began to gather and separate her hair.

"Do I get to go see my dad?"

Maudene pressed her lips together and looked away. Jenny had her answer. "I'm not going to a foster home," Jenny said, trying to fill her voice with steel. "I don't care what you say or the social worker says. I'll run away if you try and make me."

Maudene's fingers worked slowly at first and then more quickly as she wove Jenny's hair into a sleek braid. "No one is going to make you do anything." Maudene sighed, her voice unsteady. "Jenny, you have to understand that my daughter is going through a terrible time right now. My granddaughter could die, my daughter could go to jail. I can't have you stay here if you've run away from home or if you're in some kind of trouble. I'm sorry, I could get in big trouble and it could make things worse for Ellen."

Jenny rubbed her eyes with the heels of her hands. "I'm sorry. I can leave. I don't want you to get into trouble."

Maudene wrapped an elastic band around the tail of Jenny's braid and once again turned Jenny to face her. "I don't want you to have to go anywhere you don't want to go, Jenny. Just listen to what Ruth has to say. She helps kids. That's what she does for a living." Jenny wiped away the few tears that succeeded in leaking down her face and nodded. "Don't be scared. I'll stay with you the whole time if you want me to."

"I'm not scared," Jenny said with a final sniff. "I'll talk to her, but I'm not going to any foster home."

"All right then." Maudene patted Jenny on the head. "I didn't do too badly. Even after twenty-some years. Go take a look and see what you think." Jenny leaped from the chair and ran to the bathroom. She gazed at her reflection in the mirror, turning from side to side trying to catch a glimpse of the back of her head. "Here, use this." Maudene handed a gilded hand mirror to Jenny so she could better see the braid.

"It's so pretty," Jenny murmured. "If you were my mom I would let you braid my hair every single day. I'd never cut it. Ever."

"Grandma!" came a shout from the floor below.

"They're back already?" Maudene wondered out loud as she and Jenny stepped from the bathroom into the hallway. "That was a quick visit."

"Hey, Mom," Ellen said wearily.

"Is everything okay? How's Avery doing?" Maudene asked as she met Ellen in the middle of the stairs.

"She's doing okay. She still has the IV, but the doctors say she's doing better. Still has a bit of a fever though." Ellen turned to her children. "Lucas and Leah, why don't you two go and find Dolly and play with her for a few minutes. I need to talk to Grandma." Jenny stepped back into the bathroom before Ellen sent her off, as well. She wanted to hear what Ellen had to say, especially if it was about her.

"What's the matter?" Maudene asked, concern lacing her voice. "Is Avery really okay?" Jenny strained to hear what was being said.

"She's really okay. At least right now she is. Did Joe Gaddey stop by here?"

"Joe, your police officer friend?" Maudene asked. "Why would he come over here?"

Despite herself, Jenny stepped out into the hallway, joining Ellen and Maudene on the steps. "I'm not going with any policeman, Maudene!" she exclaimed angrily. "You promised!"

"Jenny, shh," Maudene hushed her just as the doorbell rang. "Just a minute." Maudene rushed down the stairs, clutching the banister for balance, and opened the front door.

Jenny looked suspiciously down at the man standing just inside the doorway. He was the tallest man that Jenny had ever seen. He was wearing gray dress pants and a short-sleeved white button-down shirt that stretched tightly across his broad shoulders. A blue-and-green-striped tie sat crookedly across his chest. The look on his face made it clear that this was the last place in the world he wanted to be.

"Hi, Joe," Ellen said. "You remember my mother, don't you? And this is Jenny, she's staying with my mom for a few days."

The man gave a weak smile and rubbed a thick hand over his face and looked back and forth among Maudene, Ellen and Jenny. "It's okay, Joe," Ellen said at last. "You can say it."

The man sighed and shook his head. "I'm sorry, Ellen. A warrant has been issued for your arrest."

Realization inched over Jenny. The man was the cop they were talking about. This couldn't be good, she thought. Cops were never good. Slowly, she began to creep back up the steps, hoping to remain unnoticed.

"What? Why?" Maudene asked confusedly, and Jenny froze midway back up the steps.

Why was Ellen being arrested? Curious, Jenny turned around and began the descent back down the steps.

"But why?" Maudene asked incredulously. "I thought they were going to let the grand jury decide and that won't happen for a few weeks."

"It's okay, Mom. I kind of figured it might happen this way."

The man shrugged his shoulders. "They're following protocol to the tee on this one, Ellen. And moving fast. Prieto is feeling the pressure. Has some child advocacy groups hollering for your arrest, and the press wants to know what he's going to do, so he moved ahead and filed charges."

Jenny watched while Maudene went to her daughter and folded her into her arms, and for a moment she forgot about her father, her grandmother and the possibility of foster care.

Ellen's face was pale and she looked as if she might start crying. "Joe, are you arresting me right now?" Ellen asked the man.

The cop lowered his head as if ashamed and pushed his large hands into his pockets. Jenny spied the gun in his holster and thought of her father. "No. When I found out what was going on, I talked it over with Prieto and he agreed to let you come to the station and surrender yourself. That way I don't have to put you in handcuffs."

"Right now? Do we have to go right now?" Ellen asked, looking around the house wildly as if trying to find an escape route.

"No. You have to turn yourself in tomorrow morning by six. That way, your booking will be done before the jail starts its regular daily duties. You'll see the judge for a bond hearing and hopefully be home before the day is over."

"Will you stay with me?" Ellen asked the man, her voice trembling with fear.

"For as long as I can." Jenny peered with interest as the police officer awkwardly patted Ellen on the back.

This cop didn't seem as bad as the ones that her dad talked about. This one seemed almost human. "You should call your lawyer right now, figure out how you're going to pay for getting bonded out."

Jenny's eyes shifted to Maudene, who was leaning against the wall for support, helpless tears streaming down her face. Jenny scurried down the final few steps and went to Maudene's side as Ellen hugged and thanked the man and Jenny watched as his face crumpled in pain.

"Oh, my God," Ellen cried out once the door shut behind the policeman. "What am I going to do?" Maudene reached for her daughter, and Ellen pulled away and ran up the stairs. Jenny heard a bedroom door slam and, in stunned silence, Maudene lowered herself into a chair, covered her face with her hands and cried. For a moment Jenny stood awkwardly behind Maudene and then began to rub her back in slow circles the way that Maudene had done for her while she was throwing up in the bathroom at the Happy Pancake. Then as Maudene's crying subsided a bit, Jenny went into the kitchen, pulled out a glass and filled it with ice and cold water, ran a clean washcloth beneath the tap. Jenny returned to the living room, where she carefully held the glass out to Maudene.

There was another knock at the front door. "I bet if you ignore it, they'll just go away," Jenny advised.

Maudene blew her nose noisily into a handkerchief. "If only it was that easy." She stood and Jenny followed her to the front door.

"Hi, Mrs. Sifkus, I'm Ruth Johnson. I work with Ellen."

"Please come in," Maudene said, stepping aside to let her in.

"Hi, Jenny," Ruth said, extending a hand to Jenny to shake. Reluctantly, Jenny held out her own hand. "You are one lucky girl," Ruth said, smiling down at her. Jenny wrinkled her forehead in puzzlement. She had been called a lot of names in her short life, but lucky wasn't one of them. "You have a lot of people very worried about you and hoping that you're okay."

"Is my dad coming?" Jenny asked hopefully.

"Can we sit down a few minutes and talk?" Ruth addressed Jenny as if she was the adult. Jenny liked that.

"Can Maudene sit with us?" Jenny thought she might like this Ruth person, but she'd still feel better if Maudene was there with her.

"Of course," Ruth assured her as they moved toward the living room sofa. "I did find out some information about your father. He is very worried about you, Jenny, and he's been trying to find you and wants to get you back to Benton," Ruth explained, and Jenny sat up straight in anticipation. Ruth held up a finger. "There's more. Jenny, you know your dad was arrested, don't you?"

"But it wasn't his fault," Jenny said in a rush. "I saw the whole thing."

Ruth nodded in agreement. "That's what your father said, as did the witnesses." Ruth paused a moment and looked kindly at Jenny. "But your father did something wrong when the police came. Instead of listening to the police officer, your father hit him." Jenny felt sick. "Your father will have to stay in jail for a while until things get straightened out. Maudene here agreed to let you stay with her for a few more days." Ruth turned to

Maudene. "All we have to do is a background check and if it's approved you'll be approved as what is called a *suitable other* in order to legally have Jenny stay with you until other arrangements are made."

Ruth turned to Jenny. "There's more. Your father needs some special help. Do you know what an alcoholic is?"

Jenny stopped listening and looked down at her feet. Once again, her toes were grimy and dusty in her flip-flops. Maybe Maudene would take her to Walmart to get a pair of tennis shoes—she couldn't wait to throw these things away.

Ruth lightly touched Jenny on the shoulder. "Jenny, do you know?" she asked again.

"My dad," Jenny said in a long, shuddering breath.

Chapter 25

I call Adam and tell him about having to turn myself in to the police in the morning. He is silent for a long time. "Adam?" I finally say.

"I'm coming right over," he says.

"No, no, someone needs to stay with Avery. I'll be okay," I insist.

"No, my mom and dad are coming right to the hospital from the airport. They'll be here in an hour. Avery is doing just fine right now."

"I want to go home," I whisper into the phone. As much as I'm appreciative of my mother and my childhood home, I want to be back in my own house, even if it's just for a short while.

"I'll meet you there at six. Bring Lucas and Leah and we'll spend the night at the house," Adam says.

My mother tells me her plans of becoming a *suitable other* for Jenny. I'm too exhausted to argue with her, though I tell her that I think it's a very bad idea.

I spend the next forty-five minutes talking to Ted Vitolo on the phone about my upcoming arrest. To say he's livid is an understatement. "There's no reason for them to do this," he says angrily. "DHS hasn't even finished its investigation—they're forgoing the grand jury and going right to charging you." He explains that since I'm being charged with a Class C felony the judge would likely order $10,000 cash or surety. "You should probably be able to get a ten percent cash surety bond for $1,000 through a bail bondsman," Vitolo says, and gives me the name of a bondsman he's worked with often. He promises to meet me at the courthouse in the morning and tells me I will be home by one o'clock that afternoon.

When I pull up in front of my own home, Adam is already there, and a strange car is sitting in the driveway. "My mom and dad's rental," he says by explanation. Leah and Lucas smother him with hugs and kisses and then trot into the house.

We eat dinner at our own kitchen table, but it is strange and sad without having Avery there. Leah and Lucas are excited to be surrounded by their own things, to play in their own yard, to sleep in their own beds. My mother plans on coming over early in the morning to watch the kids while Adam and I go to the police station.

It's difficult explaining to them what is happening, that I will being arrested for leaving Avery in the hot car. At first Adam didn't want to tell them, wanted to protect them, but I insisted. I don't want them finding out from others that their mother was arrested. Adam is wonderful. He tells them over and over it was an accident and that no matter what people say about me, I am a good mom. After answering many questions and kissing away a lot of tears, we get them settled for the night and Adam and I go into our bedroom and shut the door. We lie down on the bed and talk and cry about what was to come. We are both too exhausted to make love, but we fall asleep holding hands, something we haven't done in years, if ever.

We wake up Thursday morning well before the sun rises and don't speak as we prepare for the day. Just before five o'clock my mother arrives with a sleepy Jenny in tow. I reluctantly wake Leah and Lucas and kiss them goodbye like I promised I would. I assure them that I will see them later in the day. They both cry and I do, too.

The Cedar City Police Department is a brand-new, low-slung building situated in the heart of Cedar City. Despite the shiny tiled floor, the unscratched desks and efficiently running office equipment, a sense of desperation has already seeped into the freshly painted walls. I relish the quietness of the early morning. The lobby is nearly empty and, as promised, Joe is there waiting for us.

"Thanks for coming." My voice doesn't sound like my own. Even though Joe has already schooled me on exactly what is going to happen to me today I can't help but be terrified.

"You bet." He shakes Adam's hand and claps me on the shoulder. "You'll be fine."

Joe explains to me every step of the booking process. "They'll get started in just a minute. They like to have all the surrenders come in bright and early so they can stay on schedule for the day." Joe looks down at the floor and uncomfortably shuffles his feet. "This would probably be a good time to say your goodbyes."

Adam leads me to a corner of the room and embraces me. "It's going to be okay," he whispers into my ear. "You'll be home by this afternoon. I love you, you know that, don't you?"

"I love you, too," I whisper back, doing my best to keep my tears at bay.

The arrest goes just as Joe explained it would. It is surreal, otherworldly. Though he offers to stay with me for as much of the process as he is allowed to, I make Joe stay behind. I don't want him to see me this way. "It will all be okay," Joe assures me as he leads me through a heavy door that he unlocks with an electronic key card.

I nod and bite back the tears that threaten to fall again and begin to shiver with fear.

"Hey," Joe says, looking me in the eyes, "you're going to be fine. It will all be over in a few hours and you'll be back home." I am instantly calmed by Joe's confident words.

Before he leaves, Joe squeezes my hand and then I'm officially taken into custody by a female officer. I am surprised at how young she is, mid-twenties maybe, only a few inches taller than I am, her hair pulled back in a tight bun. The booking area is deserted and she leads me into a private spot. I know what is coming next—Joe explained it all to me the night before—but this prior knowledge doesn't make it any less humiliating.

Because I am being charged with a felony, I must be strip-searched. With trembling fingers I begin to unbutton the black wraparound dress that I pulled from my closet for just this occasion. Simple, easy to take off and put back on, professional enough for a court appearance. I fumble to untie the fabric belt at my waist while the officer stands by patiently. Goose bumps erupt on my

skin as I step out of my shoes and slide my dress over
my head. I'm painfully aware of my dimpled thighs and
the slack skin of my abdomen. And my face reddens
in shame even though the officer respectfully averts
her eyes to my nakedness. I can't help thinking about
the men and women, many the parents of children I've
removed from their care, who have stood in this exact
same spot, peeling their clothes from their bodies.

I never felt sorry for these mothers and fathers, never
gave a second thought to what they experienced during
their arrests and I know that most people feel the same
way about me. I can almost hear the comments: *She de-
serves it, what do you expect if you neglect your child?
A little embarrassment is too good for her.*

Piece by piece, the officer examines my clothing, my
dress, my bra, my underwear. She carefully checks my
pockets and runs her fingers over the seams making
sure that no contraband has been sewn inside.

When I am completely naked the officer steps forward and directs me to run my hands through my hair
to show that there is nothing hidden in my scalp. Once
again I am thankful for my short hair. I am ordered to
pull my ears forward and turn my head to show that
there is nothing tucked behind them. I am struck at how
matter-of-fact and bored the officer sounds. She gives
these exact same directions many times a day. There is
no judgment in her tone but no sympathy, either. *I'm not
like them,* I want to tell her. *I'm different. I'm a mother,
a wife, a social worker. I shouldn't be here.* I say nothing. Today, in this moment, I am no different from anyone else who has been here before me.

"Tilt your head back," the officer instructs, and I do.
She peers into my nostrils. "Open your mouth and lift

your tongue." I comply. In between each direction she gives me, one arm instinctively crosses my breasts and one drops to cover my pubic area. "Lift your arms," the officer says, and I close my eyes as she inspects each armpit. "Halfway done," she says. The first words she utters that make me feel like she sees a real person standing in front of her. But if I think the worst is behind me, I am horribly wrong.

"Lift your breasts," she says, and I blink twice, not sure if I heard her correctly. "Lift your breasts," she says again, and I do. "Open your legs," the officer says. "Squat and cough." Despite my determination not to cry, tears film my eyes and I blindly comply. "Okay, you can stand. Now show me the bottom of your feet." I lift first my left foot and then my right.

Not once during the entire search does she touch me, but still I feel dirty, violated.

The officer hands me my clothes and, turning my back to her, I quickly dress. She leads me to another area where she consults a clipboard and begins to ask me a laundry list of biographical questions. I am booked in and go through a brief medical and psychological questionnaire for safety and health reasons. I am fingerprinted, not the ink-and-paper method I recall seeing on old television shows and movies, but scanned by a computer. I am directed to stand against a wall and my picture is taken. First, face forward, then left side, then right. Mug shots. *What will happen if my children see these pictures?* I wonder. And no doubt they will in this age of instant access to information. They will be mortified. In all the terrible thoughts that have come to mind, Avery's health, my marriage, being arrested, possibly losing my job, I haven't paused to think about how all this will impact Leah and Lucas. Will their friends shun them? Will their teachers look at them differently?

The deputy uses a key card to unlock another door that opens to reveal a small, stark room with only a concrete bench running along one wall. There are no bars in this cell, only one small window inlaid in the door. "You'll wait here until you are transported over to the courthouse," the officer explains. She shuts the door and it doesn't clang or ring in my ears like in the movies. Instead, I hear a nearly imperceptible click as the lock settles into place. I sit down and, despite the stuffy, warm air, I am shivering. I try to block out the noises and the antiseptic odors that surge my way, try to bury the indignity of having to strip in front of a complete stranger. I close my eyes and think of Avery. I imagine cradling her in my arms. I think of Leah and Lucas at home with my mother and how scared they must be right now. I think of Adam, torn between returning to the hospital and waiting anxiously at the courthouse for my case number to be called.

"What have I done?" I say out loud. All it would have taken was for me to stop and listen, really listen to what Adam was trying to tell me about how he put Avery in the van for me. If I would have just paused, pushed aside all the distractions of the morning, the worry of being late, everything could have turned out differently.

Several hours later, I am still waiting. I have to go to the bathroom and, inexplicably, my stomach growls, though the thought of eating anything turns my stomach. I have lost all concept of time, I don't know if it's twelve noon or four o'clock. I do know that, by law, I am supposed to see a judge within twenty-four hours of being arrested. This means, theoretically, I could have to spend the night here. Would they leave me in this tiny room or will I be placed in a cell with others who have been arrested? I can't stay here overnight. What would Adam tell Leah and Lucas? A rope of panic coils tightly in my chest and I'm afraid I'm going to start hyperventilating. I lower my head to my knees and am trying to calm my breathing when there is a rap on the metal door and it opens. A female officer, a different one than earlier, stands in the doorway.

"It's time to go," she says. I prepare myself for being handcuffed but instead a male officer joins us, and together we move through a winding maze of hallways and locked doors until we step out into the hot July sun. Flanked on each side by an officer, we cross the street to the courthouse and I find myself in a courtroom where just two weeks ago I was sitting on the witness stand testifying in my role as a social worker in an abuse case.

I hear my name and I move down the aisle, past the courtroom gallery. Prieto is there, as are Caren and several of my colleagues from the Department of Human Services. It's not a large courtroom, but for some reason it's crowded today and I can't find Adam anywhere within the sea of faces. Today there are no friendly nods or waves. My co-workers won't even look at me. All eyes are on the floor as if searching for a lost button or coin. But of course I'm not here today to testify on behalf of a neglected, abused child or here to chronicle the many indignities they have endured. I feel Vitolo's reassuring hand on my elbow and he leads me to a small table just to the right of the judge—a judge I've chatted casually with about home and family—who is staring down at me from his bench. I turn back and finally see that Adam is sitting in the gallery, as are Joe and Kelly.

Little mercies, I think to myself. This is one of those small gifts that my mother was talking about.

The judge tells me that I am not allowed to leave the state and that I need to report to the Department of Corrections within the next twenty-four hours for a pretrial release meeting where I will be told what is expected of me pending my trial. Ted explains to me that this could include a curfew or a mental health evaluation.

In two weeks my arraignment hearing will be held. This is where the state will turn in the official trial information, the documents that detail the charges against me, lists of all the witnesses, their addresses and a written summary of their expected testimony. I will be asked to enter my formal plea, asked if I want a formal reading of the trial information.

Just as quickly as it began, the hearing is over. Ted tells me to come to his office the following day and we'll begin preparation for the trial. I thank him and go to where Adam, Joe and Kelly are waiting for me.

"Are you okay?" Adam asks, pulling me into an embrace. I nod tearfully into his shoulder but want to tell him that, no, I'm not okay, that it was awful, that I wouldn't wish it on anyone and if I ever was able to be a social worker again, I would look at my clients a little bit differently, with a bit more empathy. But I don't say anything, because no matter how harrowing being arrested, strip-searched, fingerprinted and photographed was, for what I am putting Avery through, my family through, I deserve much, much worse.

Chapter 26

Later that afternoon, even after Ellen and her husband had returned from the courthouse to their home, where Maudene was watching Lucas and Leah, Jenny knew that bad things were still happening. First, it was not finding her grandmother at the house on Hickory Street and then Ellen getting arrested. But Jenny knew there was more just around the corner. Jenny always knew when her father was going to lose a job, lose an apartment, lose a friend-girl, even before he did. When her father was working at a restaurant that specialized in chicken wings in a staggering array of flavors, he would bring home bags of frozen wings that he stuffed into an ancient deep freezer that he bought for fifteen dollars. The freezer took up most of the living room and each night, when her father came home from work, he would retrieve a bag of wings from the freezer for their supper. Jenny knew there was going to be trouble when each night her father kept bringing home the wings along with other frozen appetizers: mozzarella sticks, onion rings, French fries. People started showing up at their apartment with small wads of cash that they would hand to her father, and in return he would send them on their way with a pack of frozen teriyaki chicken wings and fried pickles.

One day while walking home from the bus stop, Jenny dug some coins out of her backpack and stopped at a convenience store and bought a newspaper. Jenny wasn't much of a reader, but she knew that newspapers had sections just for people looking for jobs, and sooner rather than later Billy would be looking for a new job. Sure enough, when she arrived home, paper in hand, her father was there. "Time for a new adventure, Jenny Penny," he proclaimed. She handed him the newspaper, went into the bathroom and slammed the door.

Even though Maudene didn't tell her much about what was happening, Jenny could tell by the look on Maudene's face that she was thinking hard about all that had been going on. Maudene also had to be thinking about what she was going to do with Jenny now that there was no grandmother to give her to. She couldn't keep hauling Jenny around town in her little yellow car and letting her stay in the white bedroom forever. Maybe Maudene was going to call the police or Ruth from DHS again and let someone else worry about what happened to her. Jenny couldn't really blame her.

Jenny knew enough to fade into the background and stay quiet. She'd learned how to do that with her mother's boyfriend, with nosy teachers, with her father's friend-girls.

Now they were just waiting—and waiting was the worst. When you were waiting for something, Jenny thought, your mind always went to the bad.

"Are you coming home with us?" Maudene asked Ellen as she pulled her car keys from her purse.

"No, no." Ellen shook her head. "We're staying right here tonight. We all need to sleep in our own beds tonight."

"Are you sure?" Maudene asked. "It's no bother, is it, Jenny?"

Jenny looked up in surprise at being consulted. Maybe Maudene wasn't going to dump her just yet. "No, it doesn't bother me a bit." She cast a glance over at Leah, whose eyes were fixed on her mother.

"Thanks, Mom. But I think we need to just stay home. Come on, guys, give Grandma a hug and say goodbye." Leah and Lucas both stood and gave their grandmother a perfunctory hug. Jenny couldn't help notice the hurt in Maudene's face. Maybe it wasn't hurt exactly, maybe more it was the feeling you get when you realize you aren't really needed. Jenny knew what that felt like.

Before she could stop herself, Jenny said, "Maudene and I can make supper for you all and bring it over tonight." Everyone's eyes swung toward Jenny who self-consciously tried to tuck her t-shirt into her shorts.

Ellen looked over at Maudene, who nodded in agreement. "That would be really, really nice. Thanks, Jenny." Jenny blushed and fingered her French braid. "Thanks, Mom," Ellen said, drawing her mother into a tight hug.

Once they were outside Ellen's home and again sitting in the car, Jenny asked, "What do you think we should make?"

"Comfort food," Maudene said and smiled without hesitation as she pulled away from the curb.

They drove in silence for several minutes until Jenny

spoke. "What's comfort food?" Jenny asked, wrinkling up her nose.

"It's food that makes you forget what you're so worried about, at least for a while." At Jenny's perplexed expression, Maudene went on. "Food that tastes so good that all your concentration goes into eating. Like fried chicken and mashed potatoes. That's comfort food."

"Couldn't we just go to KFC and pick up a bucket?" Jenny asked, running her fingers up and down the ridges of her French braid. She wondered if the braid would come undone during the night and if Maudene would braid it again for her in the morning.

"KFC has its place," Maudene said sagely, "but comfort food is best if it's made from scratch."

"Does it have to be chicken, can't it be something else?" Jenny asked, moving her face close to the vent pushing out cool air.

"Sure," Maudene said as she turned onto her street. "It just has to be homemade and taste really good. We'll read through some cookbooks and you can pick out what we should make."

Anxiety pinched at Jenny, just as it did each time she was asked to read something that might be too hard for her, but quickly eased after they arrived at the house and Maudene set three large cookbooks in front of Jenny. She was relieved to see that the cookbooks were filled with photographs of delicious, brightly colored food, lots of numbers. There were lots of words, but she just asked Maudene and she told her what they said. Jenny finally settled on a menu consisting of pot roast, garlic mashed potatoes, buttered corn and rhubarb crisp, and they spent the next few hours grocery shopping, slicing, measuring and stirring.

"Whew," Maudene said, looking around at the piles of pots and pans, the dirtied spoons and knives, the countertops splattered with oil and dusted flour and brown sugar.

"I'm sorry." Jenny hastily reached for a damp rag and began scrubbing at the counter.

Maudene laughed. "No sorries needed. This is what a kitchen is supposed to look like when you're making comfort food." She took off her glasses and rubbed at her eyes.

"I'll clean up. I do it all the time for my dad," Jenny said automatically.

"Nonsense." Maudene waved her hand dismissively. "We'll do it together."

"No, really, I want to. I *like* cleaning up," Jenny insisted. She glanced slyly at Maudene out of the corner of her eye. "I promise not to steal anything."

"Silly girl," Maudene said, smiling fondly down at her. "I'm tired though. If you don't mind I will go and lie down for a bit. And when I get up, I'm going to do *you* a favor."

"What kind of favor?" Jenny paused in her scrubbing, not accustomed to people offering such random kindnesses.

"Let's just say, you and Dolly are going to become friends once and for all."

Jenny scowled. "That doesn't sound like much of a favor."

"Trust me," Maudene said before exiting the kitchen. And Jenny, to her surprise, found that she did.

Jenny tackled the pots and pans first, scraped carrot and potato peels into the garbage and used hot soapy water and a long-handled scrub brush to wash away the

sticky bits. For a brief moment she guiltily thought of
Connie, sitting by her phone back in Benton, waiting
for Jenny to call her back. She hoped she wasn't too
worried about her and vowed to call her a little bit later.

Jenny heard a tapping noise and first thought it was
Dolly's toenails clacking against the hardwood floors.
The noise became more insistent and she realized someone was knocking at the front door. She wiped her wet
hands on a dish towel and, feeling very grown up,
peeked through the curtains to see who was there. She
found Ellen, Leah and Lucas on the front porch. Ellen
looked scared, casting furtive looks over her shoulder
and Jenny quickly opened the door.

"We had to leave," Lucas said excitedly. "The TV
people came. They were all over! We snuck out the back
and ended up going over to Kelly's house," he added.

"Jenny, where's my mom?" Ellen asked, looking
around.

"She's upstairs. Sleeping," Jenny said. "Do you want
me to go get her?"

Leah, near tears, shook her head. "Why are you even
still here?" she spat at Jenny, and stomped out of the
room and into the kitchen.

Jenny looked down at the floor, her face burning
with embarrassment.

Ellen paced around the living room, pausing only to
peer through the sheers. "She's just upset about her sister and the reporters, Jenny. She doesn't mean it. I think
we are going to have to stay here, at least for tonight."

Jenny had joined Ellen at the window, keeping an eye
out for reporters, when the house phone rang. Absent-

mindedly, Ellen answered. She was silent for a moment and then held the phone out toward Jenny.

"It's for you," Ellen said, unable to keep the surprise from her voice. "It's your father."

Chapter 27

I decide to give Jenny some privacy to talk to her father, climb the stairs and pause outside my brothers' old bedroom, the one that my mother redesigned after they had grown up and moved away. It was her respite during my father's illness, the only place my mother could get any sleep after spending long days tending to my father's many needs. I push open the door and see that this is the room where Jenny is staying. Small plastic figurines line the dresser and there is a neatly folded pile of clothes belonging to a little girl sitting on a chair. The bed is made but rumpled in places. I walk over to straighten one of the pillows leaning askew at the head of the bed and find deposited beneath it a box of chocolate-covered snack cakes. I shake my head at the strange little girl who my mother has taken into her home and return the box to its hiding spot. On a hunch, I open the bedside table and find it filled with bags of chips and cookies. I get down on my knees, lift the bed skirt, peer beneath the bed and pull out several bars of baking chocolate and a box of cereal. Jenny's a food hoarder. I've seen it before. Children who don't get enough to eat will gather and hide food, much like a squirrel does when preparing for winter. I replace Jenny's stash, move to the hallway and vow to have a serious talk with my mother about exactly what's going on with this little girl.

I tap quietly on my mother's bedroom door. There is no response and I figure she must be sleeping. I turn to leave, then stop. Never have I remembered needing my mother as much as I do right now. Growing up she was one of those mothers who moved along in the wake of her family, following behind quietly, always there, watchful, but never really a participant. Our dad was the one who got down on the ground to wrestle with us, play touch football in the yard, the one who yelled and delegated, the one who grounded us and took the car keys away. But my mother was the one I went to when I fell down and scraped my knee, failed a test, and when I came home in tears because someone had been inexplicably cruel to me. She didn't judge, she rarely scolded. She listened, hugged and always left me with a few words that I never realized was advice until later. *"I guess that tree wasn't meant to be climbed. I wonder what Mr. Hansen would say if you asked him to go over the test with you? When someone is cruel, it usually means that something hard and horrible is going on in their own lives."*

I know I should let my mother sleep, but instead, I quietly tiptoe into the darkened room. She is lying on her side beneath the covers, her face slack in sleep, one hand curled beneath her chin in the same way that Lucas does when he sleeps. She looks so old and I try not to think about how many days I might have left with her.

"It's okay, I'm awake," my mother says blearily, rising to one elbow. "Is everything okay?"

I slip off my shoes and ease myself next to her on the bed and lie down. I close my eyes, willing my brain to stop whirring, but it won't. "I'm sorry, Mom," I say. "I'm sorry you have to be part of this whole mess."

"Life can be a mess," she says simply.

"There are reporters outside my house. They all of a sudden showed up in droves. They must have heard that I turned myself in this morning. They were talking to the neighbors." My voice rises with the improbability of it all.

"Did they see you?" my mother asks, her voice still gravelly with sleep.

"I don't think so. We went out the back." I put my face in my hands. It is all feeling like way too much. Avery, the protection order, being arrested and now the press. "I have never been so humiliated in my life. Jail was horrible. I was strip-searched. Can you believe it? Exactly what do they think I was going to smuggle into jail with me?" My mother has no answer for this. "What am I going to do? What if I end up having to go to jail?" I cover my face with a pillow in shame.

I expect my mother to just pat my hand and tell me that things have a way of working out and I'll just have to trust that everything is going to be okay. But she doesn't. She sits up, plumps her pillow and leans back against the headboard. "You're already doing it. You've got the best lawyer and you're fighting. You keep fighting so you can be with Avery."

We sit in silence for a few moments and I wonder if she has fallen asleep again, but then she speaks. "You'll stay with us for as long as you need to. And if the reporters find us here, we'll go to a hotel."

I notice that my mother used the collective *us* in her invitation. Us being she and Jenny, I assume. "Jenny's on the phone with her father. What exactly is going on here? I thought that Ruth would have this taken care of by now."

"I haven't told you the full story about Jenny," she says contritely, as if she's a child caught in a lie.

"She's a runaway, isn't she?" I say. "I knew it."

"No." My mother shakes her head back and forth, causing the headboard to rattle. "It's much more complicated than that." She goes on to describe once again how she met Jenny and, in my mind, the dubious story of how she ended up in Cedar City.

"You've told me this already. Jenny gets separated from her father, takes a bus across Nebraska and Iowa by herself, gets off in Cedar City to reunite with a grandmother she never met, and you meet her at the Happy Pancake." We sit in silence for a moment. "I'm still not sure how she ended up in your extra bedroom." I'm trying to keep the exasperation out of my voice, but it's there and my mother hears it, too.

"I know I should have called someone right away, but I really thought I would be able to find her grandmother." I can't help smiling. My mother has always taken in strays. Stray cats and dogs that would stay with us until my father had had enough and insisted she find homes for them. Even the neighbors' kids would find reasons to come over to our house to hang out, and while I'd like to think it was due to my winning personality, I know my mother's bottomless cookie jar and kindness played a big part. "I tried to handle it without worrying you," she says. "Ruth called and is planning on taking Jenny back to Benton next Monday. She'll be in foster care until they work things out with her father, but at least she'll be near him."

"That's good news. I would think Jenny would be happy to be back in the same town with her dad," I say, glad that at least one of our lives is starting to get settled.

"For some reason Jenny is deathly afraid of going into a foster care," my mother explains. "I'm afraid to tell her."

"I think it's for the best. Ruth will be able to find Jenny a good foster home, at least until they figure out where her family is."

"Jenny trusts me, though," Maudene says sadly.

"I don't think we have much of a choice." I shake my head. "What a mess."

"There's more," my mother says guiltily, and I groan. "When I took Jenny to the address we had for her grandmother, I left her in the car while I went to the door. A woman answered, and I asked if a Margie Flanagan lived there. She said no, Margie had passed about a year ago."

"Okay, Jenny's grandmother died and her father is in jail. So we have to find out if there are any other relatives we can find. I'm sure Ruth can do that for us."

"No, no," my mother says, her voice tinged with impatience. "I'm not finished. The woman who answered the door was the spitting image of Jenny. She told me that Margie Flanagan was her mother. That woman is Jenny's mother, I know it. And, Ellen, I saw pictures of what that woman did to Jenny." My mother's voice broke slightly and she continued with a steely resolve that I don't think I've heard from her. "Jenny cannot know that her mother is living in this town and that woman cannot know that Jenny is here."

Chapter 28

When Jenny heard her father's voice, she couldn't help but start crying. "How are you, Jenny Penny?" he asked.

"Okay," Jenny said through her tears. "When are you coming to get me?"

"I can't be the one to come and get you, but the good news is you're coming back to Benton in a few days. Isn't that good news, Jenny?"

"I'm coming home?" Jenny sniffled. "But where are we going to live?"

Her father was silent for a moment. "The social worker told you it would be a while until we could be together, didn't she?" Jenny nodded, but couldn't speak even though she knew her father couldn't see her.

"You'll stay with a nice family for a little while, but we'll be able to talk on the phone."

Jenny froze. "What nice family?" she asked.

"It's just for a little while, Jenny. I promise," her father said earnestly.

"A foster family?" Jenny asked fearfully.

Her father's voice broke. "I'm trying to get better, Jenny, but it's hard."

"A foster family?" Jenny repeated.

Jenny had never heard her father crying before and it caused her to cry even harder. "I love you, Jenny," her father whispered.

Jenny couldn't remember her father ever saying that to her before. "Love you, too," Jenny echoed.

When they hung up, Jenny sat on the floor, sobbing. She was going to be sent to a foster home.

The timer on the oven began beeping, signaling that the rhubarb crisp they'd made was finished. Wearily, Jenny climbed the stairs and stood outside Maudene's room. She hadn't meant to eavesdrop—her father's friend-girls always told her it's rude to listen to other people's conversations. But she couldn't help but listen to what Maudene and Ellen were saying. The door was opened just a crack and she heard Ellen say her name and again there was talk of a social worker and foster care. *Traitors!* Jenny thought. And then Maudene talked about her grandmother being dead. And then she said that it was Jenny's mother who'd answered the door. Could it be true? Was her mother living in this town, just a few miles from where Jenny was standing right here and now? Was she still with Jimmy? And why hadn't she ever tried to call Jenny? So many questions spun through Jenny's head.

She crept back to the top of the stairs, being careful to make sure the floor didn't creak beneath her feet. "Maudene," she hollered. "Maudene, the oven is beeping! The rhubarb crisp is done!"

"Oh, my!" Maudene answered, tripping into the hallway. Maudene's feet were bare, her white hair was tousled from sleep and there was a crease in the delicate skin on one side of her face.

"I didn't want it to burn," Jenny explained.

"Let's go take a look," Maudene said airily. "I can smell it from up here."

Jenny followed Maudene down the stairs and with each step a plan began to form in her mind. She needed to make sure that they didn't send her away just yet and she needed to go and see for herself if it was really her mother in the house on Hickory Street. She would have to work fast. All it took was one phone call and within minutes she would be placed in the backseat of a social worker's car and on her way to some foster home. "I'll be right there!" Jenny called down the steps after Maudene, and turned around, almost bumping into Ellen.

"You okay, Jenny?" Ellen asked scrutinizing Jenny's face with concern.

"Yeah, I'm fine. I just have to grab something from my room." Jenny stepped past Ellen, slipped into the bedroom, flipped on the light and scanned the room. She couldn't quite pinpoint how she knew, but someone had been in here. She thought of her backpack, down in the kitchen, and she chided herself for letting it out of her sight. Her father's cell phone was still plugged into its charger and she grabbed it. Six missed calls, three voice mails and two texts, all from Connie. Jenny read the texts first: Call me im worried about u. And then, i talked to ur dad hes ok call me. Next Jenny listened to the voice mails, hoping to hear more news about her father.

"Jenny," came Connie's fretful voice. "Please, please call me. I'm so worried about you. I just want to know that you're okay. Please call me." The second message was much the same, but the third made Jenny sit up.

"Jenny, it's Connie. I talked to your dad. He is in jail, but he's okay. He said he's been trying to tell anyone that will listen that you are somewhere out there all by yourself. You've got to call me, Jenny," Connie pleaded. "I'll come and get you, just tell me where you are."

Jenny hated that she had caused Connie to worry so much. She should just call her, tell her she's okay and ask her to come and get her. But she wanted to see her mom, just to see if it was really her. Maybe Jimmy would be long gone and her mother would explain that she didn't really mean to leave Jenny behind. That she didn't really choose Jimmy over Jenny. Maybe he had kidnapped her mother and forced her to run away. Jenny's heart pounded with the possibilities. She just needed a little more time to figure out exactly what to do.

She pressed Send to connect to Connie and she answered on the first ring. "Jenny! My God, are you okay?"

"I'm okay."

"Listen, don't do that to me again. Please don't ignore my calls. I've been so worried about you!"

"I'm sorry," Jenny said apologetically. She did feel bad that she made Connie worry so much. "I talked to my dad, I really miss him."

Connie sighed. "I'm glad you two talked. He really got himself into a mess this time, didn't he? He's not really hurt, but it might take a little time to get all the—" she paused trying to find the right words "—legal stuff figured out," she concluded.

"How long do you think it will take?" Jenny asked, hoping that Connie could answer the question her father did not.

"I don't know for sure, but I imagine it could take some time."

"Oh," Jenny said in a small voice. "Then I guess we're not moving to Dubuque?"

"I don't think so. At least not for a while anyway," Connie answered.

"So if I go back to Benton, I really won't be able to stay with my dad?" Jenny asked, already knowing the answer.

"I don't know exactly how all this works, but I don't think so," Connie said with difficulty. "But we'll work something out. It will be okay. I'll make sure to check on you. When you get settled into your foster home you can call me anytime you want. I'll come visit to make sure you're doing okay." Jenny thought she heard Connie sniffle on the other end of the phone.

"Couldn't I just stay with you?" Jenny asked before she could stop herself. The short silence that followed was answer enough.

"It's complicated, Jenny," Connie finally said. "Do you want me to come to pick you up and bring you back to Benton? I will."

Jenny closed her eyes and waited for the ache in her chest to pass. "No, that's okay," she said finally, thinking of her mother in the white house and green shutters. "I've got to go." Before Connie could speak again, Jenny hung up and headed down the steps to help with dinner.

Very quickly, Jenny realized that someone else was in the house. An unfamiliar female voice chattered on and on from the direction of the kitchen and Jenny stood outside the door trying to listen.

"I was worried when I went to your home and saw

all the press outside. Smart thinking, coming over to your mom's house."

Jenny exhaled with relief. Whoever it was, she wasn't there about Jenny. She slipped quietly into the kitchen.

Sitting at the kitchen table was Maudene, Ellen and the stranger. She was young and pretty with long shiny yellow hair pulled back in a headband. She wore a short-sleeved yellow t-shirt, a khaki skirt and brown sandals. "Now, Ellen," the woman said. "I know you know how all this works."

"I do," Ellen said tightly.

"And I imagine it's very uncomfortable for you, but I promise I will make my visits as unobtrusive and painless as possible." The woman took a sip from the glass of iced tea sitting in front of her. "I'll interview Lucas and—" she peered at the notebook in her hand "—Leah. Talk with you, of course, and also visit with your husband. And he is where?" She looked around the kitchen as if the husband would miraculously appear.

"He's at the hospital with Avery," Ellen supplied patiently.

"Oh, who's this?" the woman asked, seeing Jenny lurking across the room. "Leah, maybe?"

"No, no," Maudene said hurriedly. "This is Jenny. I'm watching her for a few days."

"Nice to meet you, Jenny. My name is Nicole." She flashed Jenny a smile, but Jenny wasn't fooled—both Maudene and Ellen were clearly worried about this visit. "How long will you be staying?" Nicole asked.

"Just until Monday," Jenny answered, looking Nicole straight in the eyes. "I'm leaving on Monday."

Nicole nodded, still grinning as she turned back to Ellen. "As your care coordinator, I will also attend any scheduled family team meetings as well as any court hearings that might arise."

"Okay," Ellen said, fidgeting nervously. "Would you like to speak with Leah and Lucas now or do you want to talk with me some more?"

"I can visit with the kids now. As you know I will talk with each of your children individually."

Ellen pinched her lips together. "I'll go and get them," she said stiffly, rising from her chair.

Jenny was familiar with care coordinators, though they weren't called that back in Nebraska. They nosed into your family's business, wrote everything down in little notebooks and typed up long reports that strangers read. Jenny decided she wasn't going to like Nicole, but wanted to be helpful to Maudene and Ellen.

"Ellen is a very good mother," Jenny said, joining Nicole and Maudene at the table.

"Oh?" Nicole asked. "How so?"

Maudene cleared her throat. "Can I get you some more iced tea?"

"No, thank you," Nicole declined.

"Jenny, can you go on into the laundry room and see if you can find my green apron with the apples embroidered on it?" Maudene was staring hard at Jenny, so Jenny scraped her chair back from the table, even though she had no idea where the laundry room was. On her way through the living room she passed by Leah, who looked frightened.

"Don't worry," Jenny whispered as they brushed past each other. "Just don't say anything bad about your mom and you'll be fine."

Jenny trotted up the steps and found a door leading to a room she hadn't been in yet. Inside was a washer and dryer and mounds of neatly folded towels and dish-rags. Sitting at the bottom of the laundry basket was the green apron and Jenny plucked it from the pile. Jenny knew that Maudene didn't want her to come downstairs just yet, so she sat down on the tiled floor and thought about the overheard conversation between Maudene and Ellen. Her mother could be making dinner right this minute in the white house, or maybe she was folding laundry into tidy little stacks. If she left for Nebraska on Monday, she would never know for sure if it was her mother living in the house on Hickory Street. Tomor-row morning she would just go to the house and take a peek to see if she recognized the woman as her mother. And if it wasn't her mother, at least she'd know. And if it was her mother… Jenny didn't dare try to imag-ine what could happen then. She buried her face in the green apron, inhaling its freshly laundered scent and, despite herself, hope swelled within her chest.

Chapter 29

Immediately after Nicole questioned Leah and Lucas and informed me that as our care coordinator she could return to our home at any time, I took my cell phone and went up to the white bedroom, which Jenny good-naturedly surrendered. Initially I had planned on making two phone calls. One to Ted Vitolo, to talk to him about the next hearing, the second to Ruth Johnson to see how far she'd come in finding out if Jenny had any other relatives. I end up only making the call to the Ted. We talk for just a few minutes and I confirm that I'm going to meet with him the following day after I have my pretrial conference with a corrections officer.

At the dinner table Jenny surprises us by informing us that she is ready to go back to Benton and to her new foster home. "My dad told me about it last night. I'm sorry I caused so much trouble," she tells us as she forks up a mound of mashed potatoes.

My mother looks taken aback. "Really? You're really okay with this, Jenny? It's only temporary, until things get figured out with your dad."

"I'm okay. Really," she says, not quite meeting my

mother's eyes. "What time will I leave for Benton?" Jenny asks. "Will I have to take the bus back?"

"No," Maudene says quickly. "Ruth said she will drive you back to Benton and then help you get settled. You won't leave until next Monday. It's only Thursday, so we still have four days together. Does that sound okay?"

Jenny nods, her eyes fixed on her plate.

What my mother doesn't realize is all the behind-the-scenes work that goes into the reunification process. The good news is that Jenny's dad appears serious in his desire to get Jenny back. Already the state of Nebraska has opened a court case on Jenny and a court order has been drafted stating that Jenny is to be placed in a foster home in Benton. Since Ruth already has a relationship with Jenny, she volunteered to be the one to drive her back to Nebraska. She'll meet with staff from the Nebraska Department of Health and Human Services to help with the transition to foster care.

"Of course, you can call me anytime you want," my mother says, a bit flustered. "I wish I could go with you and help get you settled in, but…" I can tell she has grown attached to Jenny and isn't quite ready to say goodbye to her.

Again, Jenny shrugs as if she doesn't care, but the defeated slope of her shoulders tells me otherwise.

I am a bit suspicious of Jenny's sudden willingness to go back into foster care, but decide to give her the benefit of the doubt and see what Monday brings.

It's a low-key dinner. Leah and Lucas are exceptionally quiet after their interviews with Nicole who, I realize, when I see the faces of my exhausted children, must have interview techniques that rival the Inquisition.

After we finish eating we all work to clear the table, rinse the dishes and wrap up the leftovers. I go upstairs to make one final phone call.

"Mom," Lucas calls up to me. "Come outside! You have to see all the fireflies we're catching!"

"Be right down!" I yell back. I dial my husband's cell phone. I want to say good-night to him and Avery. I want Adam to press his phone up against Avery's ear so I can say the bedtime prayer I say with her every night. He doesn't answer, which is understandable. The nurses could be changing Avery's IV bag or he could be in the cafeteria getting something to eat. I open the bedside table and pull out the package of cookies that Jenny left behind and begin to eat one even though I am still stuffed from supper. After I swallow, I once again dial Adam's number. This time he answers. His words come in a rush and I am slow to keep up with what he is saying. "Wait, wait," I tell him. "Start over. What's happening?"

"Something is happening to Avery," he cries. "One minute she was fine, just sleeping, and then all these beeps started going off and she's shaking and won't stop. Then the room was filled with doctors and nurses. They made me leave the room." He is crying now. "Ellen, I don't know what to do. What should I do?"

"I'll be right there. I'm coming right now." I hang up the phone and run down the stairs. I don't want to scare Lucas and Leah, so I try to calm myself before I go out onto the porch. I take a deep breath and open the front door. My mother is sitting on the porch swing, Dolly asleep at her feet, watching Lucas, Leah and Jenny chasing after fireflies. They are laughing and swiping at the small, bright flashing lights with cupped hands.

"Look," Leah says, holding up a glass jar filled with twinkling lights.

"Good job, guys," I call to them. In a low voice I tell my mother that I have to go to the hospital and will call her later. "Please don't say anything to Leah and Lucas just yet. I don't want to worry them."

"Yes, of course," my mother says. "You go now. I'll take good care of them."

"I know you will." I bend down and kiss her cheek. "Thanks, Mom." I arrange my face into an animated mask and make an effort to admire each of the kids' firefly jars. "I'm just going to run to the house and get a few things. I'm sure the reporters are gone by now."

"Can I go with you?" Leah calls, lunging toward a winking glow.

"No, you stay here and have some fun. I want to see who caught the most fireflies when I get back."

"I'm going to," Jenny yells, her hair falling loose from its braid as she chases a flashing light.

"No, I am!" Lucas disagrees. Leah rolls her eyes as if she is above it all but runs to join the fray.

I try to steady my hands as I climb into the truck. Avery has to be okay. I turn on the lights, turn the key in the ignition and pull away from my childhood home. I do my best to stay within the speed limit but find myself moving too quickly through the residential neighborhood, not stopping completely at stop signs. I force myself to slow down and it feels like an eternity before I arrive at the hospital, though it takes me under ten minutes to get there.

I see no television vans or reporters at the front entrance, but it wouldn't matter if there were. This entrance is the fastest way to get to Avery. I rush through the corridors and up the elevator until I reach the PICU. I find Adam standing outside Avery's room steadying himself against the nurses' station. "What's going on?" I ask, desperately searching his face for some indication that everything is okay.

"I don't know. They are still in there. No one can tell me anything," he says, pulling me into a hug.

"It'll be okay," I say, because it's the only thing I can think of to say and because it has to be.

A nurse that I don't recognize eyes us uneasily. At first I think Avery must be in a very bad way, but then I realize she's not nervous about Avery, it's me she's worried about. Damn, I say to myself, she's going to make trouble. I pull on Adam's hand and lead him to the hallway where we are out of sight of the nurse but still close enough if we need to get to Avery right away. "What happened?" I ask again, searching his face for any answers he can give me.

"I'm not sure." He removes his baseball cap and runs a hand through his hair. "She was fine one minute and the next—" he looks around as if he can pluck the right word from air above us "—chaos."

"Look, Adam," I say, trying to get him to focus on my face. "I'm not even supposed to be here. Can you go back in there and try and find out what's happening? I'll go and wait in the cafeteria. No one can say I'm doing any harm if I'm down there." He nods, but I can tell he's nervous about returning to the PICU by himself. Afraid of what might be awaiting him there. "Call me the minute you hear anything, and if I need to I'll come right back up here." I surprise myself with the fierceness I hear in my own voice. Nothing will keep me away from Avery if she needs me. I will push past nurses, doctors, Prieto and Caren if I have to.

I watch Adam as he reenters the PICU and force myself to head to the elevator. I'm too late, though, a hospital security guard is moving my way. I pretend I don't see him and as casually as possible turn and walk in the other direction. I'll take the stairs down to the cafeteria. Hopefully, the security guard will assume I'm leaving and let things alone. No such luck. I glance behind me and see that he is still following me. He is a clean-cut, heavyset young man who can't be more than twenty-one years old. His weight slows him down and I'm able to get a head start down the steps. Instinctively, I feel his pace quicken behind me and I wonder if I can get in trouble for evading a security officer. My feet pound down the concrete steps, each footfall echoing through the stairwell. The strangeness of the situation does not escape me as I rush past a startled pair of nurses in green scrubs. Slightly out of breath, I push through the heavy metal door that opens to the first floor and crash into a wall of solid flesh. "Sorry!" Head down, I try to step past the figure, but he moves with me, blocking my way.

"Got a call about a disturbance on the PICU," he says, taking me by the arm.

"Hey," I protest, looking up at my assailant. "Joe." I hiss, "You scared me to death."

Red-faced and out of breath, the security guard joins us. "I can't believe you ran," he says angrily, sweat dripping from his temple.

"I wasn't running," I say, feigning innocence. "Were you trying to talk to me?"

"Yeah, right," he snorts. "You—" he points a stubby finger at me "—are not allowed on the PICU."

I look helplessly up at Joe. I don't think I can stand having to explain myself to this child who knows nothing about my situation. "I got it now," Joe tells the guard, flashing him his badge. "I'll make sure to get her to where she needs to go." The security guard narrows his eyes at me as if memorizing my face for the next time he catches me and reluctantly walks away, this time toward the elevators.

Joe's face breaks into a wide smile as he looks down at me. The appearance of my old friend should be comforting to me, but instead I start crying. "It's not funny. There is nothing funny about this at all."

Joe's demeanor changes immediately and the smile falls from his face. "Of course, it's not funny," he says contritely. "Come on, let's go get a cup of coffee."

"Are you sure you want to be seen with me?" I am only half kidding. Both Joe and I know I'm in violation of a protective order, nothing to take lightly.

"Ellen," he says as if I should know better. We walk in silence the rest of the way to the cafeteria while I keep checking my cell phone in case I've missed a call from Adam. It's too hot for coffee, so Joe buys me a soda and we find a table in the corner so we can talk.

Joe regards me carefully as he peels the paper wrapper from his straw. We haven't talked about it yet and I know he's debating whether or not to ask me about what happened. How I could have possibly left Avery in the car. He doesn't ask. Instead, he takes a long sip of soda through his straw. "It was an accident," I whisper. "A horrible accident." I shake my head, wondering how many times I will have to say these three words. A horrible accident.

"Avery going to be okay?" he asks, his eyes soft with concern.

I feel what little composure I have left crumbling. "They're working on her right now." I swipe at my nose with a napkin. "The doctors and nurses are doing things to her and I don't even know what because I can't be there." My voice is rising and a group of residents sitting nearby turn briefly to look at me.

"I'm waiting for Adam to call me, text me, or something. I can't stand not knowing what's happening." I look at Joe and get an idea. "You could escort me upstairs. They can't possibly think I would be any harm to Avery if a policeman is with me."

Joe reaches over to pat me on the hand; his thick fingers lie heavily against mine and I welcome the weight. "Not a good idea, El."

I know he's right. If I keep showing up at Avery's hospital bed, defying the protective order, I could be arrested again and, technically, Joe would have to be the one to read me my rights. It wouldn't be fair to him.

Joe looks thoughtfully at me as if he wants to say something but is hesitant. "You know," he finally says, "this could have happened to anyone. You have to stop beating yourself up. I've been reading up on similar situations. Accidents like this."

I don't want to talk about it. Don't want to think about other parents who come out to their car after a day of work, after working out at the gym, after church, to find a child languishing in the backseat. Or worse. I stare intently at my cell phone sitting in front of me, willing it to buzz with word from Adam that everything is okay.

"Happens about twenty-five times a year."

But not to me! I want to cry. *It shouldn't have happened to me.*

"Regular people like us." Joe looks at me earnestly. "Happened to a police officer and an accountant. To a pastor. Even happened to a doctor."

I don't want to be a member of this club. I want to go back in time. What would I do differently? So many things. Everything.

"What it comes down to is the county attorney. He or she decides if a person should be charged. And Prieto decided to charge you." Joe's hand still covers mine and I'm mindful that it could be the only thing that is keeping me from breaking into a million pieces. *Why doesn't Adam call? Please call.* "This will all be over in a few weeks. DHS will do its investigation and determine it was an accident." Joe pauses. "You'll see." But we both know that this won't be over. Ever.

My phone shakes and I clamber for it, my fingers clumsily pressing buttons. "It's okay," Adam tells me. "She had another seizure, but it's over. She's tired but she seems like she's okay."

I begin to weep, burying my face in a thin napkin pulled from the dispenser on the table. "She's okay," I tell Joe. "For now she's okay." Joe nods, relief relaxing his face, and he gets up and refills our glasses, allowing me a moment to gather myself together. This is a comforting thing about hospitals: No one looks at you twice if you succumb to tears. If anything, there are expressions of solidarity, silent transmissions saying, *I know. I know just how you feel.*

Joe comes back to the table, sets my glass in front of me. "Bet you wish you had some rum to put in that Coke." I smile at him halfheartedly, appreciative of his effort to get me to laugh. "Is Adam coming down here?" he asks. Joe and Adam are friendly but not friends. Though he doesn't come out and say anything, there are times, when I get off the phone with Joe or talk about him, Adam gets very quiet, distant. "In a little bit. He's afraid to leave Avery's side. Don't feel like you have to sit here with me, Joe," I tell him. "I'm sure you've got better things to do."

"That's okay. Nothing I can't reschedule," Joe says charitably. We both know this isn't true. Since his divorce Joe does two things—work and sleep. He has gained a little weight, his skin has the unhealthy pallor of someone who doesn't get outside or exercise as much as he needs to, but still he has a sweet, boyish face.

"I don't know what I'll do if she dies," I blurt out. "I don't think I could live through it," I say numbly.

"She's not going to die," Joe says.

"You don't know that," I say, wishing with all my heart that he did know. "What am I going to do?" I ask him helplessly. "What will I do if Avery dies?"

Chapter 30

Jenny collapsed onto the front porch with the deep satisfaction that only children seem to appreciate after completely and utterly throwing themselves into an activity. Jenny's French braid was completely unraveled and her hair lay in sweaty strands against her face and neck. Lucas and Leah stumbled to the porch, equally exhausted, but for the first time since Avery's medical crisis, they were happy. Maudene joined them outside carrying a tray of tall frosty glasses filled with lemonade. Jenny couldn't remember anything tasting so good sliding down her throat. She almost forgot, for a moment, that she would be leaving soon to find her mother, and her stomach flipped with something she couldn't find a name for.

"It's nine-thirty," Maudene exclaimed. "Time to come inside before we all get eaten up by the mosquitoes."

"I move too fast for mosquitoes to catch me," Lucas explained. "Can't we play some more?"

"Tomorrow's another day," Maudene promised, and to Jenny's surprise Jenny and Leah exchanged knowing glances. *Tomorrow is not always another day. It's not fair.* "Come on, kiddos," Maudene cajoled. "Head on inside and shower up."

"But you promised me you would make Dolly and me friends," Jenny said, trying to buy time.

"I did, now, didn't I," Maudene agreed. "Here, girl." Dolly got to her feet and stood expectantly in front of Maudene. "Sit." Dolly sat. "Shake." Dolly raised one black-and-brown-speckled paw. "Now take her paw," Maudene said to Jenny. Jenny looked uncertain. "Go ahead. Take it." Jenny reluctantly reached for the paw. "There. Now you're friends."

Jenny spent the next fifteen minutes shaking Dolly's paw and rubbing her silky back and when it was time for her turn in the shower, she didn't rush. She turned the water on as cold as it would go and stood beneath the spray until goose bumps erupted on her skin and her teeth clattered. Then she twisted the knob in the opposite direction and steam billowed around her, turned her skin a rosy pink, fogged the mirror. She wondered if her mother still looked the same, wondered if she still smelled the same. Jenny toweled off, slipped on her pajamas and wrapped her wet head, turban-style in a towel.

Jenny repacked her backpack, arranged her Happy Pancake figurines and the manila envelope carefully beneath her father's shirt. She counted her money, retrieved twenty dollars to leave on the kitchen counter for Maudene. Thanks for all that she had done for Jenny. Maudene had washed and dried Jenny's clothes and she buried her nose in her clean t-shirt, breathing in deeply the fresh scent. Maudene had made up a bed for Jenny on the sofa in the television room. It wasn't quite

the same as the white room, which Jenny had firmly
affixed in her head as the perfect place to sleep, but it
would do. Maudene had slipped a robin's-egg-blue fit-
ted sheet over the sofa cushions, covered that with a
matching sheet and a yellow blanket as soft as the rabbit's foot her father had given her. Atop it all was the
large feather pillow from the white bedroom. Maudene
even set a glass of ice water on the coffee table right
next to the sofa.

Jenny slid between the cool sheets, settled her head
on the pillow but did not switch off the brass lamp that
stood next to the sofa. The weak glow reminded her of
the fireflies. In her mind she counted the hours since
she got on the bus in Benton. It felt like a thousand, so
much had happened since she arrived. As she drifted
off to sleep she catalogued all the good things that had
happened since finding Maudene: the white room, of
course, grocery shopping, the shower, lemonade, the
feel of Maudene's hand on her forehead when she was
throwing up, fireflies, roast beef, rhubarb crisp. Jenny
sighed. It wouldn't be easy leaving, but the thought of
finding her mother sent a charge of electricity through
her. Maybe she could come back and visit. After all,
Maudene didn't live far from the house on Hickory
Street. A creak of the floorboard startled her from near
sleep; her eyes flew open and her feet hit the floor.

"I just needed to get my book," Leah announced,
scanning the room. "I can't go to sleep without reading for a while."

Jenny pointed to a book sitting on a chair across
the room.

Leah looked as if she wanted to say something but,
instead, stomped across the floor, retrieved her book,

then turned on Jenny. "She just let you stay here because you had nowhere to go. *Your* grandma died, *your* dad was in jail, your mom is who knows where."

"I do too know where my mom is," Jenny interjected softly.

"My grandma feels sorry for you." Leah's voice shook with emotion, tears brimmed in her eyes. "I'm glad you're leaving soon. She's *my* grandma, you know, not yours." She stalked out without waiting for Jenny's response.

"But she's my..." Jenny struggled to find the right word. "Maudene," she said to the empty room.

Chapter 31

Adam calls and says that Avery is doing better and he'll meet me downstairs in a little while to give me a full update.

"No more seizures," I tell Joe when I get off the phone. My knees are weak with relief. "She's sleeping. Adam is coming down in a few minutes."

"That's great news," Joe says. "I should probably get going, call me if you need anything," he says, not quite looking me in the eye.

"Thanks for sitting with me." I walk with him to the lobby doors.

"Anytime. I can come back later and bring something for you to eat. I'm sure you're tired of this hospital food."

"That's all right. I'm going to go over to my mom's—she always seems to have a feast waiting for me."

"Your mom doing okay? What's with the little girl staying with her? Who is she?"

"It's kind of a mess, and I can't even believe I'm worrying about this right now, but she's worried that Jenny's mother was abusive to her at one time and DHS is looking for her next of kin. Can you do some checking on the mother and into her past?"

Joe looks confused. "Isn't that what DHS does?"

I shake my head. "I know it doesn't make sense, but it's important to my mother."

"Sure, I'll check things out. What's the mom's name?"

"That's the problem. We don't know her name. I know the grandmother's name, though."

Joe pulls out a little notebook from his pocket. "Give me what you know and I'll see what I can do."

"The little girl's name is Jenny Briard. She's from Benton, Nebraska, but her grandmother, Margaret Flanagan, used to live over on Hickory Street. She passed away last year and my mom thinks her daughter, Jenny's mom, lives there now."

Joe stops writing and glances up at me. "You're right, this is complicated, but I'll see what I can find out."

I thank him for sitting with me and for being such a good friend. Joe gives me a friendly hug and says he'll call me in the morning.

I wait in the cafeteria until Adam comes down to find me. "She's doing better," he reports.

"Oh, thank God." I exhale heavily, and I cling to Adam with relief.

"The seizure stopped after just a minute, so they're going to adjust her medicine, continue with the IV and watch her closely." Adam rubs his eyes as he explains. When he pulls his hands away, the whites of his eyes are pink and watery. As hard as it is for me to be the absent parent, the one who has to hear of her daughter's medical crises secondhand, I know it is equally heartbreaking to be the one bearing witness to the seizures, the vomiting, the poking and prodding.

We sit next to each other, share a muffin and talk. I tell him about the reporters at our house and how much the kids miss Avery and him. He tells me that his parents say hi and send their love and will plan on seeing me and the kids tomorrow. They're staying at a hotel near the hospital. Our eyes begin fluttering shut with exhaustion and I insist that he go back upstairs and into Avery's room where at least he can lie back in the reclining chair and get some sleep. I promise that I will go back to my mother's house and check in with him later in the morning.

I try to leave. I really do. I even make it to the parking lot, but I can't leave. I trudge back into the hospital, find a quiet corner and wait for the sun to rise.

I wake at seven Friday morning still sitting in a chair in an empty waiting area with my purse on my lap, cell phone in hand. The television that hangs from the wall is tuned in to a local television station and, even though the volume is on mute, from the graphics it's plain to see that there is no relief in sight from the heat. I immediately check my cell phone for a message from Adam. There is none. I think about calling him but resist, hoping that that both he and Avery had a restful night's sleep. I know my mother, an early riser, will be up and I call her instead. As I wait for her to answer, I stand and stretch, my back aching from my few hours of sleeping upright.

When she picks up, her voice is thick with sleep. "I woke you," I say apologetically. "I'm sorry."

"It's okay." She stifles a yawn. "We stayed up late chasing fireflies. Avery is still doing okay?"

An image on the television screen catches my eye. I lower the phone from my ear and stand transfixed. It's a picture of me, the same stock photo from the newspaper article. I yank a chair over to the television, step on to it and press the volume button so I can hear what is being said, my nose nearly touching the screen. A young, pretty reporter is standing in front of the hospital in what looks like a live report. "A local Department of Human Services social worker was arrested for Child Endangerment Resulting in Grievous Bodily Harm. On Tuesday morning, Ellen Moore's daughter was rushed to a local hospital for hyperthermia, or heatstroke, the result of being left in a locked car for an extended amount of time. Temperatures soared to over ninety-five degrees on Tuesday and temperatures continue to climb. The child remains in the Cedar City Hospital. Her condition isn't being shared publically at this time."

The camera cuts to the newscasters who are seated behind a large kidney-shaped desk looking duly serious. "What can you tell us about the legal challenges this mother faces, Lindsey?" a woman with a stiff brown bob asks.

Lindsey nods before speaking. "Right now, Ellen Moore surrendered to law enforcement officials yesterday and made her initial court appearance where she posted a ten-thousand-dollar bond and was released. Her next court appearance is slated for mid-August."

"Thank you, Lindsey. This is a story that we'll continue to watch very carefully throughout the day."

"That's right, Jamie. In fact, in our next half hour, I'll be talking with a parent who had dealings with Moore through her work as a social worker. This mother calls into question not only Moore's personal judgment, but her professional record as an employee of the Department of Human Services, as well."

"We look forward to that report." Brown bob nods at the camera. "Now we go to health reporter, Darren Scott, who will share tips with us about how to stay cool when temperatures soar."

I step blindly off the chair and the weight of the day that lies before me sits heavily on my chest. I realize that my phone is still open at my side and the disembodied voice of my mother is calling out to me. I numbly return the phone to my ear. "Ellen, Ellen," my mother repeats. "Are you okay? Are you still there? Talk to me!"

"Yes, everything is okay. Avery is okay," I say. "I'm just..." I'm so many things I think to myself, *guilt-ridden, scared, angry, sad.* "Tired," I finally settle upon.

"Come home," my mother urges me. "Come home and see Leah and Lucas, take a shower, eat something. You need to take care of yourself."

"I'm worried about Adam," I tell her. "He's exhausted, he hasn't been home in days. I know he's not eating well. I wish he could go home and just sleep for eight hours. It would do him a world of good."

"I'll come up," she immediately offers. "He can come here and spend time with the kids, with you. I will stay with Avery as long as you need me to."

"Thanks, Mom. I'll tell him. His folks are in town and they're helping, too."

We disconnect and I immediately call Adam to check on how the rest of Avery's night went. There is no answer, which is no surprise, since cell phones need to remain off in the unit. I leave him a lengthy message about my mother's offer to relieve him and how Leah and Lucas would love to see him for a bit. I leave out the piece about him needing to lock himself in a quiet room and take a long nap, but know that he is so exhausted that the minute he finds himself on my mother's sofa he will fall asleep. I also omit the information about the newscast—I don't want him worrying about that, too.

I debate whether or not I should just leave for my mother's right now to give Lucas and Leah a hug, to shower and change my clothes, but then realize that in a few minutes, right in front of the hospital, near to where I parked last night in my desperation to find out what was happening with Avery, a television interview is going to occur. For me to get to my truck I will have to pass right by a reporter and a vengeful former client of mine who wants the world to know that a woman who would leave her child in a hot car certainly should not pass judgment on others. My attorney, Ted Vitolo, advised me to decline any requests for interviews, to avoid the press at all costs, to discuss what happened with no one except my husband and mother and they should, under no circumstances, speak with the press, either. He says that even those with my best interests in mind may make a slip of the tongue, do irreparable damage to my case.

I consider my options. I could call a cab to take me to my mother's, could call a friend, could walk the three miles to her home; the fresh air, the exercise would do me good. I call Joe. He says he'll be here in twenty minutes. He will come and get me and then I can thank him again for being there for me last night, for trying to make me feel better. My mother will feed him a real home-cooked breakfast, something that he hasn't had in years.

My phone vibrates and I see that it's Adam. "Avery's night went well," he says. "She ate some applesauce this morning," he declares proudly.

"That's great," I exclaim. Each step forward is a milestone.

"Are the kids there?" he asks, and I realize that he thinks I went home after he left me in the cafeteria.

"I'm still here."

"What?"

"I fell asleep in the lobby."

"Oh, El, you've got to get some rest. You're going to make yourself sick."

"We're both tired," I say. "Will you come to my mom's? She says she will sit with Avery for a while. It will give you a chance to visit with your mom and dad and see Lucas and Leah." But what I really mean is that I need my husband there with me, holding my hand, telling me that no matter what happens he loves me, he'll be there for me.

"Later. I'll come later. Once my parents get here and are settled in," he says. "Love you, El."

"Love you, too," I say, and hang up.

I contemplate finding another television in order to watch exactly what this person being interviewed has to say about me. How my situation compares to hers. How my actions two days ago impact in any way what she chose to subject her children to. My heart thumps loudly in my chest telling me I'm better off not watching the interview.

Joe has agreed to meet me once again by the cafeteria. He said he wanted to bring Avery a little something and stop by her hospital room. My kids love Joe. He loves to ply them with sugar-infused gum and sodas, rile them up and then conveniently take his leave. I don't complain too loudly though. He and his ex-wife never had children and I know he laments the fact that he may never become a father. I tell him he's still young, the right girl will come along. He just shakes his head and changes the subject.

I'm pacing the hall just outside the cafeteria when I see Adam's parents swiftly approaching. "Ellen," says Adam's mother, Theresa, drawing me into a tight embrace. "How are you doing?" she asks when she finally releases me.

"I'm okay. Thank you so much for coming," I tell her as Adam's father, Hank, kisses me on the cheek in greeting.

"Adam says Avery is doing better this morning," Hank says cheerfully. "We're hoping they'll let us see her…" He trails off apologetically. "It's crazy that they won't let you be with her," he says, shaking his head in disbelief, a gesture that reminds me of Adam.

Before I can reassure them that I'd be thrilled if the hospital personnel let them visit Avery, I see a familiar figure stalking purposefully down the hospital corridor. The woman's face is twisted into a bitter snarl and it isn't until she is right in front of me that I recognize her. Lucy Pike.

Hank and Theresa step back in confusion, not sure if they should be alarmed at the sudden appearance of this angry woman.

"How does it feel?" Lucy snarls. "How does it feel to have your kids taken away?"

"Lucy," I say, trying to keep my voice even and calm. "This isn't the place…" Before I can finish my thought she hunches her shoulders and throws herself into me. It doesn't hurt, more like knocks the wind out of me. I stumble and my shoulder strikes a wall. "Bitch," Lucy growls as I cover my head with my arms to ward off the attack. "I hope they send you to jail! I hope you never see your kids again."

Hank pulls Theresa out of harm's way and I briefly see their shocked faces in between Lucy's blows.

Two men, one in scrubs, the other in street clothes, peel Lucy off me. I touch my fingers to my face. Already my lip is swollen, my nose bleeding.

"Bitch!" she screams again. "You think you can take my kids away from me? You think you're above the law?"

Lucy is twenty-four years old but looks seventeen. She has long wheat-colored hair, stands about four-nine, weighs ninety pounds, if that. She also has sweet elfin features, a small upturned nose, high cheekbones, big blue eyes, the mouth of a sailor and an addiction to prescription pain medications. Lucy is the single mother of a five-year-old boy and a three-year-old girl that she lost custody of three months ago when, high on drugs, she set her own apartment on fire, severely burning one of the children. Obviously, the children were put into foster care.

Her face is contorted and red with rage. "You think you're better than me?"

I say nothing though I could say so much. What I don't say is: *Yes, Lucy, I made a terrible mistake, a mistake I will never, ever forgive myself for.* I bite my swollen lip to keep from speaking, but my shoulders sag with the realization that maybe I am not so different from the Lucy Pikes of the world.

"I hope they send your ass to jail. I hope your kids get put in foster care and you never see them again! See how it feels!" She is struggling against the arms that are holding her back from attacking me again. Her hair is greasy, her skin waxy and pale. Lucy was tiny to begin with but has somehow lost more weight. It's clear that she is self-medicating again, this time with something that doesn't dull her senses like hydrocodone. I suspect meth or heroin.

The two men restraining Lucy let her go and just as quickly as she appeared, she is gone. Theresa gently presses a wad of tissues to my face. "Are you okay?"

I nod. "I think so."

"What was that all about?" Hank looks around in disbelief. "Who was that woman?"

The small crowd that had formed drifts away and Theresa and Hank each take me by the arm and lead me to a bench. Concern crinkles Hank's already creased face. "Do we need to get a doctor?"

"No, no. I'm okay," I insist. My nose throbs but is no longer bleeding. "Please, you should go up and see how Avery is doing. I'm hoping that you can relieve Adam for a little while so he can get some rest." I look down and realize that I am squeezing Theresa's hands tightly and quickly release them. "Please don't tell Adam about this," I whimper. "He has so much to worry about as it is."

Theresa takes my hands back into hers. "We won't say anything, will we, Hank?" Theresa says, and Hank nods in agreement.

"Thank you," I say gratefully. We both look up and I immediately recognize the Channel Eleven reporter that I had seen on the news report from earlier this morning. A cameraman lags just behind her, his camera poised on his shoulder. "Oh, no," I whisper, and I stand. "Go while you have the chance," I tell Hank and Theresa. "You won't want to speak to the press."

Theresa gives me a hug and Hank gives my hand one final squeeze before they hurry away.

"Ellen Moore?" the reporter begins. "I'm Lindsey Wright from Channel Eleven News. Lucy Pike has given her side of events. Would you like to respond?"

What side of events? I want to scream. *Lucy Pike has no side to tell. She doesn't know me, doesn't know my family, was nowhere near when Avery was pulled from the car.* I shake my head. "No comment," I say.

Lindsey glances over her shoulder at the cameraman who has his camera zeroed in on my face. "Norman," she says in exasperation, "put that down." Norman reluctantly lowers the camera and she continues. "I'd love to hear your account of what happened." Again I shake my head. Lindsey holds up her hand. "The interview would be completely on your terms. You pick the location, the time, the scope of what we talk about."

"No comment," I repeat, and scan the corridor, wondering where Joe could be. "Excuse me," I tell her as politely as I'm able and move to walk away, though I'm not sure where I will go. She couldn't follow me into the bathroom, could she?

"Mrs. Moore, I know this is a terrible time for you. I have a little boy myself." She turns to the cameraman. "Norman, can you give us a few minutes?" Norman shrugs and wanders away. "Listen, public opinion out there is brutal." I wince at the bluntness of her words. "Surely you've seen the reports. More parents are contacting us about you. They are furious that you were released from jail and are demanding the removal of your other children from your care." I open my mouth to respond. I want to tell her about all of the successes that I've had through the years. The children, at one time in terrible home situations, graduating from high school, the parents who have gotten treatment for alcohol and drug abuse. I've done good things, too, I want to tell her, but I clamp my mouth shut and take a deep breath.

"I have nothing to say," I respond with a finality that is unmistakable even to this determined reporter.

Finally, Joe emerges from around a corner and, on seeing the reporter, a look of irritation flashes across his face. I've seen this look on Joe's face before and I grin inwardly until I see that Norman, the cameraman is filming the entire exchange I'm having with Lindsey. Joe sees it, too, and he steps between me and the reporter, hands on his hips.

"Ms. Wright," he says with forced politeness.

"Officer Gaddey," Lindsey responds with a tight smile.

"I don't believe hospital policy allows for unauthorized interviews being held in the building." Joe casts a dark glare at the cameraman, who sheepishly lowers his camera.

"Just passing through," Lindsay answers. To me she extends her hand, offering a business card embossed with her name and number. "If you'd like to talk, please let me know," she says. "Good luck to you." I take the card, knowing that I will never call her.

"You're not going to talk to her, are you?" Joe scolds me.

"No, of course not."

"Avery doing okay?"

I nod. "She's better today."

"That's great news. Come on, I'll take you to your mom's house."

"Thank you," I tell Joe for perhaps the thousandth time in the past forty-eight hours.

"Yeah, yeah," Joe says dismissively. "Listen, I got some info on that name you gave me."

"Jenny Briard?"

"Yeah. Girl's dad was arrested three days ago in Benton, Nebraska, for disorderly conduct and for assaulting a police officer. According to Billy Briard, he was attacked by some acquaintances he owed money to in the parking lot of a bus station. He was getting the crap beat out of him. Meantime, ten-year-old Jenny Briard is sitting on a bus waiting for her father to get on. He never did. When the police came, he tried to tell them about Jenny on the bus. When they didn't listen, he freaked out. Broke a cop's nose."

"She traveled all this way by herself," I say, still not believing it could be possible. As we climb into his unmarked police car, I ask, "Why didn't she tell anybody? Why didn't she get off the bus before it left?"

"Don't know, but the officer I talked to said that Briard isn't a bad guy. A drunk, but not a mean drunk. Gets jobs, loses jobs, but always seems to land on his feet."

"Such a sad story," I say as Joe drives toward my mother's house.

"There's more," he finally says. I look over at him. "The grandmother, Margaret Flanagan, died a little over a year ago." I nod. This is what my mother told me. "You are never going to believe who Margaret's daughter is," Joe says as he pulls into my mother's driveway.

"Who?" I ask. Even before the car is in Park my

mother is rushing down the steps toward us. I leap from
the car.

Dread washes over me and I wonder if something
happened to Avery in the short time I've been away
from the hospital.

"It's Jenny," my mother says. "She's gone."

Chapter 32

This morning she had risen early, arranged three pillows on the sofa beneath her blanket to make it look like she was still sleeping, slid the twenty-dollar bill and a short note that read "Thank you. Love, Jenny" beneath the covers. She picked up her backpack and, moving carefully so as to not make any noise, tiptoed into the kitchen. In the dim morning light, Jenny surveyed Maudene's kitchen one last time, grabbed two blueberry muffins from the wicker basket on the counter, gave half of one to Dolly and quietly slipped out the back door.

It had taken Jenny an hour to walk to her grandmother's house on Hickory Street and her feet ached. Though Jenny wasn't much of a reader, she had the map the woman at the gas station gave her and she easily remembered the landmarks that Maudene had passed during their drive back to Maudene's from her grandmother's home: the church with the cross atop the steeple, the gas station with the green dinosaur on the sign, the elementary school with the colorful playground equipment. Jenny looked longingly at the structure with its bright yellow spiral slide, monkey bars, firefighter's pole and arched bridges. No time for play, she told herself and allowed a twinkle of hope that maybe this could be her school, her playground.

When she finally arrived on Hickory Street, she lingered on the corner of the busy street, but quickly realized that the sight of a ten-year-old girl at six-thirty in the morning was unusual. After several curious glances from dog walkers and drivers on their way to work, Jenny took a deep breath and looked around for a place to wait, unnoticed, until she got the nerve to knock on the door of her grandmother's house and maybe, just maybe, it would open to reveal her mother.

Her grandmother's yard didn't have much in the way of landscaping, no trees with low-hanging branches to climb into, no bushy hedges to hide behind, but the home right next door did. Jenny dashed across the street and looked around to see if anyone was watching. Then she ducked into the swaying, silvery plumes of maiden grass that lined the neighbor's house. The arching foliage was scratchier than it looked and though the day was already starting warm, Jenny pulled her father's t-shirt from her backpack and tugged it over her head. She lowered herself to the ground, drew the t-shirt down over her bare knees and waited. From her shaded vantage point, Jenny wasn't able to see much of her grandmother's house and yard, but there was a window. Through the window screen Jenny had a postage stamp view of the house where Maudene said her mother lived. The room appeared to be the kitchen, with a line of cupboards affixed near the ceiling. In the gap between the top of the cupboards and the ceiling someone had placed a collection of teapots. She wondered if that had been her mother's or her grandmother's idea. She never recalled her mother drinking tea, only cups of coffee and diet soda out of a can.

The strong smell of cigarettes wafted through the window down to Jenny. Someone was home. A slim figure moved across Jenny's field of vision and, though she saw her for only the briefest of moments and couldn't quite see the woman's face, Jenny knew it was her mother. It was the slope of her narrow shoulders, the way she dipped her head, the way she brought one hand up to brush her bangs from her eyes. The time it took for the woman to glide past, the blink of an eye, the flash of light from a firefly, was all it took for Jenny to know for certain. Jenny was nearly to her feet when another shadow filled the window, this one much larger. She immediately fell back to the ground, urgently trying to pull the plants around her. Jenny held her breath as the man absently looked out the window, his eyes fixed straight ahead. He lifted a cigarette to his mouth, took a deep pull and exhaled, his face obscured in a smoky cloud. As with her mother, Jenny didn't need to see a face to know who the man was. Jimmy.

Jenny couldn't remember feeling so many emotions at one time. Not even when her father was attacked in the parking lot and the bus pulled away, sending her off all alone into the world. That was just one emotion, strong as it was, fear. Not when Jimmy would make fun of her and hit her. That was embarrassment, helplessness and the oh-so-familiar fear. What she felt now was much more complicated. There was the soaring feeling of finding her mother. The choking terror at seeing Jimmy again. The flip-flopping disappointment and anger that her mother could have stayed with the man who had hurt her so badly. And, worst of all, the hollowed-out feeling that she had nowhere left to go. Barely daring to breathe, Jenny stayed as still as she was able and prayed that Jimmy wouldn't look down. If he did, he was sure to see her.

After what felt like hours but couldn't have been more than a minute, Jimmy moved away from the window. There was the sound of muffled voices. Not the angry shouts that she remembered from her time when she lived with Jimmy and her mother. They were always fighting. Jenny remembered covering her ears or humming some made-up melody to block out the cutting words and biting remarks. What she heard now sounded, well, normal. What she imagined a regular family might sound like. Talking about what they were going to do that day, what they were going to eat for supper that evening. There was even the light, songlike laugh she remembered of her mother's followed by a deeper but equally mirthful chuckle by Jimmy. A sound she could never, ever remember hearing before. It struck her then, as she sat amidst the scratchy stems of maiden grass. Here, in her grandmother's house, the arguments, the tears, the shouting, the hitting had stopped. Every word that Jimmy had spit at her was true—she was spoiled, she was a selfish little brat that made her mother so unhappy, made them fight, made him hit her. If she was gone, everything would be okay. It had nothing to do with Jimmy. It was all her. It was Jenny.

Jenny didn't even try to stop the tears that welled in her eyes, though she bit down hard on her lip to muffle the mournful sounds that were bubbling from deep within. Her shoulders rose and fell with silent sobs, and hot tears fell, staining her father's t-shirt. Jenny licked the corner of her mouth, catching the river of salty tears that ran down her face. *This is what sad tastes like,* she thought to herself.

As the sun rose slowly higher in the eastern sky, Jenny sat frozen in place. She didn't know where to go. If she stayed, someone was sure to find her and she didn't know how to begin to explain why she was there, and the thought of Jimmy recognizing her terrified Jenny. She also dismissed the idea of going back to Maudene's house. She couldn't face Maudene after sneaking away without telling her where she was going. She was too ashamed after all the nice things Maudene had done for her. She checked her father's cell phone for the time. How could it only be 7:00 a.m.? Had she only been sitting there for half an hour? Her tailbone ached and she was already becoming uncomfortably warm.

In Jenny's mind there only seemed to be two remaining options: call Connie back and ask her to come get her or go back to the station and return to Benton the way she had come—by bus. Waiting for Connie to make the eight-hour drive seemed endless so Jenny opted for the bus station, except she couldn't quite remember how to get there. That meant asking for directions and Jenny knew that with her red, tearstained face, she was in no condition to approach anyone. She rubbed her face with the sleeve of her father's t-shirt, aware that his smell was beginning to fade from it, and Jenny feared for a brief moment that she was forgetting what he looked like. She squeezed her eyes tightly, trying to conjure him. Reddish-brown hair, eyes as blue as a robin's egg, a scrub brush whiskery face. She relaxed, eyes still shut, fixing the image firmly in her mind. She hadn't forgotten.

A shadow dimmed the already filtered light through her closed eyelids and for a moment Jenny thought a cloud had passed in front of the sun. Rain, she thought, would be wonderful. It had been so long since she felt the cool plop of raindrops on her skin but hoped it would hold off until she reached the bus station.

"Jenny?" the voice questioned, breathless and tentative.

With a spasm of alarm, Jenny's eyes popped open. Above her stood her mother. Jenny wanted to scramble to her feet and dash away, and with equal measure she wanted to throw herself into her mother's arms. Instead, she stayed put, mouth agape, returning her mother's surprised gaze. Her mother had changed some in the six years since Jenny had last seen her. She was a bit heavier around the middle, but had the same gray eyes and brown hair twisted up with a clip. Her nose looked different than she remembered. Thicker, a little off center.

"You're here," her mother said in disbelief. Jenny nodded wordlessly and dragged her eyes away from her mother's face to the window above her. "It's okay, he left for work," she said, seeing Jenny's distrustful expression. "I can't believe you're really here," she said, shaking her head, bending at the waist, hands on knees to get a better look. "Your dad okay?" she asked sharply. "Are you okay?" Jenny didn't know how to answer so she remained silent. "I remembered you talking a lot more." Her lips curved upward, showing her gap-toothed smile that fell away when Jenny didn't smile back. "You want to come inside? It's getting hot already."

Her mother offered her hand, but Jenny ignored it.

She got to her feet on her own and hooked her back-pack protectively around her shoulders. Her mother led her around to the back entrance of the house and up a set of rickety wooden steps. A stout brown-and-black dog with sharp eyes sniffed at Jenny through the screen door. Jenny released a whimper of fear and her mother placed a gentle hand on her back. "It's okay, Jenny. Roscoe is a good dog. He won't bite. Come on in." Her mother went to open the door, but Jenny cried out again. "I'll go put him in the bedroom," her mother promised. "Stay right here. I'll be right back."

In the few seconds that her mother was gone, Jenny considered running away, but she found that she was too curious to leave. She was finally with her mother again. She could ask her all those questions that she had been dying to know the answers to. *How could you let Jimmy be so mean to me? Why did you choose him? Why didn't you ever call? Did you ever miss me?*

"I forgot you were afraid of dogs," her mother said, returning to the back door and holding it open, allowing Jenny to enter. "Come on in, I have so many things to ask you." Jenny watched her mother carefully as she stepped into the house and the smell of tobacco and a vaguely unpleasant but familiar odor she couldn't quite name filled her nose. *Jimmy,* Jenny thought. *It smells like Jimmy in here.* Her mother seemed genuinely happy to see her, but she had that glazed, glassy-eyed look that her father had after a few beers and it was as if her words didn't know where they started and ended, but butted into each other. "Please sit down. Can I get you something to eat or drink?" Jenny shook her head no, though her mouth was dry. "How about a glass of water? I'm going to have a glass of water." Her mother was already reaching into a cupboard and pulled down two drinking glasses, opened the freezer, plopped in a few ice cubes and went to the sink and filled each with water. She turned back to Jenny and some of the water sloshed from the glasses onto her bare feet. With a heaving sigh, she laughed the same tinkling laugh Jenny had heard through the window. "I am so nervous. Are you nervous?"

"Yeah," Jenny finally said.

"Me, too," her mother said, tears shimmering in her eyes. "I missed you, Jenny." Jenny couldn't help it, couldn't stop herself. She threw her arms around her mother's middle, jostling the glasses, and what was left of the contents spilled over the two of them. She looked up at her mother's face, her tears dropping onto Jenny's face. Jenny poked out her tongue, catching one, and was surprised to learn that happy tears tasted just the same as sad ones.

Chapter 33

Seeing the troubled look on my mother's face, I focus my attention on her. "What happened? Where would Jenny go?"

"What's going on?" Joe asks as he steps from the car.

"I have no idea," my mother says. "After we talked this morning, I went into the TV room to check on her. She made her bed to look like she was still under the covers and left me these." She holds up a twenty-dollar bill and a piece of paper covered in a childish scrawl. Her chin is quivering with emotion, an expression I've seen on my mother's face throughout the years. When I went off to kindergarten, when she and my dad dropped me off at college, when I got married, when my brothers got married, when I had children of my own. I realize then, what my mother already knows—has known for a long time. Motherhood is a procession of goodbyes. Some bittersweet and filled with promise and hope, some gradual, a gentle prying away of your fingers from something precious, some more violent, unexpected.

I put an arm around her shoulder. "I'm sure she's okay," I soothe her; all the while my social worker alarm bells are clanging in my head. According to Joe, Billy Briard is still locked up in a county jail eight hours away.

"You say you found out who Jenny's mother is?" I ask Joe.

"Deidra Olmstead," he says grimly. I freeze. There is no possible way. When I don't say anything he continues. "She's married to James Olmstead."

I don't want him to say the next name, but know it's coming so I say it for him. "Madalyn Olmstead."

I take Joe's silence as confirmation and shake my head trying to make sense of it all. "Are you sure that Deidra is Jenny's mother? When I worked with her she made no mention of other children. There were no pictures, nothing that made me think that she had been a mother before having Madalyn."

"Hold on, got my notes right here." He pulls a small, battered notebook from his jacket pocket and flips through the pages. "Jennifer Ann Briard born in Blue Earth, Minnesota. Father, William Briard. Mother, Deidra Flanagan." He pauses. "The two never married," he explains. "This Deidra Flanagan has the same social security number as Deidra Olmstead."

A hand flies to my mother's face. "Oh, no," she whispered. "You don't think she would have gone back to her grandmother's house to find her mom, do you?"

"We can go over and check it out. Did Jenny even know that her mother was in town? I thought you said she only knew about the grandmother."

"Come inside," she says in a brusque voice. "I've got to show you something."

Leah and Lucas must still be asleep. The house is quiet, except for the sound of Dolly's feet clicking across the hardwood floors coming to greet us and the whispery riffling of pages as my mother flips through a book in search of something. "Here it is," she exclaims, holding up a photograph. "I know I shouldn't have taken it," she says apologetically, handing it to me, "but she had two more, and I thought it might be important."

"Is this Jenny?" I gasp, knowing that it is. The photograph is from an old Polaroid camera, the kind of camera that was once often used in hospital emergency rooms to document evidence.

"I found it in her backpack when I first met her at the restaurant."

In the picture Jenny, several years younger, was beaten viciously. "You think the mother did this?" Joe asks, taking the photo from my mother and examining it closely.

"James Olmstead did this," I say. "The son of a bitch did this to her. Joe, did your guy in Nebraska say if there was abuse?"

"Don't know for sure. Mom and Jenny said no. Said that Jenny fell down some stairs. No one bought the story, but the police didn't have much to go on. Human Services was called and was able to remove Jenny during the investigation and she was in foster care until her father, Billy Briard, was contacted to come get her, took one look at his little girl and, according the cop I talked to, was sure it was Olmstead. Would have killed the guy if he could have gotten his hands on him. Jenny stuck to her story about falling down the stairs but Briard threatened to file for full custody and Deidra didn't argue. She and Olmstead disappeared and Jenny's been living with her dad ever since."

"She stayed with him?" my mother asked in wonder.

Knowing that she was talking about Deidra staying with James, I nodded. "It happens more than you
would think."

"I can't believe a mother would let this happen to
her child." She presses her fingers to her eyes as if trying to rub away the image. I know my mother doesn't
include me in this particular category of mothers, that
what happened to Avery is much different, but I can't
help but feel judged. I am one of those mothers.

"Listen," Joe says, "I'll call this in and have the pa-
trols keep an eye out for Jenny. I'll let you know when I
find out something." He places the photograph back into
my mother's hand and steps from the house. "What's the
matter?" Leah stands at the top of the steps. Her hair
is messy from sleep, but her eyes are wide with alarm.
"Is Avery okay?"

"Avery's fine," I assure her. "It's Jenny. She's left.
Do you have any idea where she might have gone?"

My mother has hung up the phone and hands it back
to me. "He said he'll call us later."

"I thought her dad was coming to get her," Leah says,
but there is an uncertainty in her voice and I know she
knows more.

"No, he's not coming. He can't come," my mother
says. "Do you know anything at all, Leah? It's important."

Leah shrugs. "She said something about finding her
mom or knowing where her mom was, but I thought she
was just making it up."

"Oh, God," Maudene says weakly, and sinks into a
chair. "What if her stepfather is there?"

"Why?" Leah asks fearfully? "What's wrong? Did
something bad happen?"

"We don't know," I tell her honestly. I turn to my mother. "Can you stay with the kids while I go over to the house?" She nods. "Do you have the address? When I knew the Olmsteads they lived over on Washington Street."

"On Hickory Street," she says. She looks skeptically at me. "I don't think you should go. Joe said he'll call if he finds out anything. It could be dangerous and you've got enough going on right now."

"Mom, I've thought about Madalyn Olmstead every day since she died. I have to go."

She nods thoughtfully. "Then I'm going with you. Jenny's my responsibility. Can we call the Arwoods and see if Lucas and Leah can stay with them for a bit?"

"Okay, that should be okay. I'll give Diana a call." To Leah I say, "Can you go get Lucas up and you can spend the day at the Arwoods'." Leah quickly comes down the steps and hugs me.

"I wasn't very nice to Jenny," she whispers tearfully. "Will you tell her I'm sorry?"

"You'll be able tell her yourself." I hug her back. "Remember, Leah, you never know what a person is going through in private. Jenny's had a really hard life." She nods and I kiss the top of her head. "Now go get your brother."

I pause to hug my mother, as well. It's strange, I've thought of my father, who died over a year ago, every single day since, but I could go days without calling my mother, without giving her more than a passing thought. How lonely she must have been, what a welcoming presence Jenny Briard must be to her. In one fell swoop I've nearly lost my daughter and my mother. I am so ashamed.

Chapter 34

As her mother mopped up the water that had spilled to the cracked linoleum floor, Jenny took a moment to look around the kitchen. It was old, like Maudene's, but had few of the homey touches that Maudene's kitchen had. The grubby white refrigerator held no photographs, no recipes clipped from magazines. She had hoped, secretly, that maybe her mother would have hung up one of the many pictures she had drawn for her mother when they had lived together. There was nothing but a Chinese take-out menu held to the refrigerator with a Fred's Muffler Mall magnet.

"Sit down," her mother invited as she set a newly re-filled glass of water in front of her. Jenny sat in one of the mismatched chairs around the round kitchen table and shoved her backpack beneath her feet. Her mother sat opposite her, pushed a small plate filled with Oreo cookies toward her. "Remember how much you liked these?" she asked.

Jenny nodded, remembering. Before Jimmy came along she used to twist apart the chocolate cookies and scrape her teeth against the white filling, then nibble away at the remaining disks. It annoyed Jimmy. *Just eat the damn things!* he'd shout. It took all the fun out of eating them so she stopped. They sat in uncomfortable silence and she reached for a cookie.

"Is your dad here? I mean is he in town?"

"No." Jenny shook her head. She wasn't sure how to explain. She didn't want to rat her father out, so she quickly changed the subject. "I thought you were in jail."

Deidra's eyes widened in disbelief. "Did your father tell you that?" she finally asked.

"Yeah. He said you and Jimmy ran away, were probably in jail and not ever coming back."

A red flush crept its way up her mother's neck, but she didn't speak.

"He said if you or Jimmy ever stepped foot in Benton again he would beat the snot out of you both for what Jimmy did to me." Jenny found that once she started speaking, she couldn't stop. She was surprised at the lack of emotion in her voice; it was like she was sitting at the kitchen table telling her mother what she did at school that day. "He said that kid beaters were just about the worst thing a person could be. The only thing worse was someone who watched the guy beating the kid and not doing anything."

Deidra looked down at her lap. "You came all this way to tell me that?" Deidra finally said, looking Jenny in the eyes.

"No. I came to see my grandma. But I guess she's dead."

Deidra abruptly stood and walked to the window. Head bent low, she clutched the edge of the counter, knuckles white, trying to steady herself. "She died last year. She left me the house. I never thought I would own a house of my very own." Then she turned back to Jenny, her face pale and pinched. "Remember when it was just you and me? We lived in that little apartment in Valentine? You were about three? Do you remember that at all?" Deidra asked hopefully. Jenny squinted and looked up at the stained ceiling, trying to remember. Wanting to remember. "It was just an efficiency apartment, but we made it cute. Remember we stuck those stars that glow in the dark on the ceiling? When I put you to bed at night you had to wish on every single one of those stars."

"I think I remember that," Jenny said. "Was the blanket on the bed blue?"

"Green, I think."

"Green," Jenny agreed. "It was definitely green."

Jenny wanted to ask why she had to let Jimmy come into their lives, why she allowed the memories of Jimmy to crowd out her memories of the green blanket and the stars on the ceiling. It wasn't fair.

"Where did you say your dad was? Is he waiting outside in the car?" One hand flew up to her brow and she smoothed a few loose strands of hair back into her ponytail.

"I've been staying with a friend," Jenny answered, busying herself with twisting apart a cookie and scraping her teeth across the cream filling.

If her mother thought this was odd, she didn't say so. "How long are you in town for?"

Jenny felt something beneath her breastbone splinter. Her mother wasn't going to ask her to stay, wasn't going to pack her bags and run away with Jenny. Her mother was going to stay right here with Jimmy in the house that was now her very own. "I'm going back today," Jenny said, blinking back tears and already reaching for her backpack. "Do you think you could give me a ride to the bus station?"

Deidra gave a sad little laugh. "I own the house, but not the car. Lost my license a while back. Jimmy has the car."

"That's okay," Jenny stood. "It's not too far, I can walk."

"It's two miles from here. Too far to walk on a hot day like this. I can call a cab and I can go with you to the bus station."

"Thanks," Jenny murmured, trying to tamp back the disappointment curdling in her chest.

Her mother pulled out a phone book from an overstuffed drawer, flipped through the pages and then lifted the receiver on the light blue phone that was affixed to the wall. While Deidra dialed, Jenny covertly memorized her mother, knowing that it could be a long time before she ever saw her again. She tried to find herself in her mother's long limbs and tapered fingers, but found that she had her father's blunt, thick hands. She ran her tongue across the gap between her front teeth noting how her mother's front two teeth did the same. Their hair was the same shade of brown, their eyes nearly the same green hue.

Her mother hung up the phone, giving Jenny a shy smile. "He'll be here in just a few minutes. Do you want to stay in here or wait outside?"

Jenny shrugged. "Outside, I guess." Once on the front steps, Jenny breathed out, deeply glad to expel the unpleasant smell that coated the inside of her nose.

Deidra lowered herself onto the top step and Jenny

followed suit, their bare knees touching. "Tell me about school," her mother said. "What grade are you in now?"

"I'll be in fifth this fall."

"Do you like it? I always hated school. Never was good at reading and math," her mother recalled.

"Me, either," Jenny agreed. "The teacher is always saying 'pay attention' or 'ask if you need help.'" Jenny warmed to the topic and raised her voice in a mimicking falsetto.

"Yeah, but art class was okay. I liked to draw."

"Me, too. Art's fun. But nothing else."

"You guys still living in Benton?" Deidra wondered.

Jenny wasn't sure how to respond. They didn't really live anywhere anymore. "Dad's thinking about moving to Dubuque. It's a great town," Jenny explained as if she had visited many times. "It's right on the Mississippi River. We might buy a houseboat."

"I went there a few times when I was a kid. They have a trolley built into the side of a bluff. I went up and down that thing until I ran out of quarters."

"Maybe you could visit us," Jenny suggested, casting a sideways glance at her mother, whose eyes were fixed on the end of the street.

"Maybe," Deidra said distractedly. "There's the cab." She stood and waved to the cab that pulled up next to the curb. "You wait right here for a sec," she told Jenny. "I'll be right back."

Jenny stood, reviewed the contents of her backpack one more time and tried to think of how to say goodbye to her mother. Should she just say, *See you,* and walk away? Were hugs appropriate? Her mother seemed to like the hug she gave her in the kitchen, but maybe she was just being polite. Jenny finally settled on saying, *It was nice to see you again. Take care.* She would offer her hand to shake like she had seen her father do. She decided to forgo adding, *Shit, man, it's been way too long,* the way her dad did when saying his goodbyes.

Deidra rejoined her on the front steps. "Come on, let's go," she said breathlessly. Her mother was already moving toward the cab, purse hanging from her shoulder, a small rolling suitcase thumping down the steps behind her.

"Hey," Jenny called after her. "Hey, what're you doing?"

Her mother turned to face her, still standing at the top of the steps, a tentative smile playing at her lips. "I'm going with you, Jenny, if that's okay. I'd really like to go with you."

Chapter 35

After we drop the kids at the Arwoods' house my mother and I are back in her car, making our way to Hickory Street. I look at my watch and realize that I've missed the appointment with my attorney. I quickly dial his number on my cell and as soon as he answers begin to apologize. "I'm so sorry," I begin.

"Have you gone in for your pretrial conference?" Ted interrupts.

"I'm so sorry," I say again. "I will go over there as soon as I can. There's just something really important I need to do right now." I don't go into details. Instead, I thank Ted, promising to stop by his office as soon as I'm able. Then I call Adam to check on Avery. "She's doing fine," Adam tells me. "My parents are sitting with Avery. I ran home to take a quick nap and shower."

He says he'll call me later and we say goodbye as my mother pulls her car in front of Margie Flanagan's house. "How do we do this?" I ask.

My mother looks over at me with concern. "Have you lost your nerve, Ellen?" she asks. "I've heard about how you confront and stand up to violent men who are a foot taller and weigh two hundred pounds more than you do."

"I'm suspended," I remind her. "I'm not supposed to be invoking the name of the Department of Human Services under any circumstances."

"Yeah, but I'm not suspended. Let me explain the situation. You just stand there and look pretty."

"Funny." I smile despite myself. I forgot how funny my mother can be.

We approach the run-down house with its dead lawn and peeling paint. "Careful there," I say as we climb the crumbling front steps. My mother raps on the door and from somewhere within the house a dog barks. No one answers.

"There's no one here," she states the obvious. "Now what?"

"I think it might be time we go to the police station to officially report Jenny as missing."

She nods. "You're right. I should have called the police the first time I saw Jenny at the restaurant. I knew something was wrong the minute I saw her. I really thought I could help her."

"You have helped her, Mom," I say simply. "I should have been the one to insist we get DHS involved much earlier. I'm the one who should be sorry. I know how the system works."

"Well, in your defense, you've had a lot going on."

She's right. I have had too much going on, which is why my daughter is in the hospital.

"No one's home!" a voice calls from across the street. An elderly man wearing khaki pants, a long-sleeved t-shirt and sandals waves to us from the curb. Traffic is speeding past and he looks left and right.

Afraid that he will try and cross the busy street I call back to him. "Stay there, we'll come to you." Once there is a break in traffic, my mother and I scurry across.

"My name is Maudene Sifkus," my mother says, flashing a bright smile. "This is my daughter." I nod at the man, who barely looks my way. He has to be at least eighty-five years old. His skin hangs loosely from his face and is smattered with brown age spots. From beneath thick, unruly eyebrows his brown eyes are red-rimmed and rheumy.

"The woman and a little girl left in a cab about fifteen minutes ago. Her husband came home, saw that no one was home and then he drove away like a bat out of hell."

"Any idea where they might have been headed?" I ask.

"If that woman was smart, somewhere far away from her husband. He's a mean son of a bitch. Always yelling and carrying-on going on in that house. I can hear them way over here."

My mother narrows her eyes. "Where do you think she was going?"

"Looked like a trip maybe. She had one of those rolling suitcases and the little girl had a backpack. Looked like they were leaving for a while."

My mother and I exchange glances. "What did this little girl look like?"

"Brown hair, braid. Girl was carrying a red backpack. Didn't know there was a daughter." He shrugged. "They in some kind of trouble?"

"Thanks for talking with us," I say, dodging the question. "You've been a great help."

"This can't be good," I say once we're back in the

car. "Where would Jenny and her mom go off to in a cab?"

"The mom obviously doesn't have a car, so they can't get too far in a cab. It'd be too expensive."

"That counts out the airport, too. Tickets cost a lot of money." Then it hits me. "The bus station. I bet they're heading to the bus station."

"Then where do you think the husband went off to in such a hurry?" my mom asks, pulling away from the curb.

"To find Deidra. I just hope we can get to them before he docs."

"But how would he know where she was going? It's not like she would leave him a note if she was running away. Besides, if Deidra was any kind of mother she wouldn't want Jenny near James. He's the one who beat her so badly." My mother shakes her head trying to make sense of it all.

"I wouldn't put a lot of stock in Deidra's decision-making abilities. She married the guy."

"That's true," my mother concedes. "Star sixty-nine," she says suddenly.

"Star sixty-nine?" I ask.

"Yes, I've seen it on television. The husband comes home, sees that his wife is gone, suitcase is gone. Picks up the phone and press the star and sixty-nine and it rings that last number dialed. He finds out she's called a cab, gets the dispatcher to tell him where she's heading and he follows."

"Well, let's try the bus station. At least the bus station is a public place. James won't make a scene out in the open like that. He prefers inflicting his damage behind closed doors," I say, thinking of the photos of

Jenny and the image of Madalyn's lifeless little body still seared into my brain.

I know that James murdered Madalyn and if he got his hands on Jenny the same thing could happen to her, too.

Chapter 36

Holding on to her mother's hand, Jenny walked with new purpose into the bus station. No longer was she the girl on the fringes, trying to stay unnoticed and out of sight. She had a mother and they were going to buy two bus tickets. They would sit side by side, Jenny next to the window, unless her mother preferred the window seat, then Jenny would gladly give it up. They would look out the window, watching the scenery pass by and talk about everything and nothing. And when they were too tired to talk, that would be okay. They would sit in a cozy silence because they knew they had all the time in the world to say what they wanted to say.

And Jenny had so much to say. She wanted to know everything about her mother's life in the past six years. She wanted to know about her grandmother and even about the barky Rottweiler she left back at the house. The one thing Jenny would not discuss was Jimmy. No, she would not utter his name or even give him a passing thought.

They approached the ticket counter and she leaned into her mother the way she did with her father. Where her father was sinewy her mother was yielding and where her father smelled like tobacco and his leather belt, her mother smelled like the flowery soap you find in pretty bottles at the bath store in the mall. "Where should we go, Jenny?" her mother asked, anticipation flashing in her eyes. Jenny took a step back from her mother in surprise. She had just assumed that they were buying two tickets back to Benton. Once there, they would go to the police station, collect her father and, well, just live.

The more she thought about it, she realized that there could be problems. Her mother and father had never actually gotten married. *Just didn't work out,* her father had said flatly when she asked him. Besides, her father hated her mother. He hadn't said so in those exact words, but Jenny could tell. *What kind of woman lets a man hit her kid? She was always a little slow on the uptake.* After a while, Jenny stopped asking about her mother. Maybe her mother would live in one apartment and her dad in another. Kids at school went from house to house all the time. Some even went to more than two homes. Darrion Kush went to *three* houses.

"How about it, Jenny? Where should we buy tickets to? I've got some money saved. We can go just about anywhere. Should we go somewhere warm?" They looked at each other and laughed because there didn't seem to be anywhere in the world that could be hotter than Cedar City, Iowa.

"Alaska?" Jenny asked.

"Antarctica," her mother countered.

"The North Pole," Jenny said with a giggle.

Her mother grew thoughtful: "Georgia, maybe. I've always wanted to go to Georgia. See the mountains, see the ocean. Eat Georgia peaches." Her mother smiled widely, showing her gapped teeth.

Jenny rolled the word around on her tongue. *Georgia.* It sounded smooth and sweet like a peach.

"Georgia," she whispered, as if saying it out loud was sharing a forbidden secret.

"Two one-way tickets to Georgia," her mother said with authority to the lady behind the ticket counter.

"That will be three hundred and sixteen dollars and seventy-five cents."

Jenny's jaw dropped. "That's a lot of money," she said, thinking of the cash hidden in her backpack.

"My treat," her mother said. "I've been saving up for something like this for a long time. It's actually cheaper than I thought it would be." She opened her purse, the same bright red as Jenny's backpack, and pulled out a roll of bills secured with a rubber band. "I kept it hidden in the same place I used for hiding things when I was little."

"Where?" Jenny asked. The thought of a secret hiding place was exhilarating.

"Then it wouldn't be a secret anymore, now would it?" her mother teased as she peeled bills from the roll and passed them to the woman behind the counter.

"Bus leaves in fifteen minutes," the woman said, handing the tickets to Deidra.

"Where you going, Deidra?" came a low, smooth voice from behind them. Deidra froze in place, and a spasm of fear traveled across her face and then settled into bleak resignation.

"Where you going?" he asked again, and Jenny dared to turn her head to see who was speaking, though she could never forget that silky, dangerous voice. There stood Jimmy, just as Jenny remembered him. He was a plain man compared to her father. Not too tall, not too skinny, not too fat, not too handsome. His blond hair was cut close and thinning and he had shaved the beard that Jenny last saw him with.

Deidra covertly passed one ticket to Jenny, ruffled her hair and whispered, "Get on the bus, Jenny. I will get on in just a minute."

No way, Jenny thought to herself. *Been there, done that.*

"Hi, Jimmy," Deidra said brightly. "You remember Jenny, don't you?"

"Sure do," Jimmy said. "How're you doing, Jenny?" His tone was light and there was a smile on his face, but his eyes glinted coldly.

"Fine," Jenny answered, looking down at her toes.

"Where are you two off to?" Jimmy asked breezily.

"I'm just helping Jenny find her bus." Deidra pushed the rolling suitcase a few inches closer to Jenny.

Jimmy took another step toward Deidra. Not an intimidating gesture, but still Jenny couldn't help but notice the way that her mother seemed to shrink into herself. "I came home from work, you weren't there and when I couldn't find a note I got to worrying that there was some kind of emergency."

"I didn't leave a note because I was coming right back, Jimmy," Deidra said as if he was silly to be so concerned.

"I figured as much," he answered, his eyes never leaving Deidra's face. Jenny never saw someone staring so hard at another person and a familiar niggle of fear worked its way back into her chest. Jenny was surprised to realize that the fear wasn't really for herself like it was when she was four and Jimmy seemed so much bigger and stronger. She was afraid for her mother. "Everything okay, here?" the woman behind the ticket counter asked, eyeing Jimmy suspiciously.

Jimmy looked down at Jenny and then back at the ticket taker, whose eyebrows were raised in expectation. "Everything is fine," he replied, reaching for the rolling suitcase. "This looks just like yours, Deidra."

"It is. I gave it to Jenny," Deidra said in a rush. "All she had was her backpack and a plastic bag. I thought she'd get more use out of it than I ever would."

With one hand on the suitcase and one on Jenny's elbow, Jimmy moved away from the ticket counter. "Where you headed?"

"California," Jenny lied easily. "I was going out there to stay with my dad's stepsister for a while. My dad gave me the money."

"That's a long way for a little girl to go all by herself," Jimmy pressed.

She shrugged. "Only family I got left is my mom and my aunt Maudene. She lives in California with her kids Lucas and Leah. They have a pool." Jenny said this with such conviction that she almost believed it herself.

"Jenny," her mother said carefully. "Don't you think it's time you got on the road? Your aunt will be worried."

Jenny shook her head. "No, it's okay." She grabbed her mother's hand and squeezed tightly. "I'll go with you." Jenny tried to recall some good memories that she had from the time she lived with Jimmy and her mother. She could think of nothing.

By the time they reached the parking lot, Jimmy was walking so fast and her mother was taking such long strides, Jenny had to practically run to keep up with them. Jimmy kept shooting dark looks at Deidra and her mother seemed near tears.

"Jimmy, remember when you took us swimming at that little creek?" Jenny asked, trying to catch her breath. Jimmy answered with a noncommittal grunt. "You remember, Mom, don't you? You had that pink bathing suit. We stood in the shallow parts and tried to catch tadpoles with our hands."

"I do remember that," Deidra said with a weak smile. "You said the tadpoles tickled your toes."

"Yeah, and we had a picnic lunch, too. Jimmy, you fell asleep on the grass and got really sunburned," Jenny said brightly. "That was a fun day." Jimmy didn't respond and Deidra looked questioningly at her daughter as she opened the back door of Jimmy's car to let her in. They all knew that the day at the creek wasn't all fun. No one mentioned the part where, teasingly, four-year-old Jenny set a tiny frog on Jimmy's bare belly as he napped. Jimmy, a light sleeper, awoke with a start, and gave a shriek of fright at seeing the frog. Instead of finding it funny, Jimmy was enraged and grabbed an unsuspecting Jenny by the arm and tossed her into a deeper section of the creek. The water only went up to Jenny's waist, but she didn't know that and was certain she was drowning. Murky water filled her ears and mouth. She was sure that crawdads were biting at her toes and snakes were braceleting her ankles. Disoriented, she couldn't find her footing and was sure she was going to drown. Suddenly, her mother was there, lifting her from the water, screaming obscenities at Jimmy and rubbing her dry with a towel. "Are you crazy?" Deidra had shouted. "She could have drowned!" Jimmy had stalked away toward the car.

"You drive," Jimmy ordered Deidra.

Deidra hesitated, "But I don't have my—"

"Drive." Jimmy opened the front passenger door while Deidra slid behind the wheel. Jenny climbed into the backseat behind her mother, pulled the seat belt across her midsection and snapped it into place, setting her backpack on the seat beside her.

As Deidra drove, Jimmy reached over the backseat, snatching Jenny's backpack and pulling it into the front with him.

"Hey," Jenny protested. "That's mine!"

"Jimmy, leave her alone," Deidra pleaded. "Give it back."

"I'm just seeing what goodies she's got in here," Jimmy said casually.

"Give it to me!" Jenny shouted, grabbing futilely for the bag.

Jimmy ignored her and unzipped the backpack. Jenny prayed that he wouldn't find the stash of money she had hidden away in a sock. It's all the money she had in the world. Jenny watched helplessly while Jimmy pulled out her neatly folded clothes, her father's cell phone and her Happy Pancake figurines. His hand went in the bag one more time and emerged with the manila envelope. He lifted the dog-eared flap and pulled out the map, the letter and two of her photos. The one of Deidra and Jenny together and one of Jenny and her battered face. Jimmy held the two Polaroids by the edges and stared intently down at them.

Deidra drove on, glancing nervously at Jimmy and trying to see what he was looking at that held him so transfixed. "Turn right," Jimmy commanded.

"But the house is that way," Deidra protested.

"Turn," Jimmy snapped, and Deidra jerked the steering wheel to the right, causing the tires to shudder and squeal.

"What do you two have planned?" Jimmy asked in a low, dangerous voice.

"What? Nothing," Deidra said in confusion. "What's wrong?" Jimmy shoved one of the photos beneath Deidra's nose.

Flinching, she slammed on the brakes and tried to take the picture from Jimmy's fingers. "Oh my God, is that Jenny?"

"Keep driving," Jimmy muttered. "Take a left on Indian Ridge." He twisted around to look at Jenny, who cowered in her seat. "What are you going to do with those pictures?" Jenny was paralyzed with fear. She had never seen Jimmy so angry, even in his blackest rages. "You two going to go to the police with these or something?" He was now shaking with barely contained fury.

"No, no," Deidra insisted. "I don't know anything about those pictures. She just showed up. I was taking her to the bus station!"

"Uh-uh," Jimmy said tightly, shaking his head. "You two are up to something. Ever since Madalyn, you've been different."

Madalyn? Jenny wondered. *Who was Madalyn?*

"No, no that's not true." Deidra was crying now. "Let's just go home."

"No," Jimmy said simply. "We're not going home yet. Not until you tell me why Jenny all of a sudden shows up on our doorstep with these pictures. Turn right," he directed.

"That will take us out of town," Deidra said. "Where are we going? Jimmy, what are you going to do?"

"I'm going to find out what's going on," he spat. "I've had enough of this bullshit, Deidra. I want to know what the hell is going on."

Jenny couldn't see Jimmy's eyes, but she could see her mother's through the rearview mirror. First they were filled with complete terror and then she closed her eyes. When she opened them again something had changed. The fear in her eyes was gone, replaced with what Jenny could only describe as meanness. And this frightened her more than anything that Jimmy had said.

They were moving into a less populated section of Cedar City. There were more trees, no homes, just a scattering of businesses.

"I didn't want her here anyway," Deidra said coldly. "I never wanted her." Jenny felt like she had been punched. "Jesus, Jimmy. We left her behind six years ago. You think I want the headache of having her back? I don't know how she found me. Why do you think I was so quick in getting her back to the bus station?" She turned to Jenny, the car swerving slightly with the movement. "Why did you come here, Jenny? What made you think I would want to see you? Now look what you've done." A red flush crept up her mother's neck, and her face was twisted with anger and disgust.

Deidra sped up, passing a gas station, the last building before hitting the countryside, and swung the car onto the side of the road. "Don't stop, keep driving," Jimmy demanded, but Deidra slammed on the brakes and shoved the gearshift into Park.

"Get out!" she shouted at Jenny. "Get out of my car."

The road was deserted. No cars approached from either direction. The gas station they had passed was over the hill and out of sight.

Jenny was frozen in fear. "But I thought…"

"What did you think, Jenny?" her mother spit. "That after six years I would want you to come live with us? I thought we made it crystal clear when we moved to a completely different state without you."

"Shut up, Deidra. What are you doing? Start driving." Jimmy looked around nervously.

"No," Deidra said, her voice rising hysterically. She leaped from the car, and wrenched open Jenny's door. "Get out," she ordered, her face pinched in anger. "Get out of the car!"

There was the crunch of gravel beneath tires and Jenny turned to see Maudene's familiar car pull up behind them. On shaky legs Jenny slid from the car, her mouth agape in confusion as to how Maudene had found her. Jenny's gaze flicked to Jimmy and then to her mother, who both looked equally alarmed.

Maudene emerged from the car and reached her hand out toward Jenny. "Jenny, come here," she urged, but Jenny found she couldn't move. In a cloud of dust, the passenger-side door of Maudene's VW opened and Ellen stepped from the car and, to Jenny's surprise, said in a quiet, calm voice, "Deidra, it's Ellen Moore. Do you remember me?"

Chapter 37

As my mother and I pull into the bus station we see a small charcoal four-door car driving away. At the wheel is Deidra Olmstead and next to her in the passenger seat is her husband. A small figure sits in the back. From a distance we follow the car to the outskirts of town where it parks alongside the road.

I tell my mother to stay in the car but she is out the door before I can stop her and I carefully step from the car and try to keep my voice low and calm so as to not make an obviously stressful situation much worse.

"Deidra, it's Ellen Moore. Do you remember me?" I say again.

Deidra turns her ire away from Jenny and on me. "I remember you," she says bitterly, but her eyes are filled with fear. "Why can't you people just leave us alone?"

I glance at Jenny, who is standing just outside the car. She briefly looks at me, her face a canvas of tumult and hurt. "Mom?" she asks sadly. "Aren't we going to Georgia?"

Deidra gives a shrill laugh and shakes her head. "Stupid girl, you go on now. Go with the lady."

James Olmstead remains in the front passenger seat, his body is tense. I can tell he's trying to decide how involved he should get in this conversation.

"She's a runaway," Deidra says angrily. "She needs to go back to her dad. He has full custody."

"It's okay," I assure her. "We'll make sure that Jenny gets to her father."

"Good," Deidra says venomously. "Get her away from me."

"Jenny, come here," my mother says imploringly. "You get in the car and come with us."

Jenny is crying despairingly now and shaking her head from side to side.

Finally, James Olmstead decides to materialize from the car. "Who the fuck are you?" he asks.

He doesn't appear to recognize me and this makes me as angry as anything. I know I should keep my mouth shut, but I want him to know that I know, that I've always known. I step close to him until we are merely a breath away from each other. "I'm Ellen Moore, James." I whisper so that Jenny can't hear. "I'm the social worker that visited your home before you pushed Madalyn out of the window."

His face turns an apoplectic shade of purple and he clenches and unclenches his fists. He's itching to strike out at me. "You can't prove anything."

"No," I say, my voice quivering with fear, but I can't stay quiet. "I can't prove it. But I know it's true and I can make sure you don't hurt Jenny ever again. I know what you did to Jenny. I've seen the pictures."

I'm afraid that I might have said too much, gone too far. His hand twitches and I try not to flinch, my heart pounding so loudly I can feel it thrumming through my entire body. Instead of hitting me, he leans in even closer. I can feel his hot breath against my ear. "You will never be able to prove it," he says so quietly that I almost don't believe he's said the words, "Jenny or Madalyn." He pulls back, smirks at me, stuffs his hands in his pockets and walks casually back to the car. "Get in the car," he orders Deidra, who is trembling so violently I don't know how she will be able to drive the car.

"Mom?" Jenny says, and takes a step toward her mother.

Deidra turns away, slides into the car, turns the ignition and pulls back onto the road without a backward glance toward her daughter. The spinning tires stir up a cloud of dust and Jenny runs after the retreating car for a few futile yards, her flip-flops slipping from her feet, and stumbles to her knees on the hot asphalt.

My mother and I exchange glances. We both know that we have just been in the presence of something evil, inhuman. Wordlessly, we go to Jenny, who can't stop sobbing. Her hair is flattened against her head, slick with sweat, and her knees and palms are bloodied. My mother finally coaxes her back to the car, where she cries incoherently about Georgia, stars and Oreos. I try to steady my shaking hands by gripping tightly to the steering wheel and drive while my mother sits in the backseat with Jenny's head in her lap. The only sound in the car is Jenny's mournful weeping and my mother's gentle murmurs of comfort. A few miles down the road I see a flash of red in a ditch and swing the car to the side of the road. James or Deidra had thrown Jenny's beloved backpack out the window. Numbly, I step from the car to retrieve it. It's no worse for wear, but a few of her prized possessions have tumbled from the bag.

I locate two of her Happy Pancake figurines, a few articles of clothing, her cell phone. I always thought that one day I would come face-to-face with James Olmstead, but figured it would be in the grocery store or maybe at a restaurant. Not once did I imagine that I would confront him on the side of the road and accuse him of murdering his daughter. I lean against the car until my breath steadies, until my hands stop shaking.

When we arrive at the house, even though Jenny is nearly my height, I pick her up and carry her into my mother's home. "Upstairs," my mother says, and I trudge up the steps and carefully lay Jenny amid the blankets and pillows in the white bedroom. Jenny half-heartedly protests, saying something about her dirty feet, but my mother shushes her and gently presses a wet washcloth to her bloodied knees and palms. I watch as my mother tends to Jenny in all the ways I have forgotten that she had done for me as a child. She bandages her wounds, wipes her tearstained face, lifts a mug of cool water to her lips and sits quietly by her side.

After a few minutes, I leave the room and go downstairs to call Joe to let him know that we've found Jenny. I also call Ruth Johnson and, without going into detail about our encounter with the Olmsteads, tell her that we are in need of a social worker, one that isn't suspended, who can make sure Jenny gets safely to Nebraska as soon as possible, one who will make sure that her mother and stepfather never come near her again.

Chapter 38

Back at Maudene's house, Jenny tried to lie as still as possible in the big white bed. She tried to pretend that she was asleep, but her skin felt too small for her body and something hot and mean was writhing in her chest trying to squirm out. She didn't know the last time she had cried so hard. Not when Jimmy had beaten her so badly. Not when she was first placed in foster care and realized that her mother wasn't coming back.

Maudene was trying to be nice but Jenny wanted her to go away, just leave her alone. Finally she batted away Maudene's hand that held the antibacterial ointment that she was trying to put on Jenny's scrapes, sending the tube flying through the air. "That hurts!" she cried. Maudene had apologized and said she would come back a little later to check on her.

But that wasn't what was hurting. It was the way her mother had turned on her so quickly. One minute they were running away to Georgia together, the next her mother couldn't stand the sight of her. It would have been easier, Jenny thought, if when her mother found her sitting among the tall grass of the neighbor's house she would have told her to leave, to get the hell away. Jenny had been expecting that. But her mother had invited her into her house, had fed her Oreo cookies and asked about her life. She had hugged her and cried. She didn't understand how her mother could have chosen Jimmy over her own daughter. Again. Where would she go now? Maudene would let her stay at her house. Jenny heard Ellen and Maudene talking about temporary guardianship, which was another word for foster care. She didn't think she would mind having Maudene as a foster mom, but the thought of being in the same town as her mother and Jimmy made her stomach burn. What if she ran into them on the street or at the grocery store? What if her mother started yelling at her the way she did earlier? No, she had to get out of town.

She reached for her backpack, which Ellen had rescued from the side of the road. Jenny didn't have much in her life, but what she did have was in that bag. Everything seemed to be in its place if a little dusty, but she went through it to be sure. Clothes, Happy Pancake toys, envelope. She opened the envelope. Her grandmother's letter was still there, as was the map. The pictures of a beaten and battered Jenny were gone, but Jenny didn't mind. She never wanted to see those photos again. Even the money she had hidden in a sock was still there. She scanned her personal articles lying before her and knew that something was missing. There was scratching at the door and a long brown nose pushed its way into the room. Dolly limped up to the side of the bed, sniffed at Jenny's bandaged knees and, with surprising agility, leaped onto the bed. The dog turned around two times and plopped down next to Jenny. "I still don't like you," Jenny whispered into the silky folds of the old dog's neck. Dolly gave an indifferent yawn and closed her eyes.

Then she remembered her father's cell phone. That was what was missing. Panic clawed at her chest. That cell phone was the only connection she had left to her father, the only way she could possibly contact him. It must have fallen out when Jimmy had thrown the backpack from the car. She pawed through the contents of her backpack, reaching into the deep corners and shaking out each article of clothing. Finally she checked a zippered side pocket and with relief she pulled it out noticing a few new scratches from when Jimmy threw it into the ditch.

The more Jenny thought about all that had happened, the angrier she became at her mother, the more terrified of Jimmy she became. She hated this town. It was a horrible town where mothers left their babies in hot cars and mothers made their daughters feel like they wanted them and then said terrible things to make them go away. Jenny couldn't wait to leave. She wanted to go back to Benton, but to be with her father, not to go to some foster home, and it didn't sound like that was going to happen for a while.

Jenny's eyes burned hotly, but she knew what she had to do, who she had to call. Connie. Connie said she would come and get her if she wanted. Connie, who was the closest thing to a mother she had, even though it was only for a little while. Connie, who took her to get her nails done, who made her supper, watched movies with her, helped her with her homework. Maybe, just maybe, Connie would let her stay with her until her father got out of jail, got better. With rising hope she opened the phone, wiped away a smudge of dirt that clung to it from when Jimmy threw it out the window and pressed Send. The phone rang and rang and then went to voice mail. She disconnected and tried again but still there was no answer. Jenny sat on Maudene's bed, her legs tucked up beneath her, Dolly at her side with her head on Jenny's lap, and pressed Send over and over. No one answered. But still she tried, tears splashing onto Dolly's collar as she methodically dialed, listened, disconnected until Maudene came into the room and gently pried the phone from her fingers and pulled her into her arms and held her until no more tears would come.

Chapter 39

The first thing I do after calling Joe to let him know that we found Jenny is call Adam. "How's Avery doing?" I ask as I settle into a chair at my mother's kitchen table.

"She's doing great. They're talking about moving her out of intensive care and into a regular pediatric unit in a few days. Dr. Grant says that everything looks really good. She hasn't had any more seizures, her temp is normal, her breathing is good."

"Oh, thank God." I exhale in relief.

"Is your mom still planning on coming up to the hospital to sit with Avery?"

"You are not going to believe what's been going on this morning," I say, and explain Jenny's disappearance and finding her with James and Deidra Olmstead.

"Ellen," Adam begins, and I can tell from the tightness of his voice that he's angry. "Don't you think you need to focus your energies on our children? What if that in-home FSRP person showed up and you were off chasing those crazed parents? And where are Lucas and Leah in all this? Were they tearing around town looking for Jenny with you?"

"Of course not! I would never put them in danger!" Adam is silent. "Well, it's all over anyway," I say. "Ruth is taking care of what's going to happen to Jenny."

"Good," Adam says. "I know you're just trying to help, but we need to focus on getting our life back. That social worker from Peosta County's Department of Human Services came to see me."

"Oh?" is all I can say.

"She asked a bunch of questions about us, you. Your reliability as a mother."

"What did you say?"

"I said you are a great mother. That this was a one-time thing. That it was both of our faults."

"Thank you," I say simply.

"What is the attorney saying about everything? How did your meeting go?"

"We had to reschedule," I say, afraid of what his re-action will be.

"You mean you skipped it to go running off in search of some little girl that means nothing to us. You skipped the meeting with the man who can possibly make this whole thing go away to chase after a man who you *think* murdered his daughter while our daughter is fighting for her life! What the hell are you thinking, El?"

My eyes fill with tears. "Please, Adam, please, it's not like that," I plead. "Will you please listen to me? That little girl's life was in danger! James Olmstead is Jenny's stepfather!"

"Yeah, well, I have to go. I'll call you later. You *are* watching after Leah and Lucas, aren't you?"

"I'm just going to pick them up from the Arwoods' now. Please don't be mad. I can't stand it if you are mad at me."

"I'm tired and worried, okay? I'm worried about Avery, about Lucas and Leah, and you. Just give me a little time to work through this in my head. I don't mean to be cruel, but I have to do what's best for the kids and I'm beginning to think that I don't know what that is."

"But we do know!" I cry. "We will work through it together. The investigation has to be over in twenty days. Everything will be all right then."

"I don't know that. You don't know that. We have to look at all the options, all the different scenarios. Weigh and measure the implications of everything." I can picture Adam, sitting in the hospital waiting room, raising and lowering his hands, palms upward, as if the heft of what I have done can be weighed in ounces, pounds or tons. "Please," I cry. "I need you, Adam. Avery's getting better, I'm going to see the lawyer right now and then I'm going to pick up Leah and Lucas. It's going to be okay. I promise."

I hear Adam swallowing and I know he's trying to hold back his own tears. "Okay, El," he finally says. "I'm just tired. So, so tired. I'll talk to you later." And then he is gone.

My mother is standing in the kitchen doorway, watching, frowning. "This is all my fault," she says wearily, and comes to sit down next to me. "I should have called the police first thing when I found Jenny. I should have told you about the pictures, about her mother."

"You were doing what you thought was right," I say, patting her on the hand. "And I was, too, Mom. I know that Adam doesn't see it that way. But I couldn't live with myself if something happened to Jenny and

I knew she was with the Olmsteads. James Olmstead is an evil man."

My mother nods. "It looks like Deidra Olmstead is no prize, either. I can't believe all the hateful things she said to Jenny."

"I don't know. That doesn't make sense to me. The Deidra I remember would never have said those kinds of things. She was gentle. Stupid for staying with such an awful man. But not mean. Did you see James's face when she was going off on Jenny? It was like he was seeing her for the first time. I think it even scared him." I shake my head. "Something wasn't right there, but Ruth will get it all straightened out, I'm sure."

"Yes, it will be good to have everything settled for Jenny. She's been through so much. I wish..." My mother pauses as if what she's about to say is too crazy to say out loud, but I know what she's thinking. She wishes that Jenny could stay with her forever, but she's a seventy-year-old widow and Jenny's a ten-year-old with a lifetime's worth of baggage and somehow they have found each other.

"I do, too," I finish for her. "I wish that, too." I stand and stretch my arms above my head. "I have to go to my pretrial conference at the law enforcement center and then go see my attorney. On my way back I'll pick up Lucas and Leah. Ruth is planning on stopping by this evening to talk with Jenny." I give my mother a long hug. "You guys going to be okay?" I ask.

She nods. "Once Jenny gets up, we are going to do something fun. Bake cookies I think."

I smile. Growing up, whenever I was sad or lonely, my mother would get me into the kitchen and we would bake together. The baking was always for someone else.

A sick neighbor, new parents, to welcome a new family to the neighborhood. We'd always eat a few, of course, and then go deliver the goodies. It was my mom's way of saying, *Yes, you're feeling bad right now, but look at the world around you. There are others we need to think about.* "Save me a few," I say as I move to the front door.

I am hesitant to enter the police station, but Joe is there to greet me and leads me in the back way so I can avoid any press that may be lingering. Joe takes me through the area where yesterday I was photographed and fingerprinted. I check my watch—I hope I'm not too late. I was supposed to have my pretrial conference done within twenty-fours of my initial hearing.

Behind me I hear a commotion and three police officers are leading a woman into the station. She is wearing shorts and a t-shirt that are splattered with what can only be blood. Her head is down and she is shaking so violently that two of the officers have to hold her up, practically carrying her into the lobby. She lifts her head and flecks of blood dot her face and neck like freckles. It's Deidra Olmstead.

We see each other at nearly the same time and it takes her a moment to place me and then she is desperately trying to move toward me. "Is Jenny okay?" she asks.

"Yes," I say, trying hard to focus on Deidra's green eyes, Jenny's eyes, and not the blood. Her hair is stiff with it and a sickly, metallic smell rises from her skin. "Jenny's fine."

The officers begin pulling her away, but she continues to speak to me. "You were right." With twitching lips she smiles sadly at me. "He killed Madalyn. I think I knew it all along." She shakes her head back and forth as if trying to shake the image from her head. "He told me that she wasn't listening and he hit her. Hard. When he saw what he had done he got scared. Madalyn tried to run away from him, but he chased her into the bedroom." A faraway look comes to Deidra's eyes. "She must have known and she tried to run. He said he grabbed at her and she fell, knocking her head on the windowsill. She wouldn't get up, so he picked her up and pushed her into the window screen until it gave away and she fell out the window. He laughed when he told me and said that no one would ever believe me. And he was right. Who would believe me? So I..." She looks down at her bloodstained hands as if mesmerized.

"You really shouldn't say anything," I tell her. "Not until you get a lawyer."

She gives an angry little laugh. "We almost got away. Jenny and me. But he found us and he found the picture of what he did to her. He was going to kill her, and me, too. I know he was. He thought we were going to go to the police with that picture." Deidra is shaking so hard that her teeth are clanking together.

"I think she's in shock," I say to the officers. "I think she needs a doctor."

"I had to do it," she murmurs, trying to wipe the blood from hands on her shirt.

"Don't talk," I beg her. "Don't say another word."

"Tell Jenny I had to say those terrible things. Tell her I had to get her away from him. Please," she begs.

"I'll tell her. I promise." Someone appears with a blanket and wraps it around Deidra's shoulders and guides her through the same door that I was led through just the day before. Dizzily I stagger to a chair. I can't believe what Deidra has done. I put my head between my knees and try to steady my breathing. My phone buzzes and I want to ignore it. I can't take any more bad news, but it could be Adam with information about Avery. "Hello," I say, my head still down near my knees.

"Ellen, it's Ted. You need to come to my office right now."

"Ted, I'm at the police station right now. Deidra Olmstead just killed her husband. Can't we do this tomorrow?"

He is silent for a moment. "We can't worry about that now. You need to come over to my office as soon as you can," he says briskly, and hangs up.

Panic fills my chest. What could be happening? Was I too late for my pretrial conference? Could I be arrested for missing it? I'm terrified that he is going to tell me that for some reason my bail had been revoked and I am heading back to jail. I really tried to be so careful, making sure to stay far away from the PICU so that no one could accuse me of violating the protective order. But maybe the security guard from the hospital reported me. Each night, before Avery goes to sleep, Adam calls me and places the phone next to Avery's ear so I can say prayers with her or read her a story or sing her a song. I'm so afraid that she is forgetting me. Forgetting what I sound like, what I look like, what I smell like. Worst of all, I'm scared that Avery thinks that I have abandoned her, don't love her anymore.

Once Joe and I arrive at Ted's office, we are led into a large conference. I am shocked to see Prieto and Caren Regis sitting at the large, mahogany, boat-shaped table and it is all I can do to keep from running right out of the room. And to my surprise, so is Adam. I look at him questioningly and he shrugs his shoulders.

"Everyone already knows one another," Ted says, pulling out a chair for me next to Adam, "so let's get started right away."

"Richard, it's clear that you are determined to follow through with bringing this case to trial," Ted says, looking squarely at Prieto.

"You are correct and I'm not willing to offer Ellen a deal. However, if she pleads guilty, I will ask the judge to take into account her willingness to cooperate," Prieto says.

"That's very generous of you, Richard," Ted says, and smiles. "But not necessary. Ellen will not be pleading guilty and I'm hoping that after you hear what we have to say today, you will reconsider your decision to go forward with the charges."

Prieto simply looks at his watch. I feel Adam stiffen next me and, beneath the table, I reach for his hand. Ted slides a thick file folder across the table and in front of Prieto. "What's this?" he asks.

"Fifty-three good reasons as to why you should drop the charges against Ellen," Ted explains.

Prieto opens the file folder, flips through the pages slowly at first and then quickly. With pursed lips he looks up at Ted. I want to grab the folder, want to see what Prieto is looking at, but I wait, my heart thumping.

"These are just fifty-three affidavits from Ellen's colleagues and families that she has worked with over the years. All describing how she has made life-changing impacts on the lives of her clients." Prieto looks skeptical. "These were gathered in just the last three days,

Richard. We are confident that hundreds of others will be willing to step forward to speak on Ellen's behalf."

"Drug addicts and child abusers." Prieto gives a dismissive flip of his hand.

"Troubled people, who have successfully made significant changes in their lives with Ellen's help," Ted says with feeling. "In there you'll find rehabilitated addicts who now work to help get others off drugs and alcohol, neglectful mothers who took parenting classes and are now homeroom moms at their children's schools. There are signed documents from children that Ellen saved from horrific home lives who are now grown, attending college, who are doctors, or teachers, or social workers."

Prieto closes the folder. "Anything else?" he asks, clearly not impressed.

Caren Regis clears her throat. "The Peosta County Department of Human Services has finished their investigation of Ellen. The complete report is here." She hands Prieto the folder. "You'll see that the caseworker has determined that the neglect in this instance was confirmed..." Beside me, Adam begins to protest, but I shake my head, imploring him not to say anything because I know there is a second part to what Caren has to say. The one word that will make all the difference in the world to our family's future.

"Unfounded," Caren says, and I nearly collapse in relief. "Their investigation determined that Ellen is no danger to her daughter, Avery, or her other children. The charge of child abuse is unfounded."

"What does that mean?" Adam asks, looking at those arranged around the table. "What's happening?"

"It means," Joe says, speaking for the first time since

we arrived, "that this was a terrible, unfortunate accident that could have happened to any one of us."

Prieto is quiet for a long moment. I know he is running through the different scenarios in his head, trying to figure out how he can come out on the other side of this as the hero. "I'll be in touch." He stands, picks up the folder and leaves without another word.

"What just happened?" Adam asks.

"Prieto is going to drop the charges. It might take him a few days, but he'll drop them. We'll send him a new affidavit every few days just as a reminder," Ted says as he stands and we all follow suit.

"All those affidavits. Who?" I ask in bewilderment.

"Jade Tharp for one," Joe says. "She couldn't stand to see what was happening to you, so she came forward, wanting to help. She said you changed her life. That she couldn't stand by after she gave Avery CPR and see her kept away from you any longer. Manda Hoskins, too. She said that you saved her life and the lives of her children the day you came to her house. She felt horrible that you could lose Avery when all you were trying to do was to save her girls. It avalanched from there. It will be professional suicide for Prieto to keep on pursuing this."

It hits me then. The overwhelming support from my clients, the "unfounded" ruling by the Peosta Department of Human Services, only one thing matters. "Avery. I can go see Avery," I whisper.

"Yes, you can." Caren smiles. "The protective order has been lifted. You can see Avery whenever and wherever you'd like to."

"Thank you," I breathe, hugging Ted, Joe, Caren and Adam. Each one in turn. "Thank you."

Chapter 40

Jenny waited on the step of the front porch, Dolly sitting at her side. The Monday-morning sun was still hot, but the shade from the big tree shielded her face from the rays. Earlier Maudene had French-braided her hair and Jenny couldn't stop nervously fingering the roped plait. Yesterday Maudene had taken her to the mall to buy some new clothes for the trip back to Benton and her new foster home. Jenny had never bought clothes at a mall before and kept trying to tell Maudene that she would pay her back, but Maudene just waved her hand and told her not to worry about it. Now, four pairs of shorts, five t-shirts, a light jacket, underwear, socks and a set of pajamas were folded neatly in the brand-new suitcase at her side.

Ruth, the social worker, said she would be there right at nine and it was nearing nine-fifteen. With each passing minute Jenny's anxiety rose. It took about eight hours to drive to Benton and Jenny figured with bathroom breaks they would arrive around six o'clock that evening. Jenny wondered what her new foster family would be like. Ruth had said that they sounded like a very nice couple who had two teenage daughters of their own living with them. Ruth said that they were looking forward to meeting Jenny. Jenny wished she felt the same way.

Last night, Maudene had made a goodbye dinner for Jenny. Ellen, Leah and Lucas came, too. Jenny really didn't understand it all, but knew that the trouble Ellen was in magically seemed to have gone away. Jenny wished the same thing would happen for her, that her father would get out of jail, stop drinking and get a job so they could live together again.

Maudene told her that she would make anything that Jenny would like to eat. She had carefully flipped through Maudene's cookbooks until she came across a stained page with the corner folded down. It was the recipe for homemade chicken potpie. "How about this?" Jenny asked. "This looks good."

A smile emerged on Maudene's face. "That was my husband's favorite," she said quietly. For a minute Jenny was worried that this might upset Maudene, but Maudene began to pull ingredients from the cupboards and chattered happily about how Wes had loved her chicken potpie.

It was a happy dinner, Jenny thought. Everyone was much more relaxed, there was laughter. Jenny tried to enjoy herself, but the worry about what was to become of her ate away at her stomach. After they had eaten the potpie and the strawberry shortcake with fresh whipped cream that Jenny requested for dessert, Ellen turned serious. "Jenny, can we talk for a little bit? I have something to tell you about your mother."

Jenny scowled. She didn't want to hear anything about her mother. She was a terrible, awful person who said terrible, awful things to her. "I don't care," Jenny said with a scowl. "I hate her."

"Come on," Ellen said, pushing her chair away from the dining room table. "Let's go sit out on the porch. It's cooled off some." Jenny followed Ellen out to the porch. The sun was low in the sky and a delicate breeze wound itself through the trees. Together they sat on the porch swing, Jenny's feet lightly skimming the floor as they swayed. "I don't think that your mom said those things because she didn't want you. I think she said them because she loves you."

Jenny planted her feet on the floor, causing them to stop midswing. "That doesn't make sense," Jenny said angrily.

"I know, I know. But think about it. Your mom was going to run away with you. She had her suitcase packed and you were buying tickets to Georgia when James found you." When Jenny didn't comment, Ellen continued. "Your mom wanted me to tell you she didn't mean the things she said to you. She was just trying to protect you from James."

"You talked to my mom?" Jenny asked with confusion.

Ellen sighed. "I did." Ellen paused, gathering her thoughts. "I knew your mom for a while, Jenny. She and James had a little girl named Madalyn."

Jenny thought about this. "I have a sister?"

"Madalyn died a few years ago, Jenny." Ellen took a deep breath. "Your mother believes, and I do, too, that James hurt Madalyn so badly that she died. Your mother was afraid that James was going to hurt you and said those things to get you out of the car, away from James."

Jenny thought about this. "If he's so bad why isn't he in jail?"

Ellen shook her head. "Things don't always work out the way they should. But the important thing is that your mother does love you and wants the best for you."

Jenny had tried to tamp down the hope that filled her chest. "Can I see her?"

"No, Jenny, you can't," Ellen said gently.

Jenny sat for a long time on the porch trying to digest what Ellen had told her. In one day she found her mother, lost her mother, learned that she had a sister and learned that she had lost a sister. It was too much. Now she was once again sitting on the porch waiting for Ruth to come and take her to live with a family she had never met before.

A car appeared and pulled up to the curb in front of Maudene's house. Ruth emerged and gave Jenny a cheerful wave. Jenny stood and slid her hand across Dolly's velvety head for reassurance. A second car pulled up and parked directly behind Ruth's car. Jenny peered through the lacy leaves of the oak tree trying to see who it was. The figure that stepped from the second car was that of a woman with hair pulled up into a high ponytail. "Connie!" Jenny exclaimed, rushing down the steps, throwing herself into her arms. "You came!"

"Of course I did, silly," Connie murmured. "Of course I did."

Chapter 41

Around one in the morning Adam falls asleep in the reclining chair in the corner of Avery's hospital room. I find an extra blanket in the small closet and tuck it around him. I cannot sleep. Don't want to fall asleep. I take my place in the chair next to Avery and watch her. The hospital room is not completely dark. The light from monitors casts a ghostly aura around Avery's crib. She doesn't appear to be suffering, but every once in a while a pained expression spasms across her face and a low-pitched whimper escapes her lips. I wonder where it hurts. In her nearly parboiled organs or maybe it's her chest where Jade pressed down in quick, firm chest compressions. Maybe it's the pinch of the IV needle. Or maybe she is recalling the straitjacket of her car seat, the suffocating temperature of the van rising rapidly, her unanswered cries for me. Maybe that's what pains her.

A slice of bright light appears and then is gone as the night nurse slides deftly into the room. She turns on a small light over a counter and sees me sitting vigil. "Hi," she whispers. "Remember me? I'm Meredith, Avery's nurse tonight."

"I do remember you," I say. "Thank you for taking such good care of Avery." Meredith seems too young to be a pediatric intensive care nurse, but she moves purposefully and efficiently. I watch as she works, washing her hands, slipping on gloves, quietly lowering Avery's crib, taking her temperature, scrutinizing her IV site, checking the monitors, changing Avery's diaper, tossing out the gloves, washing her hands again and finally turning her attention to me. "She's resting comfortably," she assures me. "And she's passing urine. This is what we want—it shows us that her kidneys are functioning. If all goes well tonight we'll move her to a regular pediatric floor."

"Oh, thank God," I say with relief. "Thank you. Can I hold her when she wakes up?"

"You can hold her right now if you'd like," Meredith tells me.

"Really?" I ask in surprise. "Even if she's asleep?"

"There are worse things than waking up in your mother's arms. Sometimes that's the best medicine. I can get a more comfortable chair in here for you," she offers. "Another recliner if you'd like. Those chairs are brutal."

"That's okay," I assure her. "This is fine. I just really want to hold her." Meredith is already lowering the side of the crib. "Here, I'll hand her to you. We just have to be careful of her IV tubing and monitors." Carefully, Meredith transfers a still slumbering Avery into my awaiting arms. Immediately she snuggles more closely to me, as if even in sleep, she knows it's me, recognizes my scent, my touch, the beat of my heart against hers. "Thank you," I whisper gratefully to Meredith.

"No problem," she answers. "I'll stop back in a lit-

tle bit to see if you need anything or press the call button and I'll come running." Meredith turns to leave,
hesitates and walks back to me. "Two weeks ago," she
begins, "there was a little boy in here who was electro-
cuted when he poked a bobby pin into a light socket.
Last week there was a little girl whose neck somehow
got tangled up in a window blind cord and a little boy
who choked on a hot dog." I cannot respond. We have
safety covers on every single one of our electrical out-
lets in our home. We have trimmed our window cords
so that not even Leah can reach them. I rarely buy hot
dogs, but when I do I cut them crosswise and length-
wise so there is no chance a piece will get lodged in my
children's throats. But I understand what she is trying to
tell me. Accidents happen every day to everyday people.
She's trying to be kind, to offer some kind of comfort.
She turns to leave but before she reaches the door I call
out to her in a loud whisper. "Are they okay?" I ask.

Even in the dim light I can see her measuring her
words. "I can't comment on the specific situations," she
explains. "Some of the kids are going to be just fine.
Some are not." I want to ask if she knows if Avery will
be one of those who ends up in the just fine group, but
know that she doesn't have the answer. That none of
us do just yet.

There is something about holding a sleeping child. I
remember when Leah was an infant and I had the time
to just sit and hold her for hours at a time. It didn't matter that there were stacks of dirty laundry piling up or
dirty dishes in the sink. It didn't matter that I hadn't
swept a floor, cleaned a toilet or cooked a decent meal.
Leah didn't care. All that mattered was that I was able
to sit on the couch, cradling my newborn. I could sit

and stare at her for hours. A few years later, when Lucas was born and Leah was a busy toddler demanding my full attention, I had less time to just hold him. When Leah was taking her nap or was off with Adam, I would greedily snatch Lucas from his crib or playpen and just sit and look at him. The arch of his eyebrow, the slope of his nose, the minuscule indentation in his chin. Then when Avery came along, it was nearly impossible. When I was able to hold her, I was either feeding her or carting her from one room to another while I picked up the dirty laundry or ran the vacuum cleaner or was helping Leah with her homework or tying Lucas's tennis shoes for him. I wish I would have held Avery more. I wish I would have held that time as sacred for her as I did with Leah and Lucas. I would go back and take the time to memorize the way her dark hair curled around her ears, the curve of her cheek, the way her dimpled fingers clutched at my breast as she drank. I never paid attention. Now as I stare down at her, I try to see past the IV, see past the identification band wrapped around her ankle, the pulse oximeter attached to her foot, to memorize all that is Avery. Little mercies, I remind myself. Little mercies.

Epilogue

I never thought I would get used to the institutional smell, the sight of worn-down women in orange with the word *prisoner* inscribed down one pant leg. The Iowa Correctional Center for Women in Cravenville houses over five hundred and forty women, including Deidra Olmstead. It could have been my home, as well, if it wasn't for Joe Gaddey, Ruth Johnson and Jade Tharp, my former client and the woman who gave my daughter CPR when she was pulled from the car.

That was the first miracle. The second was Avery. Just two days after I was allowed to see her again, she was moved to the regular pediatric floor and three days after that she was discharged. I'm not so arrogant as to believe that my daughter's recovery was due to my reentry into her life. I know it had everything to do with the excellent medical care she received and the prayers that so many had thrown up to the heavens on our behalf.

Her homecoming was a wonderful day. Adam, my mother, Lucas and Leah—we all went to the hospital to bring her home. I invited Joe to join us, as well, but he declined. He said that this was a special time and we

needed this time alone as a family. I told him that he was
like family to us and he smiled, a little sadly, I think,
and said he would stop over once we were all settled in.
We gathered up all the balloons, stuffed animals, cards
and flowers that people had sent us over the weeks and
piled them into our newly purchased car. The van could
have been fixed but forever I would think of it as the
place where my daughter almost died, so we traded it
in and got an SUV. Once at home, we had cake and ice
cream and Leah and Lucas showed off the huge "Welcome Home, Avery" sign they created.

My mother stops by almost every single day and
when she doesn't, we go over and see her or talk to one
another on the phone. After taking several weeks of personal time to help me out with kids, she has returned to
work at the restaurant. I know she is sad about Jenny
going back to Nebraska, but she knows that it's the best
thing for Jenny, whose mother is now in prison at Cravenville for the murder of her husband. She pleaded
guilty to manslaughter and will serve up to ten years.
She was Prieto's new project once he figured out that
I wasn't going to be the big case for him anymore. He
initially charged her with first-degree murder and if
Iowa had the death penalty would surely have fought to
have Deidra die by lethal injection. With a little begging
on my part, Ted Vitolo served as her pro bono attorney
and as part of her defense requested the exhumation of
little Madalyn's remains. The judge denied the request.

I don't think Deidra should have to serve ten years
after what James Olmstead did to Jenny and to Madalyn, but I also know that Deidra is by no means innocent in all that had happened. She knew that James was
abusive. She saw what James was capable of doing. She

was his victim, as was Jenny, but she is Jenny's mother and should have protected her. At the very least, she should have left James after she saw the beating he gave Jenny. But she didn't. She went with him, had another child. And that child died. Deidra should have called the police, let them deal with James, but she didn't. She shot him with his own gun while he slept in their bed.

I visit Deidra every few months at Cravenville, give her an update on how Jenny is doing, which by all accounts is amazingly well living with Connie. Deidra tells me that she writes letters to Jenny every week, asking her to come and see her. I advise her to give Jenny some time, that one day maybe they will find their way back to one another.

I resigned from my job as a social worker with the Department of Human Services. I didn't have to, but thought it would be best for my family and for the department. Right now, all I want to do is be with my children. I take Leah and Lucas to school every day and then spend the day at home with Avery. I know that each minute with them is a gift. I also know that I will have to return to work one day soon. Adam's teaching and coaching salary doesn't cover all our expenses and I'm thinking about applying for a job as a social worker at a nursing home or with a hospice, but for now we are content having our family back together again.

I watch my children closely for any long-term damage that my inattentiveness, my neglect, has left behind. They seem fine, but I don't know, not for sure. Leah is a bit clingier than she used to be, Lucas is the same worrier that he has always been and Avery appears, remarkably, back to normal both physically and emotionally. I guess time will tell.

For now, I will hug my children, will talk to my mother, kiss my husband, and tell them all every single day that I love them. Each day, each hour, each minute we have together is all I have. It restores me, slowly helps me forgive myself. Leaves me a little bit less broken. It's all that I dare hope for, but it's everything.

* * * * *

Acknowledgments

My gratitude goes to so many in bringing *Little Mercies* to life.

My parents, Milton and Patricia Schmida, and to my brothers and sisters, Greg, Jane, Milt, Molly and Patrick, for their unwavering support; Dr. Ghada Abusin, Dr. Tami Gudenkauf and Jeff Doerr for their medical expertise; Chief Mark Dalsing and Natalia Blaskovich for law enforcement and legal information; Teena Williams for her honest and touching insights into the social work profession; Marianne Merola, my agent, for always being there and her encouragement; Henry Thayer for his behind-the-scenes work; Erika Imranyi, my editor, for her attention to detail and wise suggestions; and to Miranda Indrigo and the entire MIRA team for their hard work and support.

As always, my love and thanks to Scott, Alex, Anna and Grace—I couldn't do it without you.

Little mercies, one and all.

Questions for Discussion

1. Like many parents, Ellen struggles to balance her personal and professional lives. Discuss how you face maintaining that precarious balance between home and work.

2. Ellen's former client Jade steps in to save Avery's life and Ellen finds herself being seen as an unfit mother. Talk about this reversal of roles. How do you think this changed Ellen's view of the parents she works with and how they think of Ellen? Does this change your opinion of parents who might have experience in the child welfare system?

3. Discuss the ways parenthood and adult-child relationships are portrayed in the novel. Think about Jenny's relationships with her father, mother, Maudene, her father's friend-girls and Ellen's relationship with her own children and the children she works with as a social worker.

4. Ellen's distractions have catastrophic effects on her daughter's health, her family, and her professional

life as a social worker. Talk about a time when you may have had a close call in your life. How did you feel? How did the experience change you?

5. Ellen is charged with a felony and potentially faces a prison sentence. Do you think she should have to serve time behind bars? Why or why not?

6. What scenes or developments in the novel affected you most?

7. Adam quickly forgives Ellen for leaving Avery in the hot car. How would you react in a similar situation? Does Ellen deserve forgiveness? Do you think she will be able to forgive herself?

8. Maudene places herself in a precarious situation by taking a wayward Jenny into her home. Discuss the possible implications of this decision. What would you have done if faced with a similar situation?

9. How do Ellen and Jenny change over the course of the novel? Which character changes the most, which the least?

10. How did your opinion of Jenny's mother change over the course of the novel?

11. In Jenny's young life she has already faced so many obstacles: poverty, abuse, struggles with school, a runaway mother and an unpredictable father. What do you think will become of Jenny?

12. What does the title *Little Mercies* mean to you?

A Conversation with Heather Gudenkauf

Little Mercies **is an emotionally charged, ripped-from-the-headlines drama about a woman who makes an honest mistake that has life-altering consequences. What was your inspiration for this story and the characters?**

When I was a young mother I was always hypervigilant in trying to protect my children. We baby-proofed our home in every way possible. I would cut grapes and apples into tiny choke-proof pieces. Each night I peeked in their cribs to make sure they were still breathing and I always kept a watchful eye on them while they played. Over the years, like most mothers, I relaxed a bit, realizing that no matter the safeguards put into place, I couldn't always prevent the scrapes, bruises and heartbreaks that accompany childhood.

But then I heard a news story about a well-meaning and, by all accounts, a loving and responsible mother who accidently left her infant in a hot car and, tragically, the child died. This and similar stories sent me reeling.

These harrowing accounts of mothers and fathers who love their children and are constantly trying to balance work and home in order to care for their families and manage all that life tosses at them forced me to ask myself, Could this happen to me? To someone I love? From these inner conversations, *Little Mercies* emerged.

In addition to your career as a writer, you spent many years working in the education system. Why did you choose to focus this novel on a social worker, and how did your experience as an educator inform and influence the story?

Just like so many women, Ellen is a loving mother and conscientious in her professional life as a social worker. We all know someone like Ellen, in fact, many of us could be Ellen. I wanted to explore how a regular woman, trying to navigate life in the midst of a harried, unrelenting schedule, faces an unthinkable tragedy.

As an educator I've had the opportunity to get to know social workers, school counselors, teachers and other educators who work tirelessly to protect children and help families learn and grow stronger. Oftentimes, we forget that those who spend their lives serving and helping others can also make mistakes, at times with shattering results. Also, during my years as a teacher, I have met or learned about many children who share the same vulnerability, courage and feistiness as Jenny.

***Little Mercies* is told in alternating perspectives between Ellen and Jenny. Why did you structure the novel this way, versus focusing on a single perspective, and what do you hope each character will offer?**

Little Mercies is my fourth novel and like the previous three I chose to tell this story in multiple perspectives. I think that by offering alternate points of view, I give readers the chance to experience one very difficult situation through the eyes of a guilt-ridden mother and an innocent but determined child.

My hope is that readers recognize Ellen's good intentions and the sincere love she has for her own family and the families with which she works, despite her terrible mistake. She reminds us of our own frailties and the importance of having a supportive network of friends and family. Through Jenny's eyes we see a worldview filled with hope despite her challenging home life and many disappointments. We have so much to learn from the perseverance and resilience of children.

What is the significance of the title *Little Mercies*, both in the story and in the message you want to send to readers?

I think there are many times when we find ourselves hoping for the big miracles in life such as a cure to a horrible illness or picking the winning lottery numbers, but I truly believe it's the small kindnesses—the little mercies—that really get us through the difficult times. In the novel, for Ellen, the little mercies come from her family and friends who help her navigate an incredibly difficult time. For Jenny, it's the compassion of strangers that she meets along her journey who come to her aid. My hope is that readers find ways to pass little mercies on to complete strangers as well as to their loved ones. It can be as simple as a smile and a cheerful hello; it can be a shoulder to cry on or the gift of time. The possibilities are endless.

What was your toughest challenge, your greatest pleasure, and your biggest surprise as you were writing *Little Mercies*?

I'd have to say that delving into the emotional devastation that Ellen experienced in the novel was the most challenging part for me. As a mother, it's crushing to see your child suffer.

My greatest pleasure while writing *Little Mercies* was the people I met and the wonderful conversations that ensued. I tend to be a bit shy and reserved, so seeking out experts to help inform my writing doesn't always come easily to me but is always rewarding. During the course of writing *Little Mercies* I met a dedicated social worker who shared the joys and challenges of serving families. In order to learn more about the medical profession and legal system I visited with doctors, a paramedic, an attorney and the chief of police. I even got the chance to tour a police station and walk through the steps of the booking process.

As it is with all my novels, the biggest surprises come from the characters and the directions they end up taking me, and Jenny and Ellen from *Little Mercies* did not disappoint.

Can you describe your writing process? Do you outline first or dive right in? Do you write scenes consecutively or jump around? Do you have a schedule or a routine? A lucky charm?

I always begin a writing project by treating myself to a beautiful journal and spend the first month or so composing life histories for each of the characters. I describe their physical characteristics, their fears and hopes. I dream up their fictional pasts and futures even if the details don't find their way onto the pages of the book. Then I begin writing the novel in longhand. This way I'm able to write nearly anywhere and minimize distractions. Later I transfer what I've written to a computer and continue to add to the story. Sometimes the story unfolds chronologically and at times I leap to an event near the end of the book only to return to an earlier scene. The characters tend to guide the direction I go. When I've finished writing the first draft I will print off a copy and begin making revisions. I also give out a copy of the manuscript to some family members and a few friends for their input.

As for a writing routine or schedule, I write whenever and wherever I can. As I am the mother of three teenagers, my uninterrupted writing time is rare, but for me, my family always comes first. I steal those quiet writing moments whenever I can. I don't have a lucky charm per se, but if someone were to peek in on me as I was writing, I'd likely have a Diet Coke and some chocolate nearby.

Read on for a sneak peek at

Everyone Is Watching,

*the next exhilarating thriller from
master of suspense Heather Gudenkauf*

Prologue

MatthewSwimBikeRun was sitting on the sofa staring at what was unfolding on his laptop. *One Lucky Winner*, a reality show his coworkers were droning on and on about, was streaming. He had listened to them endlessly babble about the show for the past four days. From what he gathered, the contestants were competing for $10 million. Curious, he decided to tune in.

On-screen, a group of four people, dressed in the same white outfits like some kind of cult, were sitting on a fancy outdoor patio drinking wine. The fifth, a woman dressed in a white high-necked halter top, seemed to be holding court. Riveting stuff. He glanced at the comment section on the right-hand side of his screen.

They are going too far.

You think this is real? Nothing on TV is real.

Have you even been watching? It is real! And someone is going to die if they aren't careful.

This got Matthew's attention. Someone could *die*? How? Why? What was this? *Squid Game*?

He set the laptop on the coffee table in front of him, leaned forward, elbows on his knees, and examined the contestants more closely. Based on the bruised, angry faces he saw on the screen, there was some kind of drama happening. One of the women had her face buried in her hands and one of the men, fist balled, banged on the table, causing the glasses of wine to jump. At the sudden sound, Matthew jumped too.

"Speak or shoot?" the woman in the white halter top asked calmly. "The choice is yours." The man didn't respond at first. Simply stared at the woman, the muscle in his jaw pulsing.

Wait a second, Matthew thought. He knew halter top lady. Knew the host of the show, though he couldn't remember her name. They lived in the same building in New York for about a year. If he recalled, she was an intern on some big-time network show. *Wow*, he thought. *She ended up making it big. Impressive.*

That's when Matthew saw it. Sitting right in the center of the table, atop the white linen cloth, long-barreled and glinting in the candlelight.

Is that a gun? Matthew typed.

Just tuning in, huh? someone responded.

It was a gun. A Ruger with hardwood grips, and a seven-and-a-half-inch satin stainless steel barrel. This was a gag, right? Why was there a gun sitting in the middle of the table for anyone to grab?

Someone should call 911. This is getting out of control.

No! Came the swift responses.

It's fine. It's just part of the game.

I don't think so...

She's handling that asshole perfectly.

Yeah, don't screw up the show by calling the police.

Matthew had to agree. He was hooked. Let's wait and see what happens, he added to the mix.

Is that a bruise on her neck? someone typed.

I think it's just a shadow, said another.

"Speak or shoot? The choice is yours," the woman in the halter top said.

The man reached for the gun. Lifted it from the table and, despite himself, Matthew gasped.

"I choose shoot," the man said, calmly getting to his feet and pressing the gun to his temple.

OMG! Don't do it!

Someone call the police.

Someone DO something!

Just stop! You don't think this is real, do you?

Of course it's real!

Matthew rolled his eyes. The thread devolved into profanity and name-calling. *Hilarious*, Matthew thought. All these bored armchair warriors threatening to kick each other's asses.

He had to agree with the naysayers. Everyone knew there was nothing real about reality television. He took a closer look at the man holding the gun against his head and his eyes widened. Then he recognized him. What were the chances that he knew *two* people on the show?

Isn't that... Matthew began typing but stopped when the man on-screen lowered the gun from his head and extended his arm. Matthew saw himself staring down the barrel of the gun through his laptop screen. The man was aiming the gun directly at him.

Three explosions in quick succession filled the air and the livestream went black and silent. It was loaded. The gun was really loaded. Matthew covered his mouth with his hand, his heart knocking against his chest.

It was quiet. Too quiet.

Finally, comments began to appear.

What happened?

Did someone get shot?

The livestream flickered and lit up. It showed the veranda, but this time, from a different angle. All that could be seen was an upended chair lying on the stone floor. There was still no sound, no lady in the halter top, none of the other contestants could be seen.

What is that? someone typed.

Oh, Jesus.

Matthew stared, mouth agape, as a slow stream of red liquid crept across the white stone collecting in a crimson puddle.

I think it's blood.

Matthew agreed. It did look like blood. Once again, the livestream went dead.

He had shot someone. But whom? And why? Matthew felt sick. He wanted to close his laptop but couldn't tear his eyes away from the screen, half hoping the livestream would return, half hoping it wouldn't. What the hell kind of game was *One Lucky Winner* and why was it worth killing for?

Chapter 1

The Best Friend

Maire Hennessy squinted against the bright October sun as she drove down the quiet Iowa county road. The fields were filled with the stubbled remains of the fall harvest and stripped bare by heavy-billed grackles and beady-eyed blackbirds eating their fill before the cold weather set in. It made her a little sad. Winter would be coming soon, unrelenting and unforgiving.

That morning, she had packed up her girls and Kryngle, their four-year-old Shetland sheepdog, to drop them off at her former mother-in-law's home. Maire, who hadn't traveled more than a hundred miles away from Calico since she abruptly dropped out of college over twenty years earlier, was embarking on an adventure that could change the course of their lives forever. Ten-year-old Dani kicked the back of Maire's seat in time to the throbbing beat coming from her older sister Keely's earbuds. Keely, a twelve-year-old carbon copy of Maire, had the hood of her sweatshirt pulled up over her head, her red curls springing out around her sullen face, as she silently pretended to read her book.

Maire tapped her fingers nervously against the steering wheel. "You're going to be just fine," she said, turning onto the highway that would take her children to her ex-mother-in-law's home. Shar was a decent enough person. Except for the fact that she smoked like a chimney and gave birth to a shit of a son, Maire knew she would take good care of the girls while she was away.

"I don't want to go," Dani murmured. "I like my own bed. Grandma's house feels weird."

Both Dani and Keely dreaded the two weeks that they were going to stay with their grandmother, a bland, unexcitable woman with steel gray hair and stooped shoulders. There would be no movie nights, no special outings, no grand adventures, but they would be well-cared for, safe. And that's all that Maire wanted.

"I thought you liked Grandma Hennessy," Maire said. "You'll make cookies and she's going to teach you both how to crochet. You'll have a great time."

"Why are you going to be gone for so long?" Dani asked, staring at Maire through the rearview mirror, her eyes filled with hurt. A wet cough rumbled through her chest and she buried her mouth in her elbow.

That familiar cloud of worry that materialized every time Dani had a coughing fit settled over Maire.

"It's only for two weeks and it's not that I don't want to see you," she said. "You know that. I would be with you every single day if I could. It's kind of a work thing and I can't pass up the opportunity."

"You work from home," Keely said, briefly pulling out an earbud.

Maire didn't mind lying to Shar but lying to her children was different. She had the chance of a lifetime and in a way, it *was* work related. Money was involved. Lots of it.

"It's like a contest," Maire explained. "And if I win, well, that would be nice. And even if I don't, a lot of people will learn about my Calico Rose jewelry and might want to sell it."

"Like Claire's in the mall?" Dani asked.

"Yes, Claire's, Target, who knows?" The lies slid so easily off her tongue now. Dani's kicks to the back of Maire's seat slowed as she mulled this over.

"I'm sorry," Maire said. "I know it's hard." Her voice broke on the last word. Hard wasn't anywhere close to how things had been for the last year. Terrifying, humiliating, devastating, soul-crushing were more like it.

Bobby had never been much of a husband or father, but his health insurance had been a lifeline for Dani. When he lost his job at a local grain elevator and then took off with the nineteen-year-old waitress from the Sunshine Café, gone was the health insurance and any hope of child support. When the first $3,000 notice for Dani's nebulizer treatments came in, Maire ran to the bathroom and vomited. It was impossible. Too much.

Between the implosion of her marriage, the impact it had on the kids, her bank account that was dangerously low, the unpaid medical bills, the jewelry she made for her Etsy shop, and the search for a job that provided decent health insurance, Maire was exhausted.

Things couldn't go on this way. "It will get better," she promised.

Maire glanced over at Keely and caught her accusatory glare. Out of all of them, the divorce hit Keely the hardest. Despite his drawbacks, Keely was a daddy's girl, and she was suffering in his absence.

The worry never ended. At the top of the list was Dani's health. Her cystic fibrosis was stable for the moment, but she was fragile. Her last infection required a two-week hospital stay, a PICC line with multiple antibiotic infusions, therapies, and nebulizer treatments. It was so much that Maire had to put together a binder for Shar filled with in-depth directions for Dani's care, and she hoped she wasn't making a huge mistake by leaving. A lung infection that may be mild for most children could be deadly for Dani. And poor Keely. Quiet, shy Keely was getting lost in the shuffle, becoming more removed, isolated from them. Another thing to worry about.

A month ago, when she got the email about the show, she almost deleted it. Maire had been online, scanning articles about the newest cystic fibrosis research, when she heard the ping. Grateful for an excuse to tear her eyes away from the words like *Fibrinogen-like 2 proteins* and *cryogenic electron microscopy*, she tapped the email icon on her phone.

CONGRATULATIONS—YOU'VE BEEN NOMINATED, the subject line called out to her. She scanned the rest of the email. Trip of a lifetime, groundbreaking new reality show, $10 million. *Scam*, Maire thought and went back to reading about clinical trials and RNA therapy. But an hour later, she was still thinking about the $10 million. She opened the email again to read it more closely.

Congratulations, you've been nominated to take part in the groundbreaking new reality competition show *One Lucky Winner*! Set in the heart of wine country, you, along with the other contestants, will battle for $10 million through a series of challenges that will test you physically, mentally, and emotionally. Competitors will spend fourteen days at the exclusive Diletta Resort and Spa in beautiful Napa Valley. When not competing, spend your time in your lavishly appointed private cottage, swimming laps in the 130-foot pool, or head to the spa for our one-of-a-kind vinotherapy-based treatments—massages, wraps, and scrubs made from grapes grown in the La Bella Luce vineyard. As a special treat, each contestant will receive a case of La Bella Luce's world-famous cabernet sauvignon with an exclusively designed label just for you!

Maire snorted. It had to be a joke. A rip-off. She closed the email, even sent it to her trash folder, but an hour later, she pulled it up again. Ten million dollars. Maire was one month away from not being able to pay the mortgage on the house, from not being able to make the car payment, from not being able to put money in the kids' school lunch accounts, from not being able to pay for one dose of Dani's medication.

She should probably just sell the house, take the loss, start over, but this was her home, the kids' home. There was no way she was giving it up without a fight. She didn't need anywhere near $10 million to save the house, but that was what it was worth to her, and that kind of money would change her life, all their lives.

Who would have nominated her? And how did that actually work? *Hey, I know of someone who could use $10 million.* The entire thing had to be fake. The email was signed by someone named Fern Espa, whose title read Production Assistant, *One Lucky Winner.*

Anyone could send an email. Maire trashed the message again.

Then, over the next three days, the car started leaking oil, Kryngle ate a sock and had to have emergency surgery, and Dani's hospital bill came in. Her credit cards were maxed out and she'd given up on any help from her ex. Maire needed money, fast. Burying her humiliation, she called her parents and asked for a loan. It wasn't nearly enough.

Maire hung up and went to the garage, sitting in her leaky car so that the kids wouldn't hear her crying.

Maybe this was the email she was waiting for. The sign she needed to finally take control of her life. Maire wasn't a fool though. She did her due diligence. While sitting in the waiting room at the vet's office, she looked up *One Lucky Winner* and found a website and an IMDB entry—both short on details—but it clearly was a real show. She searched for the name Fern Espa and found a LinkedIn entry that looked legit. And the Diletta Resort looked amazing.

And now, under the guise of a work trip, here she was, dropping her kids off at her mother-in-law's house for two weeks, hopping on a plane to Napa to take part in some *Survivor*-type reality show for the off chance she might win $10 million. It was ridiculous, over the top, maybe even irresponsible, but it ignited a spark of hope that she hadn't felt in a long time.

"You'll be okay," Maire said to the kids as she turned onto the cracked concrete of Shar's street. Shar was waiting for them, standing on her rickety front porch, a cigarette dangling from her knobby fingers. With hail-pocked, dirty white aluminum siding and a crabgrass-choked yard in need of mowing, the home her ex-husband grew up in was grim and depressing. But her mother-in-law was a sweet woman who loved her grandchildren. Maire scanned the street. Every house was in the same state of disarray and neglect. A jolt of fear shot through her. If she didn't turn things around, they would end up living in a place like this, or worse.

Jesus, Maire thought. *I'm making a huge mistake.* She fought the urge to drive right on by. Instead, she gave the girls her bravest smile. "It's okay. We're all going to be okay."

Ten million dollars would make everything okay.